Jaylene ████ a sheltered ████ ████ ████ she busily engaged he████ ████ ████ing bath. Her clothes hung from a ████by tree, as she frolicked in the water as uninhibited as Aphrodite's child.

The vision of naked loveliness she presented was not for nature alone. Todd Kirk, a sandy-haired Confederate officer, experienced intense pleasure at his chance encounter.

"Good morning, ma'am," Todd said. He took off his hat and tipped his head toward her.

"Oh!" Jaylene cried in alarm. Attempting to cover herself, she asked, "Who are you?"

"I'm Major Todd Kirk, ma'am, and I'm seeking a place to cross the river. My men are just behind me."

"You mean there are more of you?" Now she sat down in the water, willing to brave the cold in order to gain a measure of modesty.

"Not yet . . . I must say, I've never beheld a more beautiful sight."

"Sir, you should have made your presence known."

"But, I did, ma'am. I said good morning, ma'am."

"If you were a gentleman, you would leave now and allow me to recover my dignity."

"If I were a gentleman, I would be serving in the regular forces instead of leading a band of raiders. And as for you recovering your dignity, why, ma'am, I like you just the way you are . . . with nothing covered." Todd smiled broadly at his joke.

SOUTHERN ROSE

Paula Fairman

PINNACLE BOOKS
WINDSOR PUBLISHING CORP.

PINNACLE BOOKS

are published by

Windsor Publishing Corp.
475 Park Avenue South
New York, NY 10016

Third printing: November, 1990

Printed in the United States of America

Southern Rose

CHAPTER ONE

It was called Rosecrown, and it sat on top of a small hill overlooking the Mississippi River. It was a stately mansion, supported by Doric columns, and surrounded by a beautifully landscaped lawn. Roses and honeysuckle twined thickly about the veranda, while nearby the magnolia trees veiled themselves in the morning mist. A soft breeze filled the long muslin curtains and swept through the halls and rooms with a pleasant murmur and a flower-scented breath.

Outside the house, on the neatly clipped lawn, a company of soldiers were camped and now they were stirring to the morning business as smoke from their breakfast fires drifted off into the woods. The soldiers were from the First Ohio Volunteers, part of the Union army, which, under the command of General U. S. Grant, had invaded Mississippi. General Grant and several of his staff officers were in the house, sitting down to a breakfast prepared for them by the Rosecrown servants.

"Umm, taste those pancakes," General Grant said, shoving a forkful into his mouth. "I don't know when I've had anything so good."

The other officers agreed with the general, each adding his own comment to reinforce his praise. One of the officers said nothing. He was a mere captain and hardly qualified by his rank to dine in such lofty climes as this. He stood by, respectfully, as the generals and colonels took their breakfast.

"Now, Captain Holt," General Grant said, touching a napkin to his lips. "You were saying?"

"The troupe of actors, General. I gave them a pass through our lines."

"When?"

"Last night, sir," Captain Holt said. He cleared his throat nervously. "It was quite late when they passed through here. I—I saw no need to disturb you in your sleep, sir. I was Officer of the Guard, I assumed the responsibility."

"Captain, don't you think you assumed too much?" one of the colonels asked.

"Yes," one of the other colonels pitched in quickly. "They could have been a troupe of spies. Actors indeed! And just where would they be practicing their profession?"

"At Yazoo City, sir," Captain Holt answered.

"Yazoo City? Why, that's in rebel hands."

"Yes, sir, I know," Captain Holt said. "This is a Southern troupe of actors, sir, known as the Edward Fox Players."

"Captain, I can't believe you would do such a thing," the first colonel scolded. "Whatever possessed you to issue such a pass?"

"Colonel, my orders were not to interfere with the normal travel and commerce of business, but to halt only such travelers as might be of military bene-

3

fit to the rebels. I saw no harm in letting the acting troupe pass."

"I quite agree with you, Captain," General Grant said. The others around the table looked at him in surprise, and the two colonels who had been berating Captain Holt suddenly found much to look at on their plates.

"Captain Holt . . . Tony, isn't it?"

"Yes, General."

"Tony, aren't you the officer who approached me with the idea of establishing an underground railroad to send fugitive slaves up north?"

"Yes, sir," Tony said. "We would be providing a very humane service, sir."

"We are soldiers, Captain," one of the other staff officers said. "Leave the humane services to the churches and the abolitionists."

"But, Colonel, you don't understand," Tony said earnestly. "The whole reason we are fighting this war is to provide a humane service. We are fighting this war to free fellow human beings from bondage!"

The colonel laughed. "My dear Captain, I'm afraid that the real issues are much more complicated than that. There are many social and political questions which have been posed by this war, perhaps the least of which being the question of slavery."

"I'm afraid Colonel Ellis is right," General Grant said. "It would be humane, but it might also detract from our efforts here, and in the long run the most humane thing we could possibly do for these people is to win the war. Once we have won they will all have their freedom."

4

"But, General, consider this," Tony said. "Perhaps slavery is the least important issue, but it is the simplest one. It is one which everyone with a feeling for right can understand. We could rally many to our cause."

"I don't know," General Grant said.

"And prevent slave labor from improving the breastworks around Vicksburg," Tony added.

General Grant cupped his chin in his hand. "Hmm," he said. "You may have a point at that. Very well, Captain Holt. As of now you are detached from your other duties and assigned the sole responsibility for establishing and maintaining an underground railway, such a system to function in all occupied areas."

"Thank you, General," Tony said, smiling broadly and saluting the general. "You won't be sorry, sir."

"I hope not," General Grant said. "And I hope I am not sorry about you letting the troupe of players pass during the night. What did you say they were called?"

"The Edward Fox Players, sir," Tony said. He reached into his tunic pocket and took out a flyer. "Here, sir, they gave me this."

EDWARD FOX
begs to announce
the performance by his troupe of players
of the sensational drama
ANGEL OF MIDNIGHT
The Players

Count de Stromberg	Mr. J. W. Booth
Dr. Paul Bernarr	Mr. F. Hardenburgh

John Small . . . . Mr. Edward Fox
Edna Whalen . . . . Miss Lucy Wade
and, as the Midnight Angel,
Miss Jaylene Cooper!

General Grant perused the broadsheet for a moment, pulling at his whiskers as he did so.

"Hmm, I believe I have heard of an actor named Booth. Could this be the same fellow?" he asked.

"You may have heard of Edwin Booth, General," Tony said. "I believe he is a Shakespearean actor of some note in New York. This fellow is his brother. His name is Wilkes Booth. John Wilkes Booth."

"Then there is no doubt that they are players, is there?"

"No, sir," Tony said. "No doubt at all."

"I wonder where they are now?" General Grant mused. "It might have been good to solicit them to put on a performance for us."

At the moment of this discussion the Edward Fox Players were camped but three miles south of the Yazoo River. Jaylene Cooper, the troupe's leading lady, had found a sheltered spot on the river, and there she was busily engaged with her morning bath. Her clothes hung from a nearby tree, while Jaylene, naked, stood knee-deep in bracing water, rinsing away the soap of her earlier scrub.

The picture Jaylene presented was as lovely as could be imagined. She was twenty-one, with a full head of tawny hair, shining brightly in the morning sun. Her brown eyes were almost gold, and even in the privacy of her bath they were turbulent and lusty with life. She had a fine, slender form, with highlifted breasts and long smooth legs, and she

6

frolicked in the water as uninhabitedly as Aphrodite's child.

Though Jaylene didn't realize it, the vision of lovelines she presented was not for nature alone, for other eyes had discovered the scene, and now they were watching her with cool detachment and unbridled interest.

These eyes were as blue as the afternoon sky, and they belonged to Todd Kirk, a young, sandy-haired Confederate officer. Todd Kirk was the commanding officer of Kirk's Raiders, a daring group of guerrillas who operated behind the enemy lines. Todd and his men were made of the stuff of pirates and highwaymen—a Robin Hood and his men of derring-do who had a love for adventure and fair play. Added to that was a verve for life, for clearly reflected in Todd Kirk's face at this moment was the intense pleasure he was experiencing in this chance encounter.

Jaylene was humming a little song while splashing herself with water, her beautifully curved back presented to Todd. She was unaware of his presence.

"Good morning, ma'am," Todd said. He took off his hat and tipped his head toward her.

"Oh!" Jaylene cried in alarm. She turned toward the voice, making a vain attempt to cover herself as she did so. "Who are you, and what are you doing here?"

"I'm Major Todd Kirk, ma'am, and I'm seeking a place to cross the river. My men are just behind me."

"You mean there are more of you?" Jaylene

asked. She sat down in the water, willing to brave the cold in order to gain a measure of modesty.

"Not yet, ma'am. I'm the only one here, and I must say, I've never beheld a more beautiful sight than that which I happened on a moment ago."

"Sir, you should have made your presence known!"

"But I did, ma'am. I said good morning, ma'am, don't you remember?" Todd teased.

"If you were a gentleman you would leave now and allow me to recover my dignity."

"If I were a gentleman I would be serving in the regular forces instead of leading a band of raiders. And as for you recovering your dignity, why, ma'am, I like you just the way you are . . . with nothing covered." Todd smiled broadly at his joke.

"You—you are a cad, sir!" Jaylene said. "A vile creature who disgraces the uniform you wear!"

"Now, ma'am, please don't think too harshly of me," Todd said. "If I were really as bad as all that, why, I could take your clothes and ride away."

"You . . . you wouldn't do that, would you?" Jaylene asked in a voice which had lost its challenge and was now small with the fear that he might do just what he said.

"No, ma'am," Todd said. "I guess perhaps there is a bit of Southern chivalry in me, after all." He saluted her. "If you would get dressed quickly, ma'am, I'll be leading my men across here in about three more minutes."

At the thought of an entire army coming through, Jaylene abandoned all efforts to shield herself further from Todd's gaze, and came quickly out of the water to recover her clothes. The result was that for a long uninterrupted moment, Todd enjoyed a magnificent view of her charms; then he wheeled his horse about and rode away.

Jaylene dressed quickly. She was mortified by the incident, and her cheeks flamed red as she thought of what had happened. She had been seen nude by a man for the first time in her adult life.

It was a perfectly mortifying experience. And yet, tucked away beneath the embarrassment and the shame, was a tiny feeling of pleasure. Jaylene hadn't admitted it to herself yet—couldn't admit it, for to do so would question her values—but there was no denying that it was there. For despite her embarrassment, she couldn't help but notice what a handsome man Todd Kirk was, nor did his obvious appreciation of her beauty escape her notice.

Dressed, Jaylene turned to look toward the small embankment over which Major Kirk had disappeared. She didn't see or hear anything, and she stood there for a long moment, wondering where he went, and if he would really be back. She heard only the sound of the bubbling river as it broke swiftly over the rocks, and the gentle sigh of the breeze in the trees, and the birds exchanging songs. Could it be that Major Kirk had lied to her? Was it but a ruse to get her to come out of the water, and thus expose herself to him once more?

Now the tiny spark of pleasure which had nestled deep within was extinguished by the cold anger she felt for someone who would be so ungentlemanly as to pull such a trick on a defenseless woman. Oh, how she hated Todd Kirk at this moment!

In the distance Jaylene heard a low, rumbling sound, like a prolonged roll of timpani, and for a moment she wondered what it was. Then the drumming began to swell, growing louder and louder until it was like thunder. It made her stomach quiver and it filled the trees with its pounding until finally, bursting over the crest of the embankment, she saw the source of the sound. Major Kirk was riding at the head of a column of men, bent low over his horse's neck. The horse's mane and tail were streaming out behind as it was in full gallop, nostrils flared wide, the powerful muscles in its shoulders and haunches throbbing.

Following Kirk was a flag bearer, and Jaylene saw the red, white, and blue ensign snapping in the wind. Then came the entire body of men, all urging their animals to a fast pace.

The column of men hit the water and sand and silver bubbles flew up in a sheet of spray, sustained by the churning action of the horses' hooves, until it was like rain. Jaylene watched the body of raiders cross the river, totally transfixed by the scene. Never had she seen anything more grand or glorious than that! Even the anger she had felt toward Todd Kirk was now pacified by the thrill of watching a band of mounted men cross a river at full gallop. It was positively breathtaking.

Jaylene stood there for a moment longer, listening as the thunder receded, until finally it was gone, and once again there was only the sound of the river, the whisper of the trees, and the songs of the birds. Slowly, almost reluctantly, she returned to the site where the Edward Fox Players had camped for the night.

CHAPTER TWO

"Oh, Jaylene, you missed it," Edward Fox said as Jaylene returned to the encampment. Edward Fox was Jaylene's uncle, as well as the master of the theater troupe. He was tall and very thin. He wore his white hair long, and that, plus his luxuriant white goatee and moustache, gave him a dignified air. His suit was always neat, and Jaylene never saw him without a cravat, or at least a string tie. It was as if he compensated for the somewhat suspect reputation of his profession by constantly appearing to be the perfect gentleman.

"And what did I miss, Uncle?" Jaylene asked. She accepted a cup of coffee proffered her by Lucy Wade, and joined the others, who were having their breakfast.

"The riders," Edward said. "There was an entire troop. They must have been guerrillas, and they passed by at a gallop, no doubt on their way to raid some Yankee supply station somewhere. Oh, it was a magnificent sight!"

"These fellows were much too well disciplined to be ragtag guerrillas," one of the others said. The one who spoke was John Wilkes Booth, a young man with dark hair and black, brooding eyes. He was the leading man of the acting troupe, an exceptionally handsome man who often caused the women in the audiences to swoon. "No, they were regular cavalry men, I am certain of that."

"I see," Jaylene said. "Are you an expert in military affairs?"

Jaylene spoke with the air of one who had long suffered from the young man's ego. He was perfect in every way. He was a far superior actor than his brother, or anyone else on stage for that matter. He also knew more about everything than anyone else. At least, that is what he would have everyone believe.

"I have no small amount of knowledge about things military," Booth replied.

"Then tell me, Wilkes. If you have such valuable military knowledge and experience, why is it that you are not serving in the army?" Jaylene asked.

"Oh, my dear, I am far more valuable to the Confederacy in my present situation," Booth replied easily. "With my experience I can easily judge the composition of a military unit just by simple observation. Thus, whenever we pass through Yankee lines, as we did last night, for example, I am able to look around, and bring important information to the Confederate commanders. Why, it was for just such a purpose that I consented to become a part of this small traveling group in the first place. My talents are far too great to be wasted with a road show."

"You are a talented actor, Wilkes," Edward said. "But your talents aren't wasted with us. We have an excellent company. Besides, the shows we produce bring tremendous happiness into the lives of our sol-

13

diers and civilians alike. We are helping to keep up morale, and that is very important."

"Of course it is," Booth said easily, placating the older man's feelings somewhat. "I'm sorry, I didn't mean to imply that the Edward Fox Players weren't talented. Why, any actor would be pleased to perform with anyone here." He smiled broadly.

"Thank you, Wilkes," Jaylene said sarcastically. "I appreciate your kind words about our talent. I only hope you are more adept at judging acting talent than you are at identifying military units."

"What do you mean?"

"The unit that just passed was a guerrilla unit. It was Kirk's Raiders."

"Kirk's Raiders?" Edward said with interest. "Are you certain, girl? I thought he was up in Tennessee."

"I'm certain," Jaylene said. "Major Todd Kirk spoke to me."

"I *knew* it," Edward said, pounding his fist into his hand. "They *are* going after a supply depot. Or maybe they are even going to raid the Yankee headquarters. I wouldn't be surprised if there weren't some pretty high-ranking Yankee generals back there at Rosecrown."

"I doubt that," Booth said authoritatively. "You could tell from the disposition of the soldiers on the lawn that there wasn't anyone of importance inside the house."

As the men continued to talk about military matters, Lucy gathered up the dishes and carried them down to the river to wash them. Jaylene went with her, to help, but also to be out of hearing of Booth's braggadocio.

14

"Did Todd Kirk really speak to you?" Lucy asked when the two women were alone. Lucy was not quite as tall as Jaylene, and she was three years older. She had hair so dark as to be almost midnight blue, and her eyes were large and brown and framed by lashes as delicately beautiful as mimosa. Her skin was smooth and lovely and touched with an olive cast.

Before Jaylene joined the troupe, Lucy had been the leading lady, but she accepted Jaylene not only graciously but enthusiastically. The two women were fast and dear friends, and there was no professional jealousy between them at all.

"Yes," Jaylene said. She stopped and looked back over her shoulder to make certain they were alone. "Lucy . . . he saw me bathing. He saw me naked."

Lucy gasped; then, without thinking, she blurted out, "Oh, I wish I had been bathing then!"

"Lucy!"

Lucy covered her mouth, then blushed, as if unable to believe she had said such a thing. Then her natural sense of humor spilled out in bubbles of laughter.

"Well," she said. "After all, they say he is handsome, and so dashing and romantic."

"They say Wilkes is handsome too," Jaylene said. "And I suppose he is. But when one knows him as we do, one sees beyond his handsome countenance to his unseemly character. I have glimpsed that in Mr. Kirk."

"Jaylene, did he . . . did he *molest* you?" Lucy asked.

"No."

15

"Then he took your clothes, or mocked you?"

"Well, no, he didn't do that either," Jaylene said. "But when I accused him of not being a gentleman, he made no effort to disagree with me. And he . . . he . . . " Jaylene stopped.

"He what?"

"He looked at me with such obvious enjoyment that I felt . . . used."

"Would you prefer that he looked on you without appreciation?"

"I would prefer that he not look on me at all," Jaylene said. "But since he did, I feel it was most rude of him to take such pleasure at my discomfort."

Lucy laughed. "Perhaps you are right. As such a thing has never happened to me, I don't know how I should feel. But if it does happen, I would not be too upset if it was someone like Major Todd Kirk."

"Jaylene, Lucy, hurry with your chores. We must be off soon," Edward called from the wagons.

"Here," Jaylene offered, picking up a stack of dishes. "You do those and I'll do these. I'll be glad to reach Yazoo City, where I believe we will be able to sleep in a hotel tonight."

"Umm, that will be nice," Lucy agreed, as she and Jaylene bent to their tasks.

As the two wagons of the traveling theater rolled into Yazoo City, they picked up a few cheers and friendly waves. The sides of both wagons were decorated with large banners proclaiming their identity, and travelling theater groups were a much welcomed commodity in a state strained by war.

Yazoo City had a normal population of three

16

thousand during peacetime, but the population was swollen to four times that number now. Most of the increase came from soldiers, as the army had been rolled south by Grant's advance. But there were also many civilians who had abandoned the farms and small towns in the occupied area, and they, too, had come to Yazoo City.

Everywhere Jaylene looked she saw people: soldiers standing along the boardwalks or grouped in the streets, children laughing and shouting, running along with the wagons, and men and women in civilian clothes watching them from the windows.

Yazoo City was quite close to the enemy lines, but one couldn't tell it from the mood of the people. Their spirits were high, almost festive, and everywhere there was the atmosphere of a celebration. A large banner was stretched across the main street, bearing the legend "Hurrah for Freedom," and red, white, and blue bunting decorated the poles and porch supports. There were several recruitment posters, too.

As the wagons rolled down the street, an officer stepped out in front of them and signaled them to stop. Edward halted his team, and the wagon behind him stopped as well.

"Mr. Fox, I presume?" the officer asked. "At your service, sir," Edward answered.

The officer saluted politely. "Mr. Fox, I am Captain Leighton. Colonel Culpepper's regards, sir, and he begs that you join him for lunch in his private dining room, where he will discuss the schedule for tonight's show."

"Tell Colonel Culpepper we will be delighted to

17

join him for lunch. But where is his private dining room?"

"The Lexington House has been taken over for that purpose," Captain Leighton replied.

"Very well, Captain, we shall be there shortly," Edward said.

Captain Leighton saluted again, then returned to deliver the message. The Edward Fox Players headed for the theater at the far end of the street.

There were several persons standing around the front of the theater when the wagons arrived, and they sent up a cheer for the players. As Jaylene and Lucy climbed down from the wagons, a few soldiers moved toward them, holding two large bouquets of flowers. One of the soldiers cleared his throat nervously.

"Miss Cooper and Miss Wade," the soldier said. Jaylene and Lucy smiled at them.

"If it pleases you, ma'am, we'd like you to have this," the soldier said.

The two soldiers who were holding the bouquets just stood there, still smiling. Finally the soldier who had spoken looked toward them irritably. "Well, *give* it to 'em," he said gruffly.

"Oh, uh, yeah, Sarge," one of the soldiers said. He handed his bouquet to Jaylene, and the other soldier handed his to Lucy. The remainder of the soldiers gave another cheer.

"Gentlemen," Edward said, holding up his arms. "Free passes to tonight's performance to all who help us unload the wagons and set up the stage."

There was a rush to the wagons, and in a short time they were unloaded and the sets and props were all transported inside. The soldiers worked under Edward's direction, and by lunchtime the stage was set and ready.

Edward thanked the soldiers and dismissed them, then turned to the others and rubbed his hands together. "Well, that seems to be taken care of. Now, shall we join the colonel for lunch?"

"Mr. Fox, I have some repairs to make on my costume," Lucy said. "If you think it would be all right, I would rather stay and work on it."

"I have some things to do as well," Frank Hardenburgh said. Mr. Hardenburgh hadn't been with the group long; he had just joined them a couple of weeks earlier in order to play the role of Dr. Paul Bernarr in the new production, *The Midnight Angel*. He was a small man, rather heavyset, with very little hair. He had a deep, rich voice, and once when Jaylene heard him singing she commented to her uncle about how well he sang.

"I dare say he does, niece," Edward answered. "He was once the featured singer in Carl Zerrahn's Grand Opera in Boston. He was considered one of the finest operatic singers in America, but he fell victim, as have so many others, to Demon Rum. Now he is reduced to playing bit parts and roles for traveling repertoires."

Jaylene had looked at Mr. Hardenburgh in a different light after that. She felt a degree of sympathy for him, and understood why he preferred to spend most of his time alone.

"Very well, Frank. You and Lucy stay here and the rest of us will go. It is probably best that we leave someone with the sets anyway." He looked at Jaylene and Booth. "Shall we go, then?"

The Lexington House had been Yazoo City's finest hotel until it was taken over by Colonel Hamilton Culpepper as his own private quarters. In the dining room were a dozen glistening chandeliers, and though since it was midday none of the lamps were lit, by their very sparkle they seemed to add brightness to the room.

The carpet was of floral design, its beauty all the more visible now that all the tables had been removed but one. That table was elegantly set, and Colonel Culpepper stood graciously as they approached. He was wearing a long grey coat, richly adorned in gold trim, and he ran his hand through his reddish-brown chin whiskers as Jaylene, her uncle, and Booth walked toward the table.

"Ah, how good of you to accept my invitation," he said.

"How gracious of you to offer, Colonel Culpepper," Edward replied.

A soldier dressed in a white jacket pulled the chair out for Jaylene as they sat to the table, and another set a silver tray of oysters on the half shell before them.

"What a lovely place this is," Jaylene said, looking around to admire the room. A slanting sunbeam caught one of the crystal prisms of the chandelier just overhead and projected a burst of color on the wall. Jaylene looked at the phenomena with appreciation for its beauty. "It is certainly nicer than the tents we've been eating in during our performances in the field."

"Yes, well, I'm sure you can appreciate my position," Colonel Culpepper said. "I am the military governor here, as well as the district commander. It is necessary that I live in a place befitting my sta-

20

tion. And, also that I have on hand certain delicacies, such as these oysters, shipped up by rail from the Gulf." He picked up an oyster, sucked it from its shell, smacked his lips appreciatively, then dabbed his lips with a silk napkin.

"I'm sure the officers who have served in the field enjoy this opportunity to get away occasionally," Edward said. "That alone would justify such a place."

"Oh, I assure you, sir, the field officers never dine here," Culpepper said easily. "My staff suggested that I should throw this open for them but, quite frankly, some of the field officers are every bit as boorish as the enlisted men." He took a drink from his goblet. "Umm, an adequate sherry. Won't you try some? I'll be serving a sauterne for lunch. I've had my chef prepare an excellent shrimp jambalaya. I think your palates will be quite pleasantly stimulated."

"You are most gracious, sir," Edward said.

"And correct, I feel, to keep the riffraff out," Booth added.

"Thank you. I knew you would understand my position," Culpepper said. "The townspeople do not, feeling that they have been deprived of the Lexington House, but such are the rigors of war. I remind them of the alternative. If I wasn't here the Yankees would be, and the nigras would be walking the streets as uppity as kings."

"I'm certain that I speak for all of us, Colonel, when I say that we quite understand your position," Booth said.

Booth didn't speak for Jaylene. She thought Culpepper was a pompous buffoon, with no right to

21

usurp the hotel for his own private use, but she kept her silence for this wasn't the time or place to speak her feelings. Their right to perform for the soldiers and the people was controlled by this man, and Jaylene felt that it would be doing a great disservice to the people who needed them if she did or said anything to jeopardize the show. So she merely smiled graciously, and prepared to enjoy the excellent meal the colonel offered.

"Here, you can't go in there! This is a private dining establishment!" someone yelled from the front of the building.

"Yeah? Well, tell that to the Yankees," a gruff voice answered. "They've made it a public war!"

A soldier hurried to the table with an agitated look on his face.

"What is it, Private Anders?" Culpepper asked.

"It's a field officer, sir. He insists upon seeing you."

"Tell him he must wait until after lunch."

"I'll see you now, if you don't mind, Colonel," the officer said, walking over to the table.

Jaylene, as well as the others, looked toward the intruder; then Jaylene gasped. The intruder was Major Todd Kirk.

"Well, ma'am," Todd said, a smile suddenly replacing the set expression upon his face. He bowed slightly. "It is a pleasure to see you again."

"I can't say I share the same sentiment," Jaylene said flatly.

"Major Kirk, what is so important that I can't have my lunch?" Culpepper asked. He looked pointedly at Kirk's dirty boots, which had left a small trail across the carpet.

22

"Colonel, I've brought my men in to see the performance this evening and your pickets stopped us."

"That is correct," Culpepper said. "They did so on my orders."

"For what reason?" Kirk demanded.

"I want your men to stay in the field."

"Colonel, my men are irregulars, under my command. I take my orders from General Pemberton, not from you. We have spent thirty-six days behind the enemy lines, and they deserve a rest."

"Not in my town," Culpepper said. "Your men are guerrillas, whose ungentlemanly behavior is not in keeping with the proper decorum of soldiers. I refuse to allow them to enter."

"Colonel, if my men wanted to come into this town there is nothing you could do to stop us," Kirk reminded him.

"Perhaps not, Major, but what would it avail you? If you tried to bring your men into this town by force you would turn the city into a battleground and would have gained nothing."

"And you intend to keep us out—by force?" Kirk asked.

"That is my intention, yes."

Kirk sighed, a rasping, angry sigh. Then he pointed his finger at Culpepper's face. "Culpepper, I ought to move my men down to the Jackson theater of operations and let you stew in your own juices. If we hadn't turned back the advance of General Hovey, *he* would be sitting here now, and I'd be trying to get permission from *him* to enter."

Culpepper laughed derisively. "Major, you have been of some help, but I hardly think our security is dependent upon your group of ragtag men."

Kirk smiled, but it was a smile without mirth. "Very well, Colonel. Then I take it you have no objection to my repositioning my unit."

"No objections at all," Culpepper said.

"Then I shall do so," Kirk said. He smiled again, with more mirth, as if he actually enjoyed telling Culpepper this news. "You might be interested in knowing that General Grant is headquartered at Rosecrown. That is only fourteen miles north of here." Kirk saluted, looked at Jaylene and the others and said, "Ma'am, gentlemen, *bon appétit*," then he turned and walked quickly away.

"That's what I mean by the boorishness of field officers," Culpepper said after Kirk left. Another soldier dressed in white approached the table, carrying a large serving tray. "Ah," Culpepper said. "Our meal. Please, enjoy."

CHAPTER THREE

Jaylene stood in the wings and peered through the crack in the curtain. The theater was packed solid. The front row was occupied by wounded soldiers. Behind them were the officers, behind them townspeople, and in the very back, standing in the doors, along the walls, and anywhere there was room, were soldiers.

"Don't you know it is bad luck to count the house, Jaylene?" Edward teased.

"Oh, Uncle Edward, isn't it wonderful? We have a real theater and a real stage. Oh, I just know the show will go well."

"Dear, with an audience as starved for entertainment as these people are, we couldn't force the show not to go well."

"I guess so," Jaylene said. "Still, it is nice to perform in a theater every now and then. I do get tired of the tents and warehouses and store buildings."

Edward put his hand affectionately on his niece's shoulder. "Ah, my darlin' Jaylene. You are so lovely and talented a girl, it makes no difference where you are. Be you on the grassy glade of a battlefield, or on the stage of a New York theater, you will give a brilliant performance regardless."

Jaylene looked at her uncle, and her eyes stared deep into his, trying to decide if he was serious or merely showing a little family love.

"Uncle Edward, you aren't just saying that, are you? You didn't just take me in because Papa died and I had nowhere else to go?"

"No, darlin', I'm not just saying that," Edward said. "I would have taken you to travel with me long ago, had your papa permitted it. But you know how he felt about the profession."

"I know," Jaylene said.

"You'd think the owner of one of the finest riverboats ever to ply the Mississippi would be more tolerant of the profession. Everyone said the *Delta Mist* had the finest shows afloat."

"You know why he felt as he did," Jaylene said. "It was because of Emily McLean." Jaylene twisted her mouth as she spoke the woman's name, showing by that action the bitterness she had for her.

"Yes, I know," Edward said. "If ever a man died of a broken heart, it was your father."

"I will never forgive her for treating Papa so cruelly," Jaylene said.

"The overture is about to begin," Lucy Wade whispered, and Jaylene and her uncle left the wings to go backstage. It was a rare occasion when they were able to have an overture, but there was a military band assigned to Yazoo City, and the bandmaster had volunteered its services.

The music started, and Jaylene felt a quick surge of nervousness. It was always this way just before

27

she went on, but it was a good nervousness, more like suppressed excitement than fear.

The music stopped, and the curtain opened. The set was a drawing room. John Wilkes Booth was on stage as Count de Stromberg, wearing a black silk cape lined with red. He strolled back and forth, flipping the cape back so that the red lining flashed brightly. He waited for the audience's applause to die before he spoke.

"Miss Whalen," he called. He stopped and looked stage right. *"Miss* Whalen."

Lucy Wade came on stage, and the audience applauded again. She turned quickly to the audience and made a brief curtsy before speaking her line.

"Yes, your lordship, you called?"

"Did you think perhaps it was the honk of a goose you heard?" Booth answered. It was a guaranteed laugh line, and it nearly brought the house down this time.

It would be nearly five minutes before Jaylene was due on stage, so she walked around backstage to help suppress her nervousness. She started toward the backstage door, intending to open it a bit just to get a breath of fresh air, when it was suddenly, and quietly, opened from outside.

"Well, aren't I the lucky one, though?" Todd Kirk said, for it was he who had opened the door. He stepped just inside, smiling broadly.

"What are you doing back here?" Jaylene hissed. "You aren't supposed to be back here."

"Well, actually, I'm not supposed to be anywhere in the city," Todd said. "But I did want to leave you this." From behind his back, he brought a single,

28

long-stemmed rose, fully open and at the peak of beauty and fragrance.

Jaylene was a little surprised by it. She took it and looked at it for a moment. But she was even more surprised by what happened next, for as her mind was occupied by the rose she did not ascertain his intentions and was thus unprepared when he took her into his arms and kissed her.

Jaylene struggled against him, both from anger and from fear. But the harder she struggled, the more determined he became to hold her, until finally she abandoned the struggle and let herself go limp in his arms.

Then a strange thing began to happen. The surprise changed to surrender, the fear to curiosity, and then to sweetness. Todd's lips opened on hers and his tongue pushed into her mouth. It was shocking and thrilling at the same time, and involuntarily a moan of passion began in her throat. Her body was warmed with a fire she had never before experienced, and the kiss went on and on, longer than she had ever imagined such a thing could last. Her head grew light, and she abandoned all thought save this pleasure. The rose slipped from her hand and fell to the floor, there to lie just beneath the foot she had raised as she leaned into Todd's muscular hardness.

Finally Todd broke off the kiss and Jaylene was left standing there as limp as a rag doll. She looked at him with bewilderment in her face, and he smiled, gave sort of a half-salute, then left.

It was only then that Jaylene realized what had happened. Before she was able to regain her senses, or even feel anger, it was time for her to go on, and she had to put all feelings of outrage and indignation behind her, in order to portray her role. But as she stood in the wings waiting for her cue, she realized that one sensation had not left her. His kiss was still burning her lips, making her so aware of it that she was sure it must show.

As Todd rode away from Yazoo City, he relived the kiss. He could feel the girl's soft, pliable body against his and smell her hair, more fragrant even than the rose he had given her. And he had but to shut his eyes to recall what a beautiful vision that body was, for when he had chanced upon her this morning her loveliness had nearly taken his breath away. Never in his life had he wanted anything more than he wanted that girl. And Todd was generally a man who got what he wanted.

Todd had served as a captain on General Johnston's staff during the battle of Shiloh. He was written up in the dispatches, cited for bravery, and promoted to the temporary rank of lieutenant colonel on General Beauregard's staff after General Johnston was killed. But Todd didn't want to be a staff officer, even when Beauregard dangled the prospect of permanent promotion to full colonel. Todd wanted to fight, so he resigned his commission, then raised a body of irregular forces, and was accepted by General Pemberton at his present rank of Major. His friends teased him about making his rank "the hard way," but they knew why he had done what he had done, and they respected him for it.

As Todd rode north out of town, he either heard or sensed an approaching horseman, so he moved his own mount off the road and waited in the bushes. He pulled his pistol. He was still within his own lines, though his practice of operating so deeply behind Yankee lines had taught him that being behind your lines wasn't a guarantee of safety.

Todd stroked his horse's neck soothingly as they waited, and he heard the pounding of the hoofbeats, growing louder as the rider approached. Then, as the approaching rider rounded the bend in the road, Todd could see him in the moonlight. Little puffs of dust trailed out behind the horse, colored silver by the waxing moon. The moon was bright enough that Todd easily recognized the rider, and he smiled and put his pistol away, then moved out into the road to intercept him. It was Captain Sam Shelton, Todd's next in command.

"Sam," Todd said, holding out his hand to stop him. "What is it? Where are you headed in such a hurry?"

"Todd," Sam said, reigning his horse in sharply. "We have to warn Culpepper. There's a whole army about to load onto a train up at Rosecrown. It'll be comin' down on Yazoo City tomorrow like a duck on a june bug."

Todd twisted in his saddle to look back at the town he had just left. The saddle squeaked with his movement, and he sat there looking for a long moment before he spoke. "Let's take out the trestle over Farley Creek."

"We can't do that," Sam said. "Todd, you know we have to have Culpepper's approval for that. It's in his district."

"We've asked him three times, and he's said no," Todd said. He twisted his lips into a sneer. "It'll cut off his supply of fancy goods if we do."

31

"But surely, if he knows that it'll bring the whole Yankee army to within a couple of miles of him, he'll give you permission?"

"I doubt it," Todd said. "It's my guess that he'll think we're getting nervous over nothing. No, Sam, if we are going to blow that trestle, we'll have to do it ourselves, tonight."

"You're the boss," Sam said. He smiled. "But I thought you might say that, so I've already got the men in position."

Todd laughed. "Sam, you're a good man," he said. He slapped his reins to the side of his horse and he and Sam started back up the road at a gallop.

The applause was fantastic. There had been three curtain calls, and no doubt there could have been three more had the players wanted to take them. Jaylene was exhilarated by it all, and she stood on the stage, bowing and smiling and blowing kisses to the audience. It was wonderful, and when the curtain closed for the final time, she wished it would open for another complete performance.

"Oh, Jaylene," Lucy said, running to her and throwing her arms around her. "You were absolutely wonderful!"

"Thank you, Lucy," Jaylene said. "But you were pretty wonderful yourself."

Booth cleared his throat. "Ladies, while you are busy congratulating each other, might I remind you that it was *my* performance that got all the laughs."

"It was your character, Wilkes, not your performance," Hardenburgh said.

"How would you know?" Booth asked wryly.

"You haven't drawn a sober breath in so long that you wouldn't recognize a stellar performance if you saw one."

"I'll recognize it, Wilkes," Hardenburgh said, *"if* I ever see it."

Lucy and Jaylene couldn't help but laugh, and Booth, feeling insulted, left in a huff.

"Mr. Hardenburgh, perhaps you shouldn't be so hard on Wilkes," Lucy said. "He takes everything so seriously."

"He is a small man with grandiose ideas," Hardenburgh said. "He lives in the shadow of his brother and longs to have his own recognition. In fact, he is desperate for recognition. I know the signs, I have seen it in others."

"But he is a good actor," Lucy said, "and a very handsome man."

"Handsome, is he?" Hardenburgh said. "I have no way of judging such things. But as an actor he will never be better than a journeyman."

Their conversation was suddenly interrupted by the sound of a heavy explosion. It came from some distance away, but it filled them with a sense of dread.

"I—I wonder what that was?" Jaylene asked, frightened by it.

"Cannons?" Lucy asked.

"I've never heard a cannon that big," Hardenburgh said. "Maybe I'd better go ask Colonel Culpepper what it was."

"Huh," Jaylene said contemptuously. "From what I observed of Colonel Culpepper he wouldn't come any closer to knowing what it was than we do."

33

"Nevertheless," Hardenburgh said, "I don't like the sound of that. It bodes evil for someone."

Hardenburgh hurried off to discover, if he could, the source of the sound, and Jaylene and Lucy were left alone. Lucy happened to look over toward one of the packing crates in which the sets were normally stored, and she saw the rose that Todd had given Jaylene earlier.

"Oh," she said, reaching for the flower. "What a lovely bloom!" She held it to her nose and sniffed it. "And it has such a wonderful fragrance. Jaylene, did you see this?"

"Yes," Jaylene said, cutting her eyes away in quick embarrassment.

"I wonder where it came from?" Lucy said. When Jaylene didn't answer, Lucy looked at her with curiosity, then smiled knowingly. "You know, don't you? It was given to you by someone."

"Yes."

"Who?"

"I'd rather not say."

"Oh, Jaylene, we've never kept secrets from each other. Have you a secret lover now?"

"No," Jaylene said, her face flushing in embarrassment. "At least," she added, "no one I chose. He has taken such a course upon his own."

"Aren't you going to tell me who it is?"

"Todd Kirk," Jaylene said, and even as she said his name she could feel again the dizzying sensations of his kiss.

CHAPTER FOUR

The shock waves of the explosion moved across
the field and hit Todd, making his stomach shake.
The blasts were set off by long fuses, but were timed
to go together, starting as bursts of whitehot flame,
then erupting black smoke from the points where
the charges were laid. The underpinnings of the
trestle were carried away by the torpedos, but the
superstructure remained intact for several more seconds, stretching across the creek with no visible
means of support, as if defying the laws of gravity.
Then, slowly, the tracks began to sag and the ties
started snapping, popping with a series of loud re-
ports like pistol shots, until finally, with a resound-
ing crash and a splash of water, the whole bridge
collapsed into Farley Creek.

"Now, that's the way to do it," Sam said exult-
antly. "We dropped her into the water just as neat
as a pin!"

"I suppose so," Todd said. He let out a sigh.

"Why, what's wrong? You don't sound very en-
thused about it. It was a good job, and it'll delay the
Yankees for at least a week."

"A week," Todd said. "I watched them build that

36

trestle before the war. Do you know how long it took?"

"No."

"It took six weeks. We blow it up in six seconds, and the most we can hope to get out of it is to delay the Yankees for a week. And don't forget, Sam, it was our bridge in the first place. The tracks, the bridges, the roads, everything we are destroying down here belongs to the South. What kind of war is it when we strike at the enemy by destroying the property of our own people?"

"It's a terrible war, Todd, but that's the kind we've got," Sam said. He reached over and put his hand affectionately on his leader's shoulder, then smiled, trying to cheer him up. "But look at it this way. Better to give them one bridge than a whole town."

Todd laughed. "I wonder if they'd take Colonel Culpepper in exchange for the town. If so, I would gladly deliver him to them."

"What would they do with him?" Sam asked, joining in the laughter. "If he was a fish, they'd throw him back."

Sergeant Ward, who had been on lookout, came riding up. "Major, beggin' your pardon, sir, but they's Yankee cavalry acomin'."

"Very well, Sergeant, get the men mounted. We'll ride out of here."

"Ain't we goin' to fight 'em, Major?" Sergeant Ward asked.

Todd smiled. "If the cavalry is here, that means the supply depot at Vaughan is left unguarded. We'll hit it. As long as we are in a destroying mood,

37

I'd like some of the things we destroy to belong to the Yankees."

The train stretched along the track and the engine, which was huge and black, let off occasional breaths of steam, which echoed hollowly back from the tree line. Many of the soldiers were outside the cars, lounging or talking nearby. Most of the men had no idea why they were stopped, or why they had gotten on the train in the first place. It was, they decided, the wisdom of the army to "hurry up and get on the train so you could go a few miles, then get off and wait." There were rumors of course, and some of the rumors, those which said the rebels had blown a bridge, were true.

General Grant was also standing alongside the train, looking back at the soldiers, formless shadows, but each one a human being with his own hopes and fears. As Grant was a general, he didn't depend on rumor, but was privy to the facts. He *knew* that the trestle across Farley Creek had been destroyed.

Grant had a leather case hanging around his neck. To the casual observer, it looked like the case for a pair of binoculars, but when he opened it, those standing nearby saw that it was a container for a whiskey bottle. He pulled the cork from the bottle, turned it up and took several swallows, stuck the cork back on, palmed it in securely, then replaced the bottle. He wiped his mouth and his beard with the back of his hand before he spoke.

"I don't know Farley Creek, Colonel Birdsong," General Grant said to the field commander of the operation. "Is there any way to lay a pontoon bridge across it?"

"No, General," Birdsong said. "It cuts through a gulley, and the bridge had to be built on high trestles."

"I see," Grant said. He sighed. "Well, we might as well take the train back and proceed on foot, don't you think?"

"I agree, General. And after the cavalry takes care of Major Kirk, there will be little resistance until we enter the town itself."

"The cavalry?" Grant asked, raising his eyebrows in question. "What cavalry? There are no cavalry units assigned to this operation."

"I'm talking about Colonel Potter's Third, sir. I sent orders for his men to protect the flanks of the railroad during our assault. And it's a good thing, too, for now I've sent him after Kirk and his band of outlaws."

Grant sighed. "Colonel Birdsong, I think perhaps you had best send the train all the way back to Memphis."

"To Memphis, sir? Whatever for?" Birdsong asked, puzzled.

"We are going to need to resupply if we are to sustain this operation."

"Supplies are not a problem, sir," Birdsong said easily. "We have an adequate stockpile of everything we need at the depot in Vaughan."

"You *had* everything you need in Vaughan," General Grant said. "But if you pulled Colonel Potter's Third away from there, my guess is that is exactly where Major Kirk has gone."

* * *

The Edward Fox Players were up with the morning sun the next day, loading their wagons for the journey to the next town. Their appearance here had been a successful one, a morale boost for the soldiers and townspeople alike, justifying entirely the decision of the Confederate government to allow such troupes free passage across all lines.

The town of Yazoo City was still sleeping peacefully, totally unaware of how close it had come to being a town under siege. The citizens didn't realize what a debt they owed to Todd Kirk, for the destruction of the railroad bridge and the sacking of the supply depot at Vaughan had so totally interrupted the schedule of the Union army that the attack had been canceled. But the townspeople and even the military governor were unaware of their good fortune, so the Edward Fox Players could certainly be excused for their ignorance on the subject as well, and they made preparations to move in total innocence of the events of the evening before.

"Where is Wilkes?" Edward asked. The last item was loaded in the wagon, and all the players were ready to go except John Wilkes Booth. Booth was not only not ready to go, he hadn't even been seen this morning.

"Do us all a favor, Uncle Edward, and leave without him," Jaylene said dryly.

"I second your niece's motion," Hardenburgh said.

"Come, come, we aren't being professional," Edward scolded gently. "Wilkes can be trying sometimes, but he is a young man of talent and ambition. I think we are lucky to have him in our group."

The person who was the subject of their conver-

40

sation arrived at that moment, sauntering down the street as casually as if out for a morning stroll. When he saw the wagons all loaded and ready to go he smiled broadly and came over to them.

"I'm sorry," he said. "Am I late?"

"No, for your purposes, Wilkes, I'd say you are right on time," Hardenburgh said. "After all, you managed to miss out on all the work."

"Please forgive me," Booth said. "I accepted an invitation to stay with an old friend last night. We were talking and I'm afraid I overslept this morning."

"She didn't look all that old to me, Wilkes," Lucy said, laughing.

It was no secret that John Wilkes had spent the night with a woman. He was an exceptionally handsome man, who burned upon the stage like a brilliant light. Most women were drawn to him like moths to a flame, and Booth frequently chose from among the more comely of his admirers as they traveled from town to town.

"Why, Lucy, could it be that you are jealous?" Booth asked.

"Not a bit of it," Lucy replied easily. "Just observant."

Edward gave the order for the players to mount the wagons, and with a whistle at the teams, the two wagons pulled out of Yazoo City, bound for Jackson. Jaylene and Lucy were riding on the wagon with Edward, and Jaylene crawled into the back and stretched out to take a nap.

Jaylene had no idea how long she had slept when she was awakened by voices. Some of the voices she recognized, but others she didn't. She sat up quickly

41

and crawled to the front so she could see. There were several mounted men around the wagon.

"Uncle, what is it?" she asked. "Who are these men, and why are we stopped?"

"Ah, so you are with them, Miss Cooper," one of the men said. "Major Kirk will be pleased."

"Major Kirk?" Jaylene said, anger creeping into her voice. "What does *he* have to do with this?"

"Major Kirk is my commander, ma'am," the man replied. He tipped his hat and smiled broadly, showing an expanse of very white teeth shining brightly from a tanned face. "Allow me to introduce myself. I am Captain Sam Shelton, second in command of Kirk's Raiders."

"Captain Shelton, what is the meaning of this?" Jaylene asked angrily. "Why have you stopped us?"

"Major Kirk's orders, ma'am," Sam said.

"But he has no right to stop us. What does he think he's doing?"

They heard the sound of an approaching horseman and all looked down the road to see as he rode toward them.

"You'll be able to ask the major that for yourself," Sam said. "Here he comes."

"Well, so we meet again," Todd said, reining his horse up as he reached the halted wagons. "And you've met my executive officer as well, I see."

"Major Kirk, what is all this about?" Edward asked. "I have a pass to travel anywhere I wish. I can even go through Yankee lines."

"Oh, I'm not challenging that, Mr. Fox," Todd said easily.

"Well then, why have you stopped us?"

42

"It's simple," Todd said. "I want your group to do a performance for my men tonight."

"But we can't," Edward said. "We have to be in Jackson in two days."

"You are going to be late," Todd said. "Because you aren't going anywhere until you've performed your show for Kirk's Raiders."

"What? Why, this is an outrage, sir," Jaylene said angrily. She looked at her uncle with her eyes flashing fire. "Uncle Edward, tell this—this *creature* to stand aside so that we may proceed." She looked back at Todd. "Colonel Culpepper was right about one thing, sir. You are boorish."

Todd shook his head slowly and clucked his tongue, then rode right up to the wagon so that he was just an inch or so away from her. He looked into her defiant face.

"I had hoped it wouldn't come to this," he said. "I wanted you to do the show voluntarily."

Suddenly he reached out and grabbed her, pulling her with one strong arm off the wagon and laying her across the saddle in front of him with her backside up.

"But by damn you are going to give us a show, one way or the other," he said.

"Kirk, put me down!" Jaylene yelled, though her yell was muffled by the fact that her head was hanging down, because she was thrown across the saddle like a sack of flour. "Put me down!" she shouted again, kicking her legs and flailing her hands.

"Here, go easy there," Todd said. "You'll spook Diablo. I'd hate him to throw us with you like this, wouldn't you?"

"Oh! Kirk, let me up, please!"

"Not until you promise to be a good girl," Kirk said. "I'll let you sit up, but you mustn't try to get away. Do you promise?"

"Yes, I promise," Jaylene said. "Anything, just let me up!"

Todd lifted Jaylene up and set her sideways on the saddle in front of him, as if she were riding side-saddle.

"There now," he said. "Remember your promise to me."

Jaylene put her hand to her hair, adjusting the strands that had fallen out of place during her unceremonious moment across Todd's saddle.

"What . . . what do you want?" Jaylene asked, less defiant than she had been. She had no wish to wind up like a sack of flour again.

"I told you," Todd said. "I want you to put on a show."

"Never," Jaylene said.

"Well, then I'll just keep you until you change your mind. Sam, bring 'em along," Todd said, and with that he put spurs to his horse and, with a frightened Jaylene hanging on before him, galloped away.

Jaylene could see the wagons receding behind them, and it seemed to her that they were going frightfully fast. She was afraid that she was going to fall off, and she had nothing she could cling to, so when Todd put his arm around her, she leaned into it gratefully.

Gradually she adjusted to the rhythm of the ride, and within a short time it wasn't as frightening to her. In fact, with the overhanging boughs of the trees shading the road, and the wind in her hair, it became almost pleasant, though she wouldn't let herself forget how she came to such a state in the first place. As far as she was concerned, she had been kidnapped, and she would show her kidnapper nothing but contempt.

Todd tried to speak to her, but she steadfastly refused to answer him, letting it be known that she strongly disapproved of what he did. Then, when they finally reached their destination, Todd lifted her out of the saddle and dropped her to the ground. Jaylene landed on her feet and didn't fall to the ground, but it was still an unladylike means of dismounting.

"You!" she said, brushing her clothes angrily. "You are a brute!"

"So you can speak after all," Todd said, swinging down easily. "For a while there I was afraid you had been frightened into insensibility. Here is my headquarters. Not quite as nice as Rosecrown and General Grant's headquarters, but nice, don't you think?"

Todd took in the area with a sweep of his arm, and only then did Jaylene notice where they were—in a grassy glade, bordered on one side by a bubbling brook and surrounded by giant cottonwood trees. There were several tents pitched, but the most imposing structure—only by contrast to the tents—was a log cabin which stood on the bank of the stream. Todd took her securely by the arm and led her to the cabin.

The cabin consisted of two rooms. In the front

room there was a table and a few chairs. The back room was a bedroom, with a large double bed nearly filling the entire room.

"You go in there," Todd said. "You can stay there until I decide what I'm going to do with you."

"What do you mean, what you are going to do with me?" Jaylene asked. "You are going to let me go, of course."

"Ah, my dear," Todd said, holding his finger up. "I'm going to let you go *only* if you consent to put on a performance for me."

"Then you'd better make up your mind what you are going to do with me," Jaylene said defiantly. "For I have no intention of being *forced* into performing for you."

"Ah, Miss Cooper, why must you make it so hard on yourself?" Todd asked. "After all, what am I asking? Only that you bring a little cheer to my men and to me. After all, aren't you in that business?"

"Yes," Jaylene said. "But normally our audience doesn't hold a gun to our heads."

"Neither will I hold a gun to your head," Todd said. "Nevertheless, you shall not leave here until you have performed."

Jaylene looked at Todd and smiled at him. It was a challenging smile, without humor. If this was to be a test of wills, then so be it. She turned and walked over to the bed.

"Then I had better get comfortable," she said. "For I suppose I will be here awhile."

CHAPTER FIVE

"What would I want to go for a thing like that
for?

"You just take your orders, soldier, who try to

Despite her confinement, the day was not that
unpleasant for Jaylene. She was not locked in the
bedroom, though it was some hours before she realized that. She lay on the bed until she heard the
sounds and smelled the aromas of the noon meal
being cooked, then she walked over to try the door.
To her surprise it was unlocked, and cautiously she
pushed it open.

In the front room a young soldier sat at the table,
writing on a tablet. He had been so quiet that Jaylene was surprised by his presence, and she hesitated
for a moment, wondering if she should open the
door further. Did the soldier have orders to *shoot*
her if she attempted to escape?

The soldier looked up and smiled. He was terribly
young. Jaylene guessed he couldn't have been more
than seventeen.

"Well, Miss Cooper, did you have a nice nap?
Major Kirk, he told me to look out for you."

"I see," Jaylene said. "And shoot me, I suppose,
if I give you any trouble?"

"What?" the soldier asked with a surprised laugh.

"What would I want to go'n do a thing like that for?"

"Isn't that what you do to prisoners who try to escape?"

"Prisoner? Why, Miss Cooper, ma'am, whatever give you the idea you was a prisoner?"

"What would you call it?"

"Why, ma'am, I thought you was our guest," the young soldier said. "Major Kirk, he told we'uns how decent you'n the others was to come into the field'n give the fightin' soldiers a show same as the soldiers back in the rear."

Something about the soldier's sincerity touched Jaylene, and she softened her stand. After all, he wasn't the one who had captured her. And the soldiers were the reason for the existence of the troupe in the first place. She smiled at him.

"What is your name?"

"Charlie, ma'am," the soldier said. "My name is Charlie Parker." He actually blushed. "Ma'am, iffen you don't mind my sayin' so, why I'd bet you be about the purtiest girl in the whole South."

Jaylene's smile widened. "Thank you, Charlie. It is very nice of you to say such a thing."

"I ain't sayin' nothin', only what's true," Charlie said. "When will you be givin' the show?"

"Well, I'll have to take that up with Major Kirk," Jaylene said, not wanting to commit herself. "Where is he?"

"Major Kirk took a patrol out to see'f the Yankees actually did pull back after we blowed up the railroad bridge last night. They was aimin' to capture Yazoo City, you know, but Major Kirk stopped

49

'em. Major Kirk, why, I'll bet he's the best commander in the whole war. Iffen President Davis was to make Major Kirk a gen'rul, this war'd be over in no time."

"I'm sure that Major Kirk is a wonderful man," Jaylene said sarcastically.

"Yes, ma'am, he is," Charlie said. "I'm glad you see it too." He obviously had not caught the sarcasm in her voice.

Jaylene walked outside into the sunshine and fresh air. She saw soldiers everywhere, doing their laundry, working on their equipment, eating their lunch, or just stretched out in the sun for an afternoon nap. It was an eerie sensation, seeing an army like this. She had seen soldiers up close many times, but always on the march, or in parade, or as spectators for one of the shows she had played. She had never seen them so off guard, so vulnerable, as this.

The smells of cooking permeated the air and made Jaylene quite hungry. Despite herself, she found she was hurrying to the kitchen tent, and when she got there she saw a line of soldiers moving slowly through, getting their tin plates heaped with pork chops, mashed potatoes, and apple butter.

"Here, miss, you kin git in front o' me iffen you'd like," one soldier offered.

"I don't have a plate," Jaylene said.

Before she got the sentence out of her mouth half a dozen plates were offered to her, and when she chose one, the man to whom the plate belonged smiled broadly and accepted the congratulations of the others.

"My, do you always eat this well?" Jaylene asked as she saw the food being placed on her plate.

50

The soldiers laughed.

"Did I say something funny?"

"Yes'm, though I know you didn't mean to," the soldier who was serving the food said. "You see, lots o' time we don't have nothin' to eat but johnny cakes, 'n we're might glad to have that. But sometimes we get lucky, like yesterday when we was able to help ourself to Yankee supplies. You're eatin' Yankee food, ma'am."

One of Kirk's Raiders was coming back for seconds, rubbing his stomach with satisfaction as he did so.

"No wonder them blue bellies is all so fat'n sassy lookin' all the time. Iffen I could eat this way, why, I'd soak my pants in kerosene'n go attack the devil hisself—beggin' your pardon, ma'am."

Jaylene took her plate and was escorted to a large stump which served quite well as a table. From somewhere a box was produced for a chair, and Jaylene ate her meal in relative comfort, while soldiers crowded around her, sitting on the ground, balancing their plates on their knees or laps.

"Jaylene, hello," Lucy called, and Jaylene looked up to see Lucy being shown around by Captain Shelton. "Isn't that a marvelous meal?"

"Lucy, are you all right?" Jaylene asked. "Uncle Edward and the others, where are they?"

"They're getting set up for tonight's show," Lucy said. She walked over toward the tree trunk where Jaylene was eating, and the soldiers all stood. "Please," Lucy said. "Sit down."

"What do you mean, they're setting up for tonight's show? You mean Uncle Edward is going to *do* it? He's going to let that boorish Major Kirk bully him into putting on a show?"

"Miss Cooper, Major Kirk isn't like that," Captain Shelton said easily.

"Oh, no, I'm sure he isn't," Jaylene said. "After all, he is your glorious commander. I've already heard all about that. Well, I know him for what he *really* is, and I have no intention of being in a show tonight."

"Oh, Jaylene, please don't be like that," Lucy begged. "Even if you are upset with Major Kirk, think of the others."

Jaylene looked around at the men, all with such hopeful looks on their faces, and their silent appeal, plus Lucy's eloquent plea, finally won her over. She let a sigh of resignation escape from her lips, and then she smiled.

"Oh, very well," she said. "But it's for the soldiers, and certainly *not* for Major Todd Kirk."

The soldiers let out a loud hurrah, and when others in the camp heard the cheer and inquired as to its reason, they too cheered.

Jaylene finished her meal, then joined Lucy, as Captain Shelton showed them around. Jaylene couldn't help but notice that Captain Shelton was displaying more than polite military manners to Lucy. He took long, sidelong glances at her when she wasn't looking, and on those few occasions when it was necessary for him to touch her, to assist her over some obstacle, his hand seemed to linger a bit longer than necessary. And, Jaylene noticed, Lucy was not discouraging his actions.

Jaylene mentioned it to her later that afternoon

52

as they set up a temporary stage for the performance.

"Oh, I didn't think I was letting it show," Lucy said, blushing at the remark.

"Then you *do* like him?" Jaylene asked.

"Yes."

"But how can you, Lucy? After all, he and Major Kirk actually *kidnapped* us."

"Not really, Jaylene. They just wanted us to do a show for their men, that's all. Besides . . . when I'm close to Captain Shelton, or when he touches me, something happens inside. I can't quite explain it, but I get all warm and tingly, and my blood feels like it turns to hot tea."

Jaylene nearly gasped. She hid her strange reaction to Lucy's pronouncement, but she realized, with a sudden flush, that Lucy had described the exact sensations she felt around Todd Kirk. She had never admitted it to herself, but those feelings were there, and now that Lucy had put them into words, she felt them again.

"That's . . . that's silly," Jaylene said aloud. And though it sounded as if she were speaking to Lucy, she was chastising herself.

"I . . . I suppose so," Lucy said, a little hurt by her friend's remark. "But I can't help it."

Jaylene put her hand quickly on Lucy's arm. "Oh, dear, forgive me for saying that so rudely. I didn't mean anything by it. I just meant that . . . well, you are such a wonderful person and such a beautiful girl that I don't see how anyone could be good enough for you."

Lucy laughed and hugged Jaylene. "Oh, Jaylene, you are too good to me," she said.

The rest of the afternoon passed quickly, and soon it was time for supper. After supper, they were going to put on their show. Yet Todd Kirk was not back from patrol.

Jaylene had not spoken about it, but she had spent the entire afternoon and evening wondering if Kirk would return in time for the show. But why should she be so concerned?

Finally, it was show time. The soldiers were in the audience, the stage lanterns were lit, and they were ready to begin. But still Major Todd Kirk had not appeared.

From her position in the wings, Jaylene searched the audience one more time. It was difficult to see everyone in the dark, but she was certain that he was not there. She felt a slight tinge of disappointment, then anger. If he didn't even care enough about the show to be here, why did he go to all the trouble to kidnap her in the first place?

Major Todd Kirk was a strange man, she decided. And an aggravating one as well.

Todd Kirk did not return during the performance, nor for some time afterward. In fact, he did not return until long after Jaylene had gone to bed in the big double bed in the log cabin. She had been lying in the drowsy state between sleep and wakefulness when she heard the horses return, then the voices outside. She recognized Kirk's voice, though she didn't understand what was being said.

Well, no matter. She had put on the show, and tomorrow they would leave. Surely he wouldn't keep her any longer than that. Besides, she thought, he couldn't have been all that interested in her performance or he would not have gone out on the patrol. She rolled over, fluffed the pillow, and went back to sleep.

When Jaylene awakened later, she saw that the room was brightly lit by the full moon. She sat up in bed and looked around. At first she was puzzled as to why she was awake; then she realized that she was awake because she had heard a sound. Someone had come into her room!

Jaylene's heart pounded fiercely. "Who is it?" she asked. "What are you doing in here?"

"What?" a startled male voice answered. "What am I doing here? This is my room. What are *you* doing here?"

Jaylene recognized the unmistakable voice of Major Todd Kirk. She drew the bedclothes more tightly about her, for she had removed her dress and was sleeping in her undergarments only.

"Major Kirk, you get out of here. You get out of here at once!"

Kirk stepped into the moonlight, and Jaylene could see his light blue eyes flashing brightly in his handsome face. He was smiling broadly.

"Oho, and where would you have me go, my pretty one? After all, I am the commander here, and this is my bed. I am honored that you have chosen to share it with me."

"What?" Jaylene gasped. "Why, I have done no such thing, sir!"

"Oh? Well, here you are, Miss Cooper, in my bed, while the rest of your troupe sleeps in their wagons."

55

"But—but—when we arrived you brought me here," Jaylene said. "I thought you meant me to sleep here as well?"

"I did," Kirk said. He had already tossed his hat to one side, and now he was unbuttoning the grey shirt he wore. "And I can't tell you how pleased I am that you accepted me."

"But please," Jaylene said. "You don't understand. I didn't know what you meant." Her voice broke with a catch of fear.

"Don't be frightened," Kirk said. "I'm not going to hurt you."

Jaylene watched, paralyzed by what she was seeing, but unable to look away. Kirk unbuckled his belt, then let his breeches fall. Within a moment he stood before her totally naked.

It was terrifying—and fascinating. She noticed a small smile playing across Kirk's lips.

"Now," he said, "we are even. I saw you naked in the river, and you see me naked here. I tell you, you are a very beautiful woman. Now you tell me . . . what do you think of me?"

"I . . . I wouldn't know," Jaylene said. She found the strength to turn her head away from him.

"Can't you be honest with me?"

"I'm afraid these circumstances don't permit it," Jaylene answered, averting her eyes.

Kirk laughed quietly, then reached down and put one hand on her shoulder and the other on the edge of the blanket. He started to remove it.

"No," Jaylene said, her cry short and ineffectual. She tried to pull the blanket back into place, but she couldn't.

"I'm the commander here," Todd said easily. "It will do you no good to fight me. I will have my way."

Todd pulled the blanket away and looked at her. The silken undergarment she was wearing clung to her like a second skin. The nipples of her breasts stood out in bold relief.

"I tell you again," Todd said softly, almost reverently. "You are a very beautiful woman." And this time there was so much conviction in his voice that Jaylene felt strangely moved by it.

Todd touched her nipple lightly. Never had Jaylene experienced such a sensation. His finger felt hot and cold at the same time, and a jolt of pleasure coursed through her body.

"Please," she said. "What are you doing?"

Todd pushed her back gently, then bent over her and kissed her lips. His kiss was tender, yet with an urgency that was barely held in check. He moved his hands across her body, and Jaylene felt the heat rising, as if his hands were kindling flames within her.

Jaylene shut her eyes tightly. She fought against the rising sensations. She would not succumb to them. She would not let him have his way with her! But even as she attempted to stop the wave of sensation, her emotions raced ahead, out of control.

"Please," she murmured, as she felt his hand move down along her silk-encased body, then stop between her legs at the part that was now most sensitive.

Please stop, or please go on? In truth, she didn't really know. The fire within Jaylene rose higher and higher, and soon she was unable to control her own hands, which moved as if self-guided to feel the smooth muscles of Todd's naked body.

"I'll not force myself on you, Jaylene Cooper," Todd said. "You'll say yes, or I'll not go on."

Jaylene's body ached for fulfillment. She longed to go further.

"What will it be?" Todd asked. "Shall I go on?"

Oh, yes, I want it, I want it, Jaylene thought. But no . . . what was he saying? Was he asking for her permission? Was he asking her to make it right?

"You must tell me if you want it," Todd said again.

Jaylene longed to say the words. With every fiber of her being she wanted to know the sweet surrender that would be hers if she but said the word. And yet, from some source of strength within her, a strength she didn't know she possessed, she managed to say no.

"No!" she said, and her body, which had gone limp and weak with desire, managed to find the will to resist.

"No?" Todd asked, pulling away from her, clearly puzzled by her sudden change of heart.

"Please," Jaylene said. Now, weakened by the ordeal, and shaken by her own strange, tumultuous passions, she began to cry.

"Don't cry," Todd said. He stood up and began dressing. "Please," he said. "Don't cry. I was serious when I said I wouldn't come to you unless you wanted me to."

"And what made you think I would want to?" Jaylene asked. "Did you think that because I am an actress that I am also a tramp?"

"No, no, of course not," Todd said. He was fully dressed now, and he looked down at her. When Jaylene looked into his face she saw tenderness and concern that she had never seen in any man before and, strangely, it moved her as deeply as his kisses and skilled hands had done but moments before. "I think you are the most beautiful and desirable woman I have ever known," he said.

His words went straight to Jaylene's heart, and she almost called him back to her at that moment. But from somewhere she found the strength to resist, and when he left the room, she fell back onto her pillow, crying bitter tears. Her body ached with the pain of longing, and her mind reeled with the shame of wanting. In addition, she was confused. She should hate him, but she could not. She was miserable.

CHAPTER SIX

"Halt! Who goes there?"

"It's me, Major Kirk."

"Major Kirk, sir, I thought you was in bed. What are you doin' out this time of night?"

"I'm going to make a night patrol, Sergeant. Tell the pickets to be on the lookout for me when I come back in the morning. I wouldn't want to be shot by my own men."

"Yes, sir, Major, they'll be watchin'."

Jaylene heard the conversation just outside the window, right after Todd left her room. The voices were muffled, but she could hear in the inflection of Todd's voice the same degree of denied longing, the same confusion that pulled at her own heart. How she wanted to leap out of bed and run to the door to tell him to come back! And yet she knew that she would not, for she lacked the courage.

Todd, at least, had the advantage of being able to go out on a patrol to get away from everything, to take his mind off the disquieting events just passed. But Jaylene had to stay here, to lie in the bed of torment of her own making, to face the shame of her want and the ache of her heart all alone.

When, a moment later, she heard the hoofbeats as Todd rode away, she wished that she was on the horse with him, and that they were riding away together to start a new life, somewhere away from the war and all heartbreak.

Heartbreak. Jaylene knew a great deal about heartbreak. For it was heartbreak and Emily McLean that had killed her father.

Jaylene had but to close her eyes to see again the face of her father—and of the woman she had once called her friend.

"Stand by the bow line!" Captain Cooper had yelled down from the pilot house.

"Standin' by the bow line, sir!" came the answer from a huge black man who stood on the bow, holding a coil of rope loosely by his side.

"Engine room, stand by to reverse the paddle!"

The captain's order was repeated by another man who stood on deck, shouting it into the place the stokers called the hell-hole. Then he yelled a reply back to the captain.

"Engine room standin' by, sir!"

Jaylene was eighteen them, the daughter of the master of the *Delta Mist*. The *Delta Mist* was the fastest, finest packet boat on the Mississippi. She had the most elegant passenger accommodations in service; her dining room was famous up and down the river for the food it served; and Miss Emily McLean, who entertained in the grand salon nightly, was known far and wide as "The Songbird of the River."

Emily McLean was thirty-four years old, and she was as beautiful as she was talented. Jaylene was sure she had never seen a more beautiful woman any-where, and she was proud that Emily was not only her friend but her teacher as well, for Emily had dis-covered Jaylene's talent, and was developing it on the stage of the *Delta Mist*.

There was also a very special relationship be-tween Emily McLean and Jaylene's father, and it had been going on for the last four years. At first Jaylene did not know about it; then, when she found out, she was hurt and even a little jealous. But grad-ually she learned to accept it, then to relish it. The fact that her father and Emily seemed to be flaunt-ing convention didn't disturb her. They were in love. It didn't matter that they weren't married. They were in love, and that was all that was neces-sary.

"Emily, are you going ashore in Natchez?" Jay-lene asked. She and Emily were standing in the grand salon, looking through the glass at the dock-ing procedure as the *Delta Mist* headed for the bank at Natchez.

"Reverse the paddle!" Jaylene heard her father yell, and the order was repeated by the man on deck. The boat shuddered as the paddle wheel stopped, then started beating at the river in the opposite direction of the drift of the boat. Jaylene felt herself leaning slightly, as the forward motion of the boat was checked sharply.

"Secure the bowline!"

The boat bumped lightly against the bank, and then stopped. The whistle sounded, a bell rang, and several people cheered.

Emily had been watching the proceedings with

Jaylene, staring through the window as if deep in thought.

"Well?" Jaylene asked again. "Are you?"

This time Emily heard Jaylene and she turned toward her. "I'm sorry, dear. What did you ask me?"

"I asked if you were going to go ashore in Natchez?"

"Oh . . . uh . . . yes. Yes, I'm afraid I have to," she said.

"Good, good, then I won't have to go alone. Oh, we'll have great fun. I know where there is the most divine hat shop, and we can—"

"I'm going to have to go alone," Emily said, interrupting Jaylene.

"What? Why?" Jaylene asked.

"It's just something that I have to do," Emily said. "Excuse me."

Emily turned and walked out of the grand salon, leaving Jaylene standing there, puzzled by her odd behavior. Emily was always ready to go ashore with her. What was bothering her today?

Jaylene was more than surprised by Emily's strange behavior. She was a little hurt by it as well, but she put it aside, for it was difficult to feel any emotion save excitement when the *Delta Mist* docked at a major river town. Besides, if Emily said she had something to do, then she must have, because Jaylene knew that Emily would never lie to her.

Jaylene weaved her way through the passengers until she reached the area marked "For crew only," then slipped through the gate to go on up to the pilothouse. She had lived on board riverboats for most of her eighteen years, ever since her mother had died of pneumonia when Jaylene was four.

"Well, darlin', now that the work is done you've come to the wheelhouse, have you?" her father said as Jaylene stepped inside. He was forty-two, a ruggedly handsome man, broad of shoulder and narrow of hip, with eyes the same shade as Jaylene's. He was relating from the docking, and he sat on a cushioned bench, smoking a pipe.

"Is working what you call it when you hit the bank so hard as to break all the dishes in the salon?" Jaylene teased.

"Oh?" her father asked with a raised eyebrow. "Well, I'd like to see another captain on the river make a more gentle landing."

"There are none who could, Dad, and you know it," Jaylene said, giving her father a hug.

"Now, that's more like it," her father said, squeezing his daughter affectionately. "But say, what are you doing up here? Not that I don't appreciate a visit now and then, you understand, but generally when we dock you and Emily are off on some adventure together, and I'm left all alone."

"I don't know," Jaylene said.

Captain Cooper laughed. "You don't know? You don't know what?"

"I don't know why Emily and I aren't off on some adventure. I asked her if she wanted to go, and she said that she had something else to do."

"Well, I'm sure she did," Captain Cooper said easily.

"But Dad, that's not like Emily. She was acting so mysterious . . . she didn't even say she'd meet me somewhere later on or anything."

66

"Well, she's one of those showpeople," Captain Cooper said. "And showpeople are different from everyone else. You ought to know that, darlin', you're a showperson yourself now."

"Nevertheless, I'm not that different," Jaylene said. "And I don't understand what it is Emily has to do."

"Never mind about it, girl. Like as not it's something that's important only to her."

"I'm sure you're right," Jaylene said. She smiled. "Besides, I have no right to monopolize all of her time anyway. I need to save some for you."

"Now, I'd say that is mighty generous of you, daughter," Captain Cooper said.

"Of course, if you and Emily were . . ." Jaylene started, then she blushed and stopped in midsentence and looked away. She stared through the window of the pilot house for a long time, looking out over the river and the steady current and the quick-flowing logs which were being swept downstream. There was an awkward silence, which was finally broken by her father.

"If she and I were married, were you going to say?"

"Yes," Jaylene said quietly. "Uh, I was just going to say that if you were married you'd have all the time together you wanted."

"I see. And that would make you feel better, wouldn't it?"

"A little," Jaylene admitted. "I wouldn't have to pretend that I didn't overhear some of the things I overhear."

"Come here, darlin'," Captain Cooper said, and he opened his arms in invitation. He held her close

67

to him. "I know you don't understand, sweetheart. But you have been very tolerant of your old dad, and I want you to know how much I appreciate it. You let people say anything they want to say. It doesn't bother me a bit. I've got the love of the two finest women in the world—my daughter and Emily. I couldn't ask for anything more."

"Then neither will I," Jaylene said. "I tell you what, I'll just go ashore by myself, and I'll have a fine time."

"No you won't," Captain Cooper said.

"What? Why?"

Captain smiled broadly. "I'll go ashore with you. *We'll* have a fine time," he said, correcting her.

"Good," Jaylene said enthusiastically. "I'll just run down to my cabin and get dressed. Oh, can we eat ashore? I heard some of the passengers talking about a nice restaurant in town."

"Philippe would be awfully upset if he knew you preferred to eat ashore," Captain Cooper said.

"Oh, I don't prefer it, Papa, and you know it," Jaylene said. "But I do like to do something different every now and then."

Captain Cooper laughed. "I know, darlin'. I was just teasin' you, that's all. Now, you go and get ready. We'll have a fine time."

And they did have a fine time. They ate in the nicest restaurant, walked all through the town looking at the beautiful houses, and even went to the hat shop to buy a new hat for Jaylene. In fact, it was dark by the time they returned to the *Delta Mist.*

"Oh, won't Emily be sorry she didn't go with us now?" Jaylene said. "I wonder if she is back? I'll show her my new hat."

"And when will you wear it?" Captain Cooper teased. "You have a dozen more just as pretty."

"Oh, no I don't," Jaylene said, touching the hat and preening a bit. "This is the most beautiful hat I have ever seen. And Emily will agree with me, you'll see."

They were walking down the companionway toward Jaylene's room, and they passed Emily's cabin.

"I wonder if she's home?" Jaylene said quietly. She tried the door and it was locked. "That's funny, she's not back yet."

"Maybe she's in her cabin asleep," Captain Cooper suggested.

"Well then, we'll just wake her and have a party," Jaylene said. "To celebrate my new hat." She smiled broadly. "I have a key to her door. We'll go in and wake her."

Before Captain Cooper could say anything, his daughter had already unlocked the door and swung it open. "Surprise!" Jaylene called out, stepping inside.

But the surprise was on Jaylene and her father, for there in the bed was Emily and some man Jaylene had never seen before. And they were making love.

"Oh, Jaylene, Virgil, oh, my God, no!" Emily gasped. She made a desperate attempt to cover herself with a blanket.

"Virgil?" the man said. "So this is Virgil Cooper, the one you are so in love with?"

"Emily . . . what?" Jaylene said, feeling her knees weaken and her head spin. "What is going on?"

Jaylene heard her father give a gasping sob. She

turned to look at him, and never had she seen a greater look of pain on anyone's face.

"Papa, oh, Papa, I'm so sorry," Jaylene said.

"Virgil, please, you don't understand," Emily said.

"I understand perfectly," Captain Cooper finally managed to say. He took a deep breath, then let it out audibly, slowly. "Madam, please be off this boat within the hour, bag and baggage."

"Please, Virgil."

"One hour, madam," Captain Cooper said. He turned and walked quickly away.

"Jaylene, go to your papa," Emily pleaded. "Beg him to listen to me, to let me explain."

"Explain? Explain what? That you are a whore?" Jaylene said coldly. "I hate you for what you have done to Papa, Emily McLean. And I will hate you for the rest of my life."

Jaylene turned and left then, hearing Emily's pitiful pleas, as well as the mocking laughter of the man who was with her.

Emily did leave the boat that night, and Jaylene never saw her again. Her father took up drinking shortly after that. He had always been a heavy drinker, but never had he drunk as much as he did then. He spent days in drunken stupors, and the *Delta Mist* had to rely on the experience of the rest of the crew.

But the character of the *Delta Mist* changed. The first thing Virgil Cooper did was to dismantle the stage in the grand salon, and give orders to Jaylene that never again would she be in another show.

The *Delta Mist* was no longer the happy ship it

used to be. Passengers found it more difficult to be gay around a sullen captain.

Captain Cooper's moodiness caused the loss of business, and the loss of business made Captain Cooper even more sullen, so that it was a vicious cycle. He became moodier and moodier, and more and more distant from Jaylene. Then, one dark and moonless night, Virgil Cooper slipped, or stepped, over the edge of the boat. No one ever knew whether he did it on purpose or not, for the river's current caught him up and he was gone in an instant. The *Delta Mist* tied up for the night and searched far into the next morning, but they couldn't find him. It wasn't until three days later that his body washed ashore in the small Missouri town of Commerce.

Jaylene had no idea how deeply into debt her father had sunk until after his death, for it was then learned that the *Delta Mist* had been mortgaged from her keel to the top of her great twin stacks. Jaylene was left without a penny to her name.

That was when her uncle stepped into the picture. Edward Fox, the owner of a small traveling theater, offered Jaylene a job and the protection of a loving relative, and Jaylene jumped at the chance. She was anxious to get back into show business anyway, because it was a business she loved with all her heart.

And it was a business in which she might again encounter Emily McLean. Jaylene very much wanted to do that, for she felt that she had a score to settle with the woman who had so deceived her father.

* * *

Jaylene drifted off to sleep thinking about her father and Emily, and as she had no idea how long she had been asleep, she had no idea what time it was when the door to her room opened again.

The sound of the door closing awakened her, and she turned to see what it was. The moon, which had been so bright earlier in the night, had now set, and it was very dark. She could make out the form, though not the features, of the person who had come in.

Kirk! she thought. He had returned from his night patrol, and now sought to finish what he started. Jaylene took a quick breath, intending to tell him that she had not changed her mind, that she had said no and she meant it, but, oddly, no sound came from her lips. Why couldn't she speak? Was it because she really wanted him? Was it because she wanted him to make love to her so badly that she dared not speak for fear he would leave again?

No, she thought. *No, it isn't like that at all.*

The intruder came to her bed and, despite herself, she felt a rising heat, a quickening pulse, a tingling sensation of want, and she knew that she wouldn't send him away this time.

Then, out of the darkness, a hand appeared, and a handkerchief was clasped over her face. For a quick instant that which had been desire turned to confusion, then to fear! A sickeningly sweet, cloying sensation overtook her, and she felt her head spinning . . . spinning . . . until all was black.

Then Jaylene was dreaming, and in the dream she was with Todd Kirk. The lips that touched hers were Todd's lips, and she felt her arms go around Todd's shoulders. She could feel him, but she couldn't see him, and everything moved with sweet slowness.

Jaylene knew she should resist what was happening to her. She should fight, but how could she fight against a dream? Wasn't this merely the longings and desires of her own heart? What harm could come from giving in to the hungers of the spirit, if it was in mind only?

Then something more began to happen. The sweet tenderness of her dream gave way to a rising sensation unlike any she had ever experienced before. Her blood stirred, and a hot, surging fire flamed in her loins, sweeping upward, consuming her whole body in searing wonder, bursting over her like a fountain of color in exquisite delight.

And then, as the passion receded, she saw Todd's face once again, floating in a lavender fog, until the fog closed over everything, blotting out all, until the dream was gone, and she was sleeping peacefully once more.

CHAPTER SEVEN

The morning light spilled in through the high window of the log cabin, carrying with it the rich aromas of bacon frying in the pan and breakfast campfires. The noises of the awakening camp drifted in, and Jaylene found herself slowly abandoning sleep. She stretched luxuriously and felt a warm, sweet ache in her loins. For a moment she drifted with the delightful feelings and thought languidly of the dream she had had the night before.

It wasn't a dream!

Jaylene suddenly realized that the strange events of the night before had really happened! The dull ache in her own body was proof of that. She sat up in bed and felt her cheeks burning in shame. She looked down at herself, examining her hands, arms, body and legs, seeing if she could discern any difference, because she was not the same woman who had gone to bed last night. She was not a virgin.

Jaylene swung her legs out of bed and walked over toward the door which separated the bedroom from the small room out front. She was aware of the soreness in her limbs and, even as she thought of it, she was cognizant of a new dampness between her legs. She opened the door and peered through. Todd Kirk was sitting at the table, and he saw the door crack open.

"Good morning," Todd called, smiling brightly. "I've sent for our breakfast. It will be here soon."

Jaylene slammed the door shut in anger. How *dare* he sit out there awaiting breakfast with her, as if nothing had happened last night!

Jaylene heard a knock on the door.

"Miss Cooper? Miss Cooper, hurry and get dressed. I think your Uncle Edward wants to leave right after you eat," Todd said.

Yes, Jaylene thought. *Yes, leave. It would be wonderful to get out of this accursed place, and away from this beast of a man.*

Jaylene dressed quickly, then went into the other room. Breakfast was just arriving. Todd stood and pulled out a chair for her.

"It is good of you to take your breakfast with me," Todd said. Jaylene took her seat without so much as a word. "I also didn't get a chance to thank you last night for performing for my men."

"I'm sure you didn't get a chance," Jaylene said. "You were terribly *busy*." She twisted her mouth on the word busy.

Todd was a little surprised by her tone of voice, and the expression on his face registered his surprise.

"Look," he said. "I know you must wonder why I went to all the bother to get you to perform and then not even show up myself, but I really was busy. And, as I said, I was only looking out for my men."

"I'm sure of it, Major Kirk," Jaylene said coldly. "But I wasn't referring to the fact that you were

77

missing at the performance, and you know it. I was talking about later."

Todd looked down at his plate in quick shame.

"Yes," he said contritely. "I guess there is no way I can apologize for that. I acted like a scroundrel, and I admit it. I can't expect you to forgive me."

Tears began to slide down Jaylene's cheeks. "That's all you can say?" she said. "After what you did, you sit there and say you acted like a scoundrel but there is no way you can apologize? What about me? My life has been ruined by your act."

"Ruined?" Todd asked, looking up in confusion. "Miss Cooper, I hardly think that my momentary indiscretion ruined your life."

"Momentary indiscretion, you call it? You came into my room and you raped me, but that is only a momentary indiscretion?"

"Raped you? What are you talking about? I didn't rape you."

"Then I would like to know what it was," Jaylene said. "You drugged me with some foul-smelling potion, and while I was in a stupor you had your way with me. Did you not mean it, earlier, when you said you would heed to my wishes?"

"Miss Cooper, what on earth are you talking about? I didn't drug you, and I certainly didn't rape you. I'll admit that I was not on my best behavior last night. I . . . I had no business to disrobe before you. But I told you I would not force myself upon you, and I did not. I left your room, as you well know."

"Yes," Jaylene challenged accusingly. "You left it, only to return later in the night, when I was asleep. Then you had your way with me."

"I assure you, madam, if you entertained a lover during the night, it was not I."

"How dare you deny it?" Jaylene said, now weeping openly. "Do you think I could be *mistaken* about such a thing?"

"Yes, madam, if, as you say, someone did come to your room. I was gone for the entire night."

"Who went with you?"

"No one. I went alone."

"I see," Jaylene said. She dabbed at her eyes with the napkin. "How terribly convenient that must be for you. As you were alone, there is no one who can deny your story."

"Nor confirm it," Todd said. "So you will just have to take my word for it."

"Take your *word* for it? You forget, Major Kirk, I am the wounded party. *I* was the one raped. And *I* know it was you."

Todd's breakfast was only half eaten, but he stood up anyway and looked across the table at Jaylene.

"I will not carry on with this conversation," he said. "I am going to check on your uncle now. I suggest you eat quickly and join him. I imagine he is most anxious to be on his way."

"Thank you," Jaylene said, standing as well. "But I've had about all of your hospitality I can take. I've no wish to place myself any further in your debt."

Jaylene left the log cabin, and saw her uncle's two wagons drawn up and ready to go. Several of the soldiers were gathered around the wagons, and Wilkes Booth was regaling them with stories. Captain Shelton was astride his horse next to the first wagon, talking to Lucy Wade, who was smiling and flirting back.

"So, niece," Edward called. "You are ready to go now, are you? Very good, we will get underway."

"Are you all right?" Lucy asked, as Jaylene approached the wagon.

Why did she ask that? Jaylene wondered. Did the fact that she was no longer a virgin show in her face? She wished she had a mirror.

"Yes, I'm fine," Jaylene said. As she climbed into the wagon, she noticed Booth and Hardenburgh looking at her, as if they, too, could discern some difference in her appearance. She knew she would not be able to hide her shame long. But she knew, too, that she would not be defeated by this. She would hold her head up, no matter what. "Let's go," she said. "I'm anxious to quit this place."

Todd Kirk watched the wagons leave. He was hurt by Jaylene's bitter indictment of him, but he was confused too. Did she actually believe he had come to see her in the middle of the night? Or had someone else come?

"Charlie," he called to the young soldier who had been left in charge of Jaylene.

"Yes, sir?"

"Did anyone come to see Miss Cooper last night?"

"When, sir?"

"After I left. In the cabin, did anyone come to see her?"

"Oh, no sir," Charlie said.

"You are positive?"

"Yes sir," Charlie said. "I slept in the front room,

Major. If anyone had come, I would have known it."

"Thanks," Todd said.

"Why'd you ask that, Major? Was Miss Cooper afraid, 'cause she thought she wasn't bein' protected last night?"

"No," Todd said. "No, I was just wondering, that's all."

So, he thought, *nobody came to see her after all.* But then, that wasn't too surprising. After all, she had not only insisted that someone came, she had insisted that it was *he* who came, and Todd knew that was wrong. And, as she herself had said, it wasn't something a girl was likely to be mistaken about. She wasn't mistaken, Todd decided. She was merely lying. Though why, and to what purpose, he had no idea.

Jaylene sat on the seat of the wagon, watching the wheel turn. She had been staring at it for so long that it had become almost hypnotic, and she could see the patterns the spokes made as they interrupted the light and threw shadows on the ground. The roadbed was covered with a fine, dry powder, which adhered to the steel rims of the wheels for perhaps one half-revolution, then streamed off into small rooster tails of dust. It was soft, easy going for the team now, but in rain it would turn into mud with nearly the consistency of quicksand, and the road would become all but impassable.

Tiger lilies, morning glories, and chicory blossoms decorated the roadside, while in the trees singing cardinals and an inquisitive pair of indigo buntings provided splashes of vivid red and bright blue color. The sky overhead was crystal blue, with only a few white cotton balls of cloud. It was an exceptionally lovely day, and yet Jaylene was oblivious to it all.

Why had Todd denied it when she challenged him this morning? Surely he didn't think he could do such a thing and get away with it, did he? And why did he come back after he said he would not force himself on her?

"Jaylene," Lucy finally said, breaking the silence. "You have been so pensive this morning."

"I'm sorry," Jaylene said. She sighed. "I suppose I am just glad to leave."

"Did you really think it that bad?" Lucy asked. "I thought it quite pleasant."

"They had no right to kidnap us."

"Oh, Jaylene, you aren't being fair," Lucy said. "They didn't really kidnap us. And besides, those boys probably needed our show more than the people we normally perform for. I was glad to do it."

"You are just struck with Captain Shelton," Jaylene accused.

Jaylene was angry with Todd Kirk, and she was angry with herself. As a result she spoke the words much more sharply than she intended, and Lucy looked quickly at the ground in confused hurt.

"I . . . I do like him," she admitted.

Jaylene realized then how it had sounded, and she smiled and put her arm around the other woman's shoulder, pulling her close.

"Lucy, don't mind me," she said. "I didn't mean that the way it sounds. I'm sure Captain Shelton is a fine man, especially if you like him. But you are so fine that I can never be convinced that *any* man is good enough for you. Will you forgive my shortness?"

"Of course," Lucy said. "Though I wish you had gotten to know Major Kirk as I did Captain Shelton. He is such a handsome man that I just know the two of you would make a wonderful couple."

Edward chuckled. He had been quietly driving, and obviously listening to their conversations.

"You know," he said. "It has been my observation that God made woman into a matchmaker. Women do not like the natural order of things. They must pair everything and everyone off."

"Oh," Lucy gasped. Then she giggled and put her hand over her mouth as if to hold back the bubbles of laughter. "Mr. Fox, sometimes you are so quiet that I just forget you are there."

"I'm not here," Edward said. "You girls just go right on talking."

"You'd like that, wouldn't you, Uncle Edward?" Jaylene said. She too laughed. "That way you'd have all the latest gossip. You are worse than any old woman about such things."

"What gossip?" Edward asked. "When King David entertained Bathsheba, that was gossip. Today it is Biblical history."

"Well, I can assure you, Uncle, nothing we may say or do will ever be considered history," Jaylene said.

"No," Edward agreed. "Not what we say or do, but what we *see* will be written about by historians for years to come. This is a great war, my dear. It is a war with implications for all mankind."

83

"I know," Jaylene said. She sighed. "And history will treat the South poorly, I'm afraid, no matter how the war comes out."

"Why do you say such a thing?" Edward asked.

"Because we are fighting this war to protect the right to own slaves. Uncle, Papa paid the Negroes on his boat. They were all free men. And you've never owned slaves either. Besides, I don't even believe it is right to own another human being."

"The great myth of this war, Jaylene, is that the Yankees are fighting to free the Negroes," Edward said. "Nothing could be further from the truth. In fact, the majority of the people in the South do not own slaves."

"Then why are we fighting?" Jaylene wanted to know.

"We are fighting for the right to be free of Federal interference," Edward said. "And every Southerner, slaveowner or not, believes in that principle. That is what future historians will record."

"Lucy," Jaylene said. "You lived in a house in which there were slaves, didn't you?"

"Yes," Lucy said quietly.

"Well, what do you think? Were they mistreated? Don't you think it is evil?"

"They weren't mistreated," Lucy said. "But I don't think it is right to keep other people in bondage, whether they are mistreated or not."

"There, you see, Uncle?" Jaylene said. "Lucy agrees with me. Now if we could only get our governments to agree."

"Perhaps some day they will, my child," Edward said. "Perhaps someday they will."

84

CHAPTER EIGHT

the Jaylene said, "Oh, yes, I did. Did you see
ing. She held up the rose.
Lucy ... "That the ... ... "Something?" She

The Edward Fox Players were a smash in Jackson. They also played in Brandon, Canton, Kasciusko, and Durant. It was in Durant that the roses began to arrive.

Jaylene had left the stage after the final curtain call, and when she returned to the dressing table she saw a single long-stemmed rose there. It was identical to the rose Todd Kirk had given her in Yazoo City.

"You may retrieve your rose, Major Kirk," she said. "I don't want it."

"What?" Lucy asked, calling over from her dressing table. The theater had been set up in a warehouse, and the dressing rooms were nothing but canvas-divided partitions behind the makeshift stage. Lucy's dressing room was next to Jaylene's.

Jaylene looked around her room, though as it consisted of only a table, a chair, and a couple of boxes, there was no way anyone could be hiding there.

Lucy pulled the canvas door aside and peeked in. "Did you say something?" she asked.

"No," Jaylene said. "Uh, yes, I did. Did you see this?" She held up the rose.

"Oh," Lucy said. "Isn't that beautiful?" She walked over to take it.

"Do you have any idea how it got here?"

"From one of your admirers, I suppose," Lucy answered. She held the bloom to her nose and sniffed. "Umm, it smells so good. It isn't fair," she teased. "Why should you get a rose and not me?"

"You can have that one," Jaylene said.

"Oh, no, that wouldn't be fair to you, and it wouldn't be fair to whoever gave it to you."

"I don't care to be fair to whoever gave it to me," Jaylene said.

"Why not?" Lucy asked, puzzled by the strange remark. "After all, he was just trying to be nice. It's probably some poor young soldier who is homesick."

Jaylene looked at Lucy for a moment, then she smiled. "Yes," she said. "Yes, I'm sure you are right. It probably is some poor homesick soldier, and not who I thought it was at all."

"I don't understand," Lucy said. "Who did you think it was?"

"Nobody," Jaylene said. "I was just imagining something, that's all." She took the rose back and sniffed it. "It is a lovely thing," she said.

The Edward Fox Troupe went from Durant to Lexington, and there she found a single rose on her pillow when she went to bed that night. This time there was no mistaking the source of the rose. She knew it came from Todd Kirk.

There were four more towns after that, and four more performances, followed by four more roses.

87

And yet not once had she seen him. His ghostly presence at first confused, then angered, and finaly, despite all legitimate reasons to the contrary, intrigued her.

What kind of man would follow her about so religiously? And how was he able always to remain unseen? How did he get into her very bedroom undetected?

How indeed? How had he gotten in on the night he raped her? For she still considered that incident rape. And, when she thought about it again, she grew angry again, and his mysterious appearances seemed less romantic to her.

Then one night they received a strange request. While passing through the Union lines at Winona, something they did routinely, they were asked to perform a show for the Union soldiers.

"I say no!" Booth said. Edward had called them all together to relay the request of the Union commander. "They are the enemy, and he would be providing aid and comfort to the enemy."

"They are soldiers," Lucy said.

"Enemy soldiers," Booth scoffed.

"Human beings, like our own soldiers," Lucy said. "I say we perform for them."

"Wilkes, we don't have much choice," Edward said. "We are dependent upon the good graces of the Yankee commander for a pass through his lines. If he doesn't grant it, we'll be stuck here."

"I say do it," Jaylene said. "After all, we owe a debt to the theatrical profession."

"Besides," Edward said, "if you just stop and think about it, Wilkes, think of how much good you can do for the cause. You'll be able to observe the

Yankees at close hand and report back to Colonel Culpepper."

"Yes," Booth said, his eyes shining brightly at Edward's suggestion. "Yes, you are right. This is an excellent opportunity for such a thing. Very well, Mr. Fox, you may count upon my cooperation."

"And you, Mr. Hardenburgh?"

"Sir, would you ask that I perform for the Czar of Russia, I would do so. I am an actor, sir, not a politician or a warrior. I care little for anything save the theater."

"Good," Edward said. "Then it is agreed that we shall perform for the Yankees. Jaylene, come with me, dear. We'll tell Captain Holt."

"Captain Holt?"

"He is the liaison officer for General Hovey. We met him once before. When we required a pass through the lines at Rosecrown some weeks ago, it was Captain Holt who provided us with one."

"Oh, yes, I remember him," Jaylene said.

"That's good, because he certainly remembered you," Edward said with a chuckle. "He asked about you. That's why I want you to come with me. I'm sure your presence will help smooth any difficulty which may arise."

Jaylene laughed at her uncle's remark, but she accompanied him just as he asked. She didn't really remember Captain Holt. Oh, she remembered the incident, but she remembered nothing about the man. It would be interesting to see someone who could remember her so vividly after such a brief encounter.

The City Hall of Winona had been taken over by General Hovey, and one of the rooms of the City Hall functioned as Captain Holt's office. Jaylene followed her uncle into the office. An intense young man was sitting at a desk, discussing something in quick, urgent terms with another, equally intense young man. Jaylene and her uncle had to stand by quietly until the conference was ended.

Behind Captain Holt, pinned to the wall, was a large map of Mississippi. There were several routes marked in red, leading northward, out of the state. She studied it for a moment, puzzled by it. Why would a Union officer in an occupied town deep in the Confederacy have a map which showed routes out of the state? She walked over to get a closer look, then she saw the legend at the bottom.

"Why, this is a map of all the underground railroads," she said aloud.

"Oh, my God, I thought that was covered!" Captain Holt said. He jumped up quickly and jerked the map down, tearing it in his haste.

"Well, what did you do that for?" Jaylene asked, puzzled by his strange behavior. "Do you think I am a spy?"

"That isn't inconceivable, madam," Captain Holt said. "And a great many lives depend on this. Innocent lives."

"Runaway slaves, you mean," Jaylene said.

"Yes," Captain Holt replied. "I consider them innocent."

"So do I, Captain," Jaylene said easily.

"You do?"

"Absolutely."

"Well, I . . . I'm glad to hear that," Captain Holt said. "Oh, forgive my manners. Please, will you and your father sit down?"

"I'm the girl's uncle," Edward said. He sat in one

of the chairs offered by Captain Holt. "But I accept your kind invitation nevertheless."

"My name is Tony Holt," he said, sticking his hand toward Edward. "I know both of you. You are becoming quite well known in this part of the country." Tony smiled broadly, and it was only then, with the tension of the meeting somewhat eased, that Jaylene was able to see how handsome a man he was. "Your, uh, profession must be terribly exciting," he went on.

"It has its moments," Edward agreed.

"Well, tell me, did you come to a decision about our request? Will you perform for us?"

"We don't have a choice, do we, Captain Holt?" Jaylene asked.

"What? Why, of course you have a choice. I've only asked you to perform, Miss Cooper. I certainly have no right to order you to perform."

"I know, but if we don't, you'll keep us prisoner here. Am I right?"

Captain Holt looked genuinely surprised.

"No, Miss Cooper. Whatever gave you such an idea?" He opened a drawer and pulled out a piece of paper. "Here, you can have the pass now, if you wish. It is already written out for you."

"Captain Holt, I'm sorry for making such an accusation," Jaylene said. "It's just that we recently had a similar experience with another commander. Only he wasn't the gentleman you are. He ordered us to perform for him, and kept us prisoner until we complied."

Captain Holt laughed. "Miss Cooper, you'll find no such coercion here. I very much want you to perform—but only if you want it."

91

Only if you want it. Oh, she had heard those same words before, though from another man, and under vastly different circumstances. Then, as it developed, he didn't mean what he said, for even after she said no, he took advantage of her. Was Captain Holt going to do the same thing? For one quick moment, she thought to put him to the test, but instead she heard herself saying, "We'll be glad to perform for you, Captain."

"Thank you," Captain Holt said, smiling broadly. "Thank you very much. Just tell me what you need in the way of help, and I'll have men assigned to build a stage, or anything you want."

"That's very nice of you, Captain," Edward said. "Perhaps you could send a couple of carpenters down to the wagons. I'll show them what I need."

"They'll be right there," Captain Holt promised. As Jaylene and her uncle got up to leave, Captain Holt walked with them from his office all the way out to the front steps. "Oh, Miss Cooper," he said. "Uh, I know this may be presumptious of me, but . . . I was wondering if you would have dinner with me tonight? Oh, and of course you too, Mr. Fox."

Edward laughed. "Don't worry about me, my boy. You don't want to eat with me, I know."

"But you are perfectly welcome," Holt insisted.

"Thank you, Captain, but you take it up with Jaylene. Oh, and would you be so kind as to escort my niece back to the hotel? I have just seen an old friend I want to visit with."

"I would be delighted," Holt said, smiling broadly at the unexpected opportunity. He offered his arm to Jaylene. "And now, Miss Cooper, will you consider my invitation?"

92

"Won't that be a little difficult?" Jaylene replied, taking his arm and walking along with him. The street was crowded with soldiers in blue uniforms. Jaylene wondered how the citizens of Winona felt at being occupied, for it was literally a city under occupation. All city laws and ordinances had been superseded by military orders.

"How would it be difficult?"

"Well, after all, I am performing tonight," Jaylene replied.

"I see. But that is not difficult at all. We'll merely dine after the show. I know everyone eats their evening meal early down here, but at home we often dine much later."

"And where is your home?" Jaylene asked.

"Boston."

"My, you are a long way off. You must get homesick."

"Yes, I do. It isn't easy to fight in a war that is more than a thousand miles away."

Jaylene looked at a mother walking down the sidewalk, clutching her little boy close to her, eyeing nervously the Yankee soldiers who were leaning against a storefront.

"On the other hand, it isn't easy to fight a war in your own home either," she said quietly.

"Oh, excuse me," Holt said, apologizing sincerely. "I guess I didn't think of how that must have sounded. It was terribly callous of me."

Jaylene realized that Holt's apology was sincere, and she softened. "I know you didn't," she said. "I guess the answer is that war isn't easy for anyone."

"I agree with you on that."

"Tell me, Captain Holt. . ."

93

"Can't you call me Tony?"

"All right, Tony," Jaylene said. "Have you left someone behind? A wife or a sweetheart, perhaps?"

Tony laughed. "A sweetheart," he said.

"I see. And how do you think she would feel about my having dinner with you tonight?"

"I think she would approve," Tony said, and his smile grew broader. "She is my mother."

Now it was Jaylene's turn to smile. "Very well, Captain, since you think your mother would approve, I accept your kind invitation."

"Wonderful, wonderful," Tony said.

"Cap'n Holt, sir, wait a moment," someone called, and Jaylene and Tony turned to see a private running down the street after them.

"What is it?" Tony asked.

"The general asked me to give this to you," the private said, handing a paper to Tony. Tony opened it, read it, frowned, then stuck the note in his pocket.

"Is something wrong?" Jaylene asked.

"No, not really," Holt said. "I had hoped to walk with you to your hotel, but something has come up which needs my attention, and I must see to it right away."

"That's all right, I can walk the rest of the way by myself."

"I really don't like you to go unescorted," Tony said.

"Then perhaps I can be of assistance. I'm always ready to help a lady in need," a new voice said.

Jaylene and Tony turned toward the voice, and Tony smiled. "Yes, you will do nicely," he said. "Miss Cooper, I want you to meet the new engineering officer who has just been assigned to our staff. Captain Bill Coleman, this is Miss Jaylene Cooper, one of the actresses who will perform for us tonight."

"I'm very pleased to meet you," the smiling young man said pleasantly.

Jaylene said nothing, for she was in temporary shock. The man Tony had introduced to her as Captain Bill Coleman was Todd Kirk.

CHAPTER NINE

"I think perhaps I had better see you to your room," Todd said.

"No thank you," Jaylene replied. "That was the

"I want to thank you for not giving me away," Todd said, as he walked along the plank sidewalk with Jaylene.

"The only reason I didn't give you away was because of my loyalty to the South," Jaylene hissed. "Otherwise, varmint that you are, I would tell in a minute."

"That would mean I would be hanged," Todd said. "You would let that happen?"

"Let it? I would stand by and chortle in glee," Jaylene said angrily.

Todd chuckled. "Remind me never to get on your bad side."

"You *are* on it, you—you—" Jaylene said, exasperated and frustrated by the fact that she couldn't give full vent to her emotions here.

When they reached the hotel a moment later, Jaylene turned toward Todd and put a forced, obviously insincere smile upon her face. "Thank you so much, Captain—Coleman," she set the name apart pointedly, "for your company. I will be all right now."

"I think perhaps I had better see you to your room," Todd said.

"No thank you," Jaylene replied. "That won't be necessary."

"I think it is," Todd said, not asking, but wording it in such a way that she knew he was insisting upon it.

"Very well," she said coolly. "If you must."

They walked through the crowded lobby and up the carpeted stairway, then down the hall to the room that was Jaylene's.

"We are here," Jaylene said quietly. "You can go now."

"No," Todd said. "I have to talk to you."

"We have nothing to talk about," Jaylene said.

"Miss Cooper," Todd said, with the air of one who was getting a little impatient with an irritable child. "I don't know what your problem is, but I have a big one. I am wearing the uniform of a Union officer, and that means if I am caught I will either hang or be shot. But it is important that I do this, for the Yankees have plans to dig a canal which would bypass Vicksburg. Do you know what that would mean?"

"No," Jaylene said. "Not really."

"I didn't think you did. It means, Miss Cooper, that Vicksburg and General Pemberton's army will fall, and complete control of the Mississippi River will pass to Yankee hands. It might mean the loss of the war."

"I see," Jaylene said.

"I'm not sure you do," Todd said. "Or you wouldn't be subjecting me to this danger. Now, will you let me in, please?"

Jaylene opened the door, then she and Todd stepped inside, and Todd, after looking up and down the hallway, closed the door behind them. He locked it, then gave the key to Jaylene.

"I need your help," Todd said.

"Why should I help you?"

Todd sighed. "Then let me say that the South needs your help."

"I won't spy," Jaylene said.

"You don't have to spy," Todd said. "All you have to do is warn the others in your troupe not to give me away if they see me. That's all I'm asking."

"Very well," Jaylene said. "Your secret is safe. But I will not let you put my uncle or any of my friends in danger."

"They won't be, believe me," Todd said.

"Why should I believe you?"

"Because you have my word."

"Your word? Ha! It won't be any better this time than it was last time."

"Miss Cooper, why do you insist that I came back to your room, when you and I both know I didn't?"

"Because you and I both know that you *did*!" Jaylene said. "Don't you think I would know something like that?"

"Believe me, Miss Cooper, if I made love to you, you would know it."

"I do know it," Jaylene said.

"No, you don't," Todd said. He grabbed her, and as his move was sudden and unexpected, she was unable to resist him. He kissed her with hot, hungry lips, and the effect was so searing that it took her breath away. Twice before she had been kissed by this man, and each kiss had burned into her soul with the heat of a branding iron. Then, as her head started spinning with the sensations of the kiss, she remembered that *he hadn't kissed her when he returned that night.*

Jaylene felt Todd's tongue, first brushing across her lips and then forcing her lips open and thrusting inside. It so took her breath away that she was unable to struggle, and Todd took that opportunity to begin undressing her.

Jaylene was in a dream world. She was both an observer and a participant in what was going on. She saw him taking off her dress, and within a moment she felt the gentle kiss of air against her naked skin. A part of her mind told her that she should protest, that she should resist what was happening to her, but she couldn't.

Todd quickly removed his own clothes, and she saw him naked again, as she had in his cabin, but this time she didn't have the strength to resist. He came back to her, lifted her, then carried her over to the bed where he gently laid her down.

"Jaylene, I have wanted you more than I have ever wanted any woman," he said in a tightly constricted voice. His hands moved gently across her smooth skin, spreading fire wherever they went. "I have waited for you longer than I have ever waited for any woman."

And now Jaylene noticed something else. She had been aroused during the visit of her nightlover, but not to this degree. What she was feeling at this moment was much more intense than anything she had ever felt. There was as much difference between what she was experiencing now and what she had felt before as there was between the flickering of a candle flame and a roaring inferno.

"Jaylene, I have followed you all over the country, until I've nearly driven myself mad over you," Todd said. "Didn't you find the roses? Didn't you know they were from me?"

"They . . . they meant nothing to me," Jaylene managed to gasp, though she could scarcely get the words out. She had to say them, she had to make some fight to preserve her honor, and yet, as Todd's hand reached along her thighs the heat and dampness of her desire showed him that she was fully as desirous of him as he was of her.

"Please," Jaylene said. "Please, don't go on."

"No, Jaylene," Todd said. "I won't give you the option this time. This time we play by my rules."

Jaylene began to cry, though her body trembled with fire under his touch. She was not sure whether she was crying from fear or desire, for all emotions had fused into one under the searing heat of her own passion. Then, in an instant, Todd was over her and thrusting himself into her.

Jaylene responded to him with a passionate embrace, and when he moved his mouth over hers, stifling her cries with smothering kisses and a darting tongue, she took him eagerly, arching her back to meet him.

And then she felt it, for the first time in her life, a total, unqualified sexual fulfillment. Never had she known anything could be like this, and she felt like a rose on a silver catapult, vaulted to the stars and beyond, becoming a blazing comet to light up the heavens.

As Jaylene was experiencing rapture beyond expression, she heard a small groan escape from Todd's lips, and felt convulsions of pleasure rack his body. For one brief instant it seemed that she could feel as he felt, and the pleasures he was experiencing were telegraphed through to her as well. And when, a moment later, he rolled off her, it was as if she could still feel the pleasure of him with her. He lay beside her for a few moments, and for a while they were both silent. Finally, Todd spoke.

"Do you still think I came to see you the other night?" he asked.

"Oh, no," Jaylene said, almost dreamily. "This was so much more wonderful, so much greater than . . ." She stopped in mid-sentence. *What was she saying? She couldn't let him know how she felt, how she enjoyed it. She couldn't give him that advantage, that satisfaction.* "I . . . I don't know what to think," she finally said.

"Yes," Todd said. He raised up on one shoulder and looked down at her. She lay on her back with the arm nearest Todd thrown back, over her head. Her nipples, so recently flushed with love, were distended, protruding like tightly drawn rosebuds. Her mane of tawny hair seemed to glow in the sunlit room. "You know what to think," he said. "You know it wasn't me."

"Then who was it?" Jaylene asked.

"Perhaps it was no one," Todd suggested. "Perhaps it was a dream."

"No," Jaylene said. "One doesn't lose one's virginity in a dream. Someone came to my bed that night, and with a scented handerchief drugged me into insensibility. Then whoever it was took advantage of my condition."

"That may be so," Todd said. "But why did you think it was me?"

"Because," Jaylene said, "I . . . I saw your face. You seemed to be floating in a lavender fog, but you were there. I know you were there."

"I wasn't, Jaylene." Todd laughed quietly. "It is just that you wanted me so badly that you imagined it was me."

"You think I wanted you?" Jaylene said, piqued by the arrogant statement.

"Of course you did. You wanted me more than anything in the world, Jaylene. I could see that."

Jaylene sat up, and as a pillow was the only thing she could grab, she clubbed him with it.

"Why, you—you arrogant, conceited, boorish oaf!" she said, punctuating her remarks with the pillow. "How dare you take such an attitude with me? I turned you away, don't you remember? Yes, and I tried to turn you away this time as well, though you raped me anyway."

"Rape?" Todd asked. "Jaylene, how could you call what just happened rape? You were as willing a participant as I."

"It was not I who barged into your room, sir, nor forced myself on you. I may have responded to your lovemaking, but I was confused and beguiled by your seduction. Now, unless you intend to force yourself upon me further, sir, you will leave and allow me some time to compose myself."

"I'll leave, Jaylene," Todd said, dressing himself quickly. "And if you actually believe that I raped you, then I apologize."

"Of course I believe it," Jaylene said. "What else am I to believe?"

"You might believe it was an act of love," Todd said easily. "For, in fact, I do love you." He blew her a kiss, then quickly left the room.

CHAPTER TEN

"Then you are . . ."

"I am Marian, the one called the Midnight Angel," Jaylene said.

"And now I suppose you would scorn to touch me with your fingertips," Booth, as Count de Stromberg, said.

"Count, why do you speak so?" Hardenburgh, as Dr. Bernarr, challenged.

"Yes, we owe much to her," Edward, as John Small, said.

"And though she could have done otherwise, she treated me as her own dear sister," Lucy, who was portraying Edna Whalen, said.

"I am sorry," Count de Stromberg said. "I take back the unkind thought. Does that put it right?"

"No," the Midnight Angel said. "Not until I have made a name for myself, won something from fame which fortune has denied me."

"What proud words!" Dr. Bernarr exclaimed.

"Worthy words, from," Edward turned to face the audience as he mouthed the last of his line, to make certain that they heard the dramatic conclusion, "The Midnight Angel."

Jaylene thrust her arms upward, as if in appeal to the heavens, and every other member of the troupe assumed a rigid pose in a grand tableau as the curtain descended to thunderous applause.

"Bravo," the audience yelled. "Bravo, bravo, bravo!"

"Listen to them," Lucy said in a loud stage whisper. "I believe the Yankees enjoyed it fully as much as our own boys."

"Shhh," Edward hissed. "Hold the tableau, the curtain is coming back up."

The curtain was lifted again and the players were still in the same position, holding rigid expressions on their faces, making what Edward liked to call a living portrait. This was his specialty, and he was very proud of the tableau curtain calls.

The applause grew louder and the audience rose from their seats as they continued to cheer. The curtain descended one more time, and this time the players broke the tableau and prepared for their final bows. The curtain rose again, and one by one the actors stepped forward to receive their due.

A long-stemmed rose was tossed to Jaylene when she stepped forward, and she looked up to see Todd smiling at her. For an instant she considered throwing it back at him, but she knew she wouldn't be able to answer the questions which would arise over such an unseemly act.

Tony Holt was in the audience, and he walked down toward the stage just as Jaylene caught the rose.

"Well, it didn't take long for you to make an impression on Bill Coleman, did it?" he asked. "Perhaps I made a mistake in allowing him to escort you to the hotel."

"Bill Coleman?" Jaylene asked in confusion.

Tony laughed. "Ah, then perhaps it is all wishful thinking on his part. After all, if he didn't even impress you sufficiently to allow you to remember his name, then I have no cause for regret."

"Oh, oh yes," Jaylene said. For a moment she had forgotten the name Todd was using. Silently she scolded herself, for that could be very dangerous for him. "I remember him now."

"Though not as well as he remembered you, I see. Though I wonder why he gave you only one rose?"

"Perhaps he could only find one," Jaylene suggested. "If you'll wait right here, I shall be ready to join you for supper in a moment." Jaylene was eager to get the subject away from Todd, lest she slip and say something that shouldn't be said.

"I won't go away, I promise," Tony said.

Tony watched Jaylene disappear behind the curtain. Never had he seen a more beautiful woman. From the moment he first saw her, weeks ago at Rosecrown, she had been on his mind, and he had hoped desperately for an opportunity to see her again. When the troupe came to Winona he could scarcely believe his good luck. And when she agreed to go out with him, he considered his luck even better.

Of course, nothing would ever come from this. She was, after all, an actress, and in Tony's society actresses were but one small step removed from prostitutes. He had told her this afternoon that his mother would approve of her, but that wasn't true.

110

If his mother knew he was seeing an actress socially, she would be extremely upset.

But so what? Tony asked himself. After all, he had his own life to live, and his mother and the entire Holt family, the Boston shipping empire Holts, couldn't live it for him. Besides, he had no intention of marrying her, or even getting involved with her. She was just a pleasant diversion. Still, he could just hear his mother's voice now.

"Tony, you must never forget who you are, and what your family represents. We are one of the finest families in America, and we cannot jeopardize our position by careless indiscretions. You must weigh everything you do against how it will look to others. You are fortunate to have been born a Holt, and there are many advantages to be gained from it. But there are responsibilities too. Awesome responsibilities, and you must never overlook them."

Tony didn't forget them; they colored his entire life. When other children fought, or played in the dirt, Tony held onto the principles of decorum drilled into him by his mother. In college, while other students participated in pranks, Tony held onto the principle of hard work, taught him by his father. In fact, it wasn't until the war began that Tony dared to defy his parents.

Andrew W. Holt, Tony's father, owned one of the largest shipping fleets in America, so it was only natural that he would secure a naval commission for his son, and he even provided, at his own expense, a vessel to be used by the U.S. Navy for the blockade force. Andrew thought that would be preferable to army duty, where Tony would have to slog through the mud.

But Tony had become an ardent abolitionist during his days in college, and he felt that he could better serve the cause of abolition in the army, so he disdained the naval commission his father had secured for him, and accepted a commission in the army instead. It had been his one act of defiance, and by that act he had, he felt, become his own person.

Seeing Jaylene was another defiant act. Though in truth this act was not motivated by a need to be defiant. It had another, more basic, and much more powerful motivation. Tony was seeing Jaylene because he had never been attracted to any woman as strongly as he was to her.

Backstage, Jaylene was removing the last of her stage makeup. The dress she had worn on stage was off, hanging in the wardrobe next to the dress she had selected to wear out for the evening. She was in her chemise, and as she leaned over toward the mirror, the chemise fell low, exposing the tops of her breasts. It was a most enticing sight, and many of the soldiers who were now returning to their tents to dream of the beauty they had seen tonight would have given a month's pay to be there.

But it wasn't just the soldiers who could derive enjoyment from such a scene, for even now a brooding figure stood in the shadows looking at the form Jaylene was displaying. His breath was coming in short gasps, and he found himself sweating, and his blood ran hot as he remembered the sublime joy of having known this woman. Oh, her smooth skin, her tender flesh, the sweet ecstasy of her body, nude beneath his!

112

Jaylene's observer looked around to ensure he was alone, for only if there was no chance of unwanted interruption would he be able to enjoy Jaylene's sweet flesh again. He stuck his hand in his pocket and felt the bottle, cool, round, and reassuring. He tried to tell himself that he didn't need the bottle, that he had but to assert himself, but the bottle was too reassuring, and he knew that he couldn't, or wouldn't try anything without it. Slowly he pulled the bottle from his pocket and started through the shadows toward her, feeling his heart beating faster, enjoying this sensation of fear and excitement. Oh, it was going to be good this time. It was going to be so good.

But before he reached her, he knocked over an unseen chair, and he turned and bolted back into the shadows like a rat frightened from its prize.

Jaylene, who had no idea she was being watched, heard the sound as well, and she looked around, startled by it.

"Who is it?" she called out. "Who is in my dressing room?" She reached for the dress and held it in front of her.

"Lucy!"

"Yes," Lucy answered from the next room. "Is something wrong?"

"No . . . I guess not," Jaylene said. "I thought I heard something, that's all." She took one more quick look around the room, then slipped into her dress and left to meet Tony.

Tony smiled as Jaylene approached him. The garish stage makeup was gone, and her costume had been changed to street dress, yet even in street dress without makeup her beauty was dazzling.

"I'm all ready," she said. "I hope you didn't have to wait too long."

"It would have been worth ten times the wait," Tony said. He looked at her with obvious appreciation. "Miss Cooper, you are an exceptionally beautiful woman."

"You are most kind," Jaylene said, taking his arm in her hand.

Todd was waiting outside when Jaylene and Tony left the building. He stepped back into the shadows to ensure that he wouldn't be seen, watched them until they were well out of sight, then hurried through the darkened alleyway to the back door of the City Hall. Earlier in the afternoon he had unlocked a door which normally remained locked, and now he slipped through it.

The door opened into a large storeroom which was being used to house the city and county records, moved here to allow the building to serve as a military headquarters. The records were stacked on tables, chairs, and even in piles on the floor, so there was very little room for Todd to move, but because he had been here earlier in the day he was able to pick his way through the clutter without making any undue disturbance.

Todd crossed the room and opened the other door just a crack. The hallway outside was brightly lighted by gas lamps, and when Todd peeked through the door he saw two soldiers standing guard at the far end. They were outside General Hovey's office, and the fact that they were lounging against the wall, rather than standing in a more military posture, told Todd that General Hovey was gone. If Hovey was gone then his staff was also gone, and that meant that these two soldiers were probably the only two people Todd would have to worry about.

"Did you get to see either one of the women in the show?" one of the soldiers asked the other.

"Naw. Lee, he seen one of 'em, though. Said she was a real purty thing, with hair the color o' corn silk, 'n eyes as gold as a nugget."

"Gold eyes? I ain't never heard o 'such," the other soldier commented. "Lee must be crazy."

"They was really brown, Lee said. But such a brown as he ain't never seed before."

"Law, what a purty sight she musta been then. Did you hear tell as if they was plannin' on havin' another play tomorra, so's you'n me could see?"

The first soldier laughed. "Now, do you actually believe they would have a special play just for us?"

"Us, 'n all the others what missed 'cause o' performin' their duty."

"All that missed it total'd up don't amount to enough to put on a special show for," the first soldier said.

"It don't seem no way fair, do it?"

"It ain't meant to be," the first soldier said. "Lissen, you keep an eye open, 'n I'll slip into the genrul's office here 'n get a couple o' his fine cigars. Iffen we'uns is gonna stand guard tonight, they ain't no reason why we can't enjoy us a good smoke."

"I don't know," the secnd soldier demurred. "You think we'll get caught?"

"Naw. Who's gonna come back here tonight? Like as not we won't see a soul for the rest of the night."

The first soldier opened the door to the general's office and slipped inside. The second soldier, instead of looking out for him, was so fascinated by what he was doing that he stuck his head in the door to watch. That gave Todd the opportunity he was looking for, and he slipped adroitly down the hall and into Tony's office without being seen.

Once Todd was inside the office, he looked back toward the two guards and saw them lighting up their cigars. That was a lucky break for him, because he intended to light a candle, and one of his fears had been that the guards might smell the candle, even if they didn't see it. But with both guards smoking, the possibility of them smelling the candle was remote.

Todd lit the candle, then stuck it on the edge of Tony's desk and began rifling through the papers.

"Plan for the Removal of Contraband Slaves, to include Routes, Way Stations, and Cooperative Citizens."

Todd looked at the paper he held in his hand. It was a detailed description of how to evacuate all the slaves in Mississippi. If carried out, Todd knew, it could have a demoralizing effect, for with all the men gone to war, the brunt of the Southern economy was being carried by the slaves. Colonel Hamilton Culpepper, Todd knew, would be especially glad to see such a paper, for he was currently mobilizing all the slaves within his district to form a labor battalion.

Todd put the paper back down. Culpepper would

just have to do it on his own, for Todd had no intention of providing him with this information. In fact, it wasn't even for this material that Todd had come, and he shoved it and the other papers regarding the underground railroad aside.

Todd was looking for the civil engineering drawings of the proposed canal around Vicksburg. That was what was important, for if Todd could prevent the canal from being built, then Vicksburg's defenses would be greatly strengthened.

Finally Todd saw an envelope marked *Canal*, and quickly he opened it. Inside he found a slip of paper.

"Received of Captain Tony Holt, all papers dealing with proposed canal project." The note was signed Chauncey Anders.

"I'm tellin' you, I saw a light under the door," Todd suddenly heard one of the soldiers say, and to Todd's surprise, the voice was right outside the door.

Todd doused the candle with his fingers, then managed to duck down behind the desk, just as the hall door opened and the soldier stepped in. A bar of light spilled in from the hall and cast long, grotesque shadows on the wall beside the desk, and as Todd sat there, holding his breath, he could see the gigantic shadow of the soldier and his rifle projected against the wall.

"Anybody in here?" the soldier called.

"D'ya expect 'em to answer ya?" the other soldier said.

"I don't know. All I know is I seen a light."

At the moment there occurred a propitious happening for Todd. A flash of lightning illuminated

117

the room as bright as day for an instant, before it faded. The soldier who was standing in the doorway laughed.

"It was lightnin' I seen," the soldier said. He closed the door, and Todd could hear him outside, talking to the other soldier in obvious relief.

"I tell you, I'm just as glad it was lightnin'. I sure didn't want to go runnin' into no Reb in there."

"Now what Reb would be in there in the first place?" his partner asked. "Any Reb spy as might try 'n sneak in here would head straight for the general's office, you know that."

"Yeah, I reckon you're right. Oh, we'd better get into the general's office n' close the windows. It's commencin' to rain, 'n the general wouldn't like it much if his desk 'n all his papers got wet."

"You're right. In fact, if they do get wet, we're liable to find ourselves pullin' this here guard for the rest of the war."

Todd watched until both soldiers disappeared into the general's office, then used that opportunity to make good his escape. His mission had not been an unqualified success, but neither was it an unqualified failure. He didn't know where the Yankees intended to build the canal, but he knew who was going to be in charge of the operation. Now all he had to do was to get to Chauncey Anders.

CHAPTER ELEVEN

The wagons were loaded with all the Edward Fox Players but one, and they were ready to leave Winona. The one player who had not yet arrived was John Wilkes Booth.

"As usual, we find ourselves waiting for Booth," Hardenburgh said, making no effort to hide his irritation with the actor. "Were that man's talent as great as his ego, I've no doubt that our little troupe would be playing before the crowned heads of Europe now."

"Perhaps he has found another *friend* to keep him occupied," Lucy suggested.

"Admittedly, Mr. Booth is often tardy," Edward said. "But seldom is he this late. I wonder if he is all right."

Jaylene had not joined in the conversation, because, in truth, she was so lost in her own thoughts that she didn't care whether Booth was there or not. Her thoughts were on yesterday, and the events that had taken place then. She was not consumed with guilt or shame. After all, she could lose her virginity only once, and having lost it, could never recover it. Thus, it was pointless to dwell on that subject.

But even as Jaylene considered with such detached logic the loss of her virginity, she thought of Todd Kirk, and the passionate moments she had spent with him the day before.

Had he been the one who raped her in the night? It *had* to be Kirk who had come, for she had clearly seen his face. Why did he deny it?

But wait. She had *not* seen his face. It had been dark, and she had been able to make out the form but not the face of the intruder.

No, that's not right. The face was there, before her, floating clearly in a lavender fog, detached and observing.

That . . . that can't be, she suddenly realized. And then she knew the truth. She had not really seen Kirk. She had only imagined that she saw him, or dreamed that she saw him, for she was, in fact, unconscious. Yes . . . that was it. She was unconscious, because she had been drugged with some sweet-smelling, overpowering perfume, and while in such a stupor she had dreamed of Todd Kirk. Such dreams, she knew, were not uncommon in drug-induced sleep.

Why did she dream of Todd Kirk? Did she dream of him because she *wanted* it to be him?

No, she told herself. No, she would not accept that!

But then she remembered yesterday afternoon. He had seduced her, forced her to make love and . . . Jaylene stopped. No, she told herself with a sudden flash of honesty. She had not been forced into it. She had wanted it, and as she recalled it, she could recall only the pleasure of the moment.

And on the night she was raped, she could recall

the pleasure of that moment too, a pleasure which was induced and intensified by her mental transference of the rapist into the person of Todd Kirk.

During these moments of honesty, Jaylene also recalled the pleasure she had felt at being seen by Kirk on that morning she bathed in the river. And, even now, she began to feel quiet stirrings of desire, and her cheeks pinkened in embarrassment, as if someone could read her thoughts.

Good Lord! Did that mean she was in love with Todd Kirk?

No. No, she could not accept that either. But then what did it mean? Was she a woman moved only by the passionate side of her nature? Perhaps, for last night while dining with Tony Holt she was unable to still a disturbing idea that crept unsummoned to her consciousness: how would he be as a lover?

"Here comes Booth at last," Hardenburgh suddenly said, and his voice was a welcome interruption to the unwelcome thoughts that tumbled through Jaylene's mind.

"Wilkes, must you forever keep us waiting?" Edward inquired. His voice reflected his displeasure.

Booth smiled grandly, removed his hat, and bowed.

"Forgive me, Mr. Fox. Forgive me, one and all, for any inconvenience I may have caused you. However, you will take heart, I am certain, in the realization that this is the last time you will ever have to wait for me."

"Could it be, Wilkes, that you are bent on changing your ways for the better?" Lucy asked.

"Madam, one who possesses my sterling qualities

may find improvement difficult," Booth said. "No, it is not my ways which are changing, but my locale. I am herewith tendering my resignation from the Edward Fox Players."

"What?" Edward asked, genuinely surprised by the unexpected announcement. "What do you mean?"

"I mean I quit."

"But you can't do that, Booth. We have ten more shows scheduled."

"You will have to find a new Count de Stromberg, I'm afraid."

"You know we can't," Edward said. "Not here, and at this late date. You can't leave us now, Booth. That would be most unethical."

"I'm sorry," Booth said, though the tone of his voice did not sound in the least apologetic. "But you see, I have just been invited to play the lead role in a new play."

"But you have the lead role in this one," Edward said.

"My dear sir, ladies," Booth said, looking at the others. "Do you for one moment believe that what we have been doing would pass as theater?" He laughed mockingly. "Look at yourselves. A drunken has-been," he pointed to Hardenburgh, "an aging never-was," this sobriquet he dealt to Edward, "and two pretty girls, one with no talent and the other with no brains."

"You are being unnecessarily cruel to those who took you in," Jaylene said.

"I'm not being cruel, madam, I am being honest," Booth said.

"Where will you be going?" Edward asked.

"To a real theater," Booth said. "A theater in which my talent can achieve its true status. I'm going to Washington, to play at Ford's Theater. I'm certain you have heard of it. There, such players as Edwin Forrest and James Hackett have trod the boards, and I shall join them."

"And Edwin Booth," Edward said. "Your brother has played there quite often, has he not?"

"So what if he has?" Booth challenged. "Perhaps if I am seen in the same theater where my brother has played, my real talent will get the recognition it has long, and justly, deserved."

"What makes you think you are going to play at Ford's Theater?" Hardenburgh asked.

"I have received a personal invitation from John Ford," Booth said. "He owns the theater."

"So you are going to Washington, are you?" Jaylene said. "The capital of the Union. And you have so often espoused your dedication to the Confederacy."

"I assure you, madam, my dedication to the Confederacy is greater than any of yours." Booth suddenly got a brooding, smoldering look in his eyes. "And I may yet strike a blow for the South which shall be noticed throughout the land."

"I say good riddance, sir," Hardenburgh said. "Edward, there are plays we can do without him. Let us be gone from here and not concern ourselves over his loss."

"I agree, uncle," Jaylene said. She looked pointedly at Booth. "And I, for one, do not think leaving Mr. Booth here is a very great loss anyway."

Booth smiled. "I'm sorry you feel that way," he said. He looked at her for a moment, staring deeply, and Jaylene suddenly got the strangest feeling that he was looking at her as if she were naked. "Jaylene, I have something for you," he said mysteriously. He took a package from his inside jacket pocket and handed it to her. It was neatly wrapped and tied with a ribbon.

Jaylene couldn't have been more shocked had he suddenly slapped her in the face. What was the reason for this parting gift? She had certainly not been one of Booth's admirers. Why was he giving her a present? She began to undo the ribbon.

"No," Booth smiled. "Not now. Undo it later, please."

"Wilkes, I don't understand," Jaylene said. "Why are you giving me a present?"

Booth smiled mysteriously. "Let's just say it is a little token of my esteem," he said. "And it commemorates something we shared."

"Well, I . . . I thank you," Jaylene said. She was puzzled by the gift, and didn't quite know how to respond.

"Goodbye," Booth said, turning and walking back toward the hotel.

"What did he give you?" Lucy asked, almost immediately.

"I don't know," Jaylene said. "I don't even know *why* he gave it to me."

"Perhaps he has long been a secret admirer of yours," Lucy teased.

"Perhaps he has been the giver of the roses," Edward suggested.

Jaylene was surprised by Edward's comment. She had not realized that he knew about the roses.

"You *knew* about them?" she asked.

125

"My dear, everyone in the troupe knew about them," Hardenburgh said. He sighed. "Were I a bit younger, and not the old reprobate you see before you today, it might have been I who sent them. But alas, I cannot claim that honor. Nor, sir," he said, addressing himself to Edward, "would I credit that scoundrel Booth with such romantic ingenuity."

"It is not Booth, Uncle," Jaylene said.

"Do you know who it is?" Edward asked.

"Yes," Jaylene said. "And in truth, he is as big a scroundrel as Booth."

"Maybe there is something about you which attracts scoundrels," Edward teased with a wink.

"Oh, I truly hope not," Jaylene said. "I should not want to live the rest of my life avoiding such characters. But enough of that, Uncle Edward. Our problem is, what do we do now? Without Booth, we have no play."

"Don't you worry about it, darlin'," Edward said, patting his niece on the hand affectionately. "Mr. Hardenburgh is correct when he says we can find a new play without Booth."

"Mr. Fox, wait a moment!" someone called, and when Jaylene looked toward the one who shouted, she saw Tony Holt approaching them.

"Captain Holt, is something wrong?" Edward asked. "Has our pass been revoked?"

"Your pass? No, of course not," Tony said. "I just didn't want to let you get away without telling you goodbye, and thanking you again for the performance."

"You are most kind," Edward said.

"I understand Mr. Booth is not going with you."

"That's right."

"What will you do without him? Don't you need him in your play?"

"We will go into immediate rehearsal for a new play," Edward said. "I shan't let the troupe be destroyed by one man's defection."

"Where will you go now?"

"I think I will go to Yazoo City," Edward said. "They have a real theater there. It would be a good place to learn a new play."

"Yazoo City? Isn't that where Colonel Culpepper is?"

"Sir, I'll not give you information which may harm the South," Edward said.

"No, nor would I ask you to," Tony said. "But I know that Culpepper is there and I know also that he is rounding up Negroes to build the defenses around Vicksburg. If you are not an avid pro-slave person, you will tell any Negro who is seeking help to come to Winona. We will help them escape."

"For humanitarian reasons, Captain Holt? Or to prevent the defenses from being constructed?" Edward asked.

Tony smiled. "My motives are humanitarian," he said. "The motives of the Union army may be more pragmatic."

"I will help," Jaylene volunteered. "I am a Southerner—but I hate slavery."

"Thank you, Miss Cooper," Tony said. "I appreciate that." He stepped back from the team and looked up at the sky. "It rained last night, and I believe it's going to rain tonight. I hope you find a dry place by then."

* * *

It did rain that night and the two wagons pulled off the road for the night's encampment. The evening dinner had been restricted to dried beef and a can of brandied peaches because the rain was too heavy to start a fire.

Lucy and Jaylene shared one wagon, while Edward and Hardenburgh shared the other. Though the wagons were less than ten feet apart, the driving rain kept everyone inside under the protective covering of the canvas, so that it seemed as if Jaylene and Lucy were completely alone.

"Look out the back for me," Lucy said. "I'm going to take off these wet clothes and I don't want either of the men to come over here unexpectedly."

Jaylene laughed. "You know Uncle Edward and Mr. Hardenburgh. I doubt that either of those two would go out in a rain like this, even if the wagons were on fire."

"You're right," Lucy said. "I guess I was thinking more about Booth. I never did trust him. I used to feel him looking at me sometimes and it would make me shiver. I even felt that way when he was nowhere around, as if he were hiding somewhere to watch me change clothes."

"I know what you mean," Jaylene said.

"What did he give you?" Lucy had removed her dress and was stripping out of her undergarments. She was, Jaylene noticed, a beautiful woman, with smooth, golden, unblemished skin and well-formed breasts.

"Oh, I forgot all about that," Jaylene said. She began rummaging through a pile of quilts and blankets until she found the small package Booth had given her, and opened it.

"Well? What is it?" Lucy asked. "I'm curious."

Jaylene held up a handkerchief embroidered with the initial B. "It is this," she said. "One of his handkerchiefs."

"He gave you one of his handkerchiefs?" Lucy asked with a small laugh. "Why would he do such a thing?"

"I don't know," Jaylene said, clearly as puzzled by the strange gift as Lucy. "Perhaps he is so vain that he wanted me to have something to remember him by. As if I could ever forget him, badly as I want to."

"Smell it," Lucy suggested. "Perhaps it has the perfume of one of his ladies."

Jaylene laughed. "You are impossible," she said. She held the handkerchief up to her nose and took a deep breath.

Jaylene was nearly overcome with a sweet, cloying smell, and her head began to whirl. She gasped, her eyes fluttered, and she dropped the handkerchief and held on to the side of the wagon to keep from passing out.

"Jaylene, what is it?" Lucy asked in alarm, moving across the wagon quickly to see to Jaylene.

"What?" Jaylene asked, looking at Lucy as if wondering what the nude girl was doing, holding her and talking to her in such an urgent voice. She was dizzy and for a moment unable to come to her senses.

"Are you all right?" Lucy asked anxiously.

"Yes," Jaylene said. "Yes, I'm fine. I just grew very dizzy for a moment."

"Maybe it's because you're hungry. We didn't have much for supper."

"No," Jaylene said. Now her senses had returned, and she looked at the handkerchief. "No, that wasn't it at all. It was the handkerchief." She picked it up again, and this time sniffed it very cautiously. "Yes," she said. She handed it to Lucy. "Here, sniff it, but be careful, for this handkerchief is soaked in some sort of sleeping potion."

Lucy sniffed it, then held the handkerchief away from her face and looked at it with surprise and a little apprehension.

"You are right," she said. "Jaylene, why would Booth give you a handkerchief treated in such a way?"

"I don't know," Jaylene said. "I don't have any idea why he would . . ." Suddenly Jaylene realized the significance of the handkerchief, and she shuddered with a cold chill.

"What is it?" Lucy asked, for she had seen Jaylene's strange reaction.

"It was Booth," Jaylene said. "I accused Todd Kirk, when all along it was John Wilkes Booth!"

"What are you talking about?"

"Oh, Lucy, I am so ashamed," Jaylene said.

"Why are you ashamed?"

"I'm . . . I'm no longer a virgin," Jaylene said. "Do you remember the night we were kidnapped by Kirk's raiders?"

"Yes," Lucy said.

"Something happened that night. I didn't understand it clearly until now." She told of the mysterious visitor in the night, and of the handkerchief that was placed over her face to render her insensible. "And now, smelling the handkerchief, I recognize what happened. It was Booth who came into my room, and he left the handkerchief with me so that he could brag of it. Oh, how I hate him for his cruel and insensitive act!"

"It was a cruel act," Lucy said. "But how could you have suspected Major Kirk? Surely you were able to tell that it wasn't him."

"No," Jaylene said. "You must remember, I was insensible, or nearly so. But in truth, I was aware of what was going on, even though unable to stop it."

"And despite this awareness, you thought it was Major Kirk?"

"Yes," Jaylene said. "Oh, Lucy, you are my friend. I can confess to you things I dare not say to another soul. I . . . I wanted it to be Todd Kirk. Can you understand that?"

Lucy smiled warmly, and only then did she begin to dress again in dry clothes. "Of course I understand," she said. "Do you not remember me telling you that I wish it had been *me* your major had seen washing in the river?"

"Yes, but you don't know all of the story," Jaylene said. "For yesterday afternoon, I allowed Todd Kirk to seduce me in my hotel room."

"Oh?" Lucy replied.

"Yes. And it was wonderful," Jaylene said. "Oh, Lucy, I won't lie to you, and I can't lie to myself any longer. It was the most wonderful thing I have ever experienced." Jaylene clasped her hands and closed her eyes in rapture at the memory. "Have you . . . have you ever . . . ?"

"Been known by a man?" Lucy asked.

"Yes. Oh . . . forgive me. I know it is an indelicate question."

Lucy put her hand on Jaylene's and squeezed it

131

lightly. "Between us, Jaylene, there can never be an indelicate question."

"But I had no right to ask," Jaylene said.

"You had every right. After all, haven't you told me your most intimate secret?"

"I suppose so," Jaylene said. She let out a breath of air, then laughed nervously. "I never thought I would tell anyone such a thing."

"I am thrilled that you would tell me," Lucy said. "For it bonds our friendship with a tie which can never be broken." Lucy looked down into her lap and was silent for a long moment. Only the drumming of rain against the canvas wagon cover intruded into the silence. And then, Jaylene saw with a start, Lucy was crying, for tears tracked down each cheek.

"Lucy?" Jaylene asked. "Lucy, what is it?"

"I . . . I want to tell you something," Lucy said. "I've wanted to tell someone for so long . . . but I have been too frightened. And yet I don't wish to keep it to myself any longer."

"You can tell me."

"I am afraid," Lucy said.

"Afraid? Of what are you afraid?"

"I'm afraid that after you hear my story, you won't think the same of me."

"Lucy, how can you think such a thing?" Jaylene asked. "I'm hurt that you would have so little regard for me as to think that anything you say could alter my feelings for you."

"Oh, I hoped you would say that," Lucy said. "For I want to tell you, Jaylene. I truly want to tell you."

Jaylene reached out protectively and put her

arms around her friend. "Then you may tell me without fear of recrimination. I promise you."

Lucy accepted the affectionate hug, then straightened up and wiped her eyes, smiling apprehensively through her tears.

"In order to tell the story, I shall have to go back to my father's funeral," Lucy said. "For when father died, Tamara Gilbert died as well."

"Tamara Gilbert?" Jaylene asked. "Who is Tamara Gilbert?"

"I am," Lucy said easily. "Or, at least, I was."

"I don't understand."

"Then lean back and listen," Lucy said. "For I shall tell you a story which will forever put me in need of your protection. Are you certain you want to assume such a responsibility?"

"I am sure," Jaylene said.

Lucy sighed, and brushed an errant strand of hair from her face, then began talking.

"The night before my father's funeral was a night like this one, with steadily falling rain. It continued to rain into the next day as well, and the black dirt of Magnolia Hills turned to mud. Even the horses had to struggle through the mire, pulling their hooves free only with great effort."

As Lucy talked, in a clear and eloquent way, finally able to share her story with another, Jaylene listened, and so expressive was Lucy's story that Jaylene could picture the events as they unfolded, so that it was not as if she were only hearing the story, but rather as if she were present herself.

CHAPTER TWELVE

The preacher who was conducting the funeral dragged the eulogy on and on while the mourners hoped the rain would stop. But the point was finally reached when the mourners prefered the rain to the sermon, so the great oaken doors were swung open and the pallbearers bore Amon Gilbert's casket to the wagon.

A girl sat in the wagon beside her father's body. She was a striking girl with long, flowing black hair, deep dark eyes, and a flawless complexion. She held an umbrella, which did little to stop the slashing rain, and her black dress hung heavy with water. She looked at the train of wagons and buggies following them, noting with some pride the many neighbors who had turned up for her father's funeral.

The Negroes who had belonged to Amon Gilbert struggled through the mud on both sides of the road. They made a pathetic little army of blacks. They were singing some hymn which, with their own embellishments, was barely recognizable; nevertheless, it was mournful and hauntingly beautiful.

"Miss Tamara," Ezra Putnam said, clearing his

throat. The girl lifted her head and looked at him. It was the first word spoken to her since they had left the church. "I want to express the regrets of all your neighbors over your father's dyin'. It was truly a sad thing."

"Thank you, Mr. Putnam."

Putnam put his hand on the girl's leg and squeezed it affectionately. It may have been intended as a gesture of comfort, but it was too intimate a gesture, and she pulled away, not sharply but resolutely. He didn't touch her again, and she rode in unmolested silence until they reached the grave.

The grave where Amon Gilbert was to be laid had been dug by two Negroes while the funeral service had been going on in the church. Now they stood by the hole as the cortege approached, leaning on their shovels and peering at the procession with eyes which looked out from mud-caked faces.

The grave was half-full of water. When the coffin was lowered, it floated, as if Amon Gilbert were reluctant to leave the land he, and his father before him, had built into one of the finest plantations in Mississippi. Putnam motioned to the two gravediggers, and they began to shovel dirt on top of the casket, finally forcing it down.

"Miz Tamara," one of the blacks said, approaching the wagon respectfully. "I've carved out a headpiece for your papa, till you gets a fancy rock one. Do you s'pose it'd be all right if I put it on the grave?"

The man held up a marker inscribed simply: *Amon Gilbert—Born March 5, 1814—Died February 10, 1858.*

"Thank you, Troy," the girl said. "I think it is

beautiful, and I'd be proud to have it marking Papa's grave."

"What are you aiming to do now, Miss Tamara?" Putnam asked.

"Do?" Tamara replied. "Why, I'm going to continue on here at the plantation. What do you mean, what am I going to do?"

"Miss Tamara, now that your pa is gone, you don't have anyone to look after things," Putnam said. "Don't you think it would be best if you came to live with the missus and me and let me handle the plantation for you?" Putnam put his hand on her again and looked at her with eyes that were very deep, with red dots far at the bottom. "I'd treat you like one of my own."

"No," the girl said. She shivered, from the suggestion and from the touch. "I have Alva and Troy. And soon Marcus will return and when he does, I will be married. I'm not worried."

"Alva and Troy are both black, Miss Tamara," Putnam said, speaking slowly as if explaining something to a child. "And Marcus is in Memphis."

"I *know* Alva and Troy are black, Mr. Putnam. But they will watch out for me."

"Well, don't you fret none about it," Putnam said, as if not hearing a word she was saying. "We'll work something out for you." He reached his hand over to squeeze her leg a third time, and she pulled it away from him again, this time more sharply.

The wagons and buggies were once more filled with people as the procession started back to the big house that dominated Magnolia Hills. The house servants had been working all morning, and by the time the mourners reached the house they found

138

food prepared and plates set out on every available table and sideboard.

From the conversation at the table it was hard to realize that the people were gathered for the purpose of mourning. But funerals ranked right behind weddings as social events, and the families who saw each other only occasionally were now able to exchange all the latest gossip. The dinner was gay and noisy, and now and then a trill of laughter rent the air, only to be cut off by a quick, embarrassed shush as someone realized that the mood was supposed to be solemn.

After the dinner Putnam stood up and called for the attention of the men.

"Gentlemen, I think it is about time we came to some agreement about Miss Tamara."

"What agreement?" the girl asked quickly.

"There, there, Tamara, honey. Don't you worry about it any. The men folk will think of something," Ellen Putnam said, as she patted Tamara's arm. Ellen was Putnam's wife. Where Putnam's features were bony and hawkish, Ellen's were full and round.

"I don't want them to think of something," Tamara protested. "I don't need their help."

"Don't worry about it, child," Ellen said. "You won't be a bother to them at all. Come on with us. I had your girl, Alva, fix us up some sassafrass tea. There's nothing like a little sassafrass to keep the chill from settin' in on a body."

Tamara was coaxed away by the good neighbor ladies and given a seat in a rocking chair. A cup of tea was put in her hand and she sipped it absently, straining to hear the conversation of the men who were across the hall in the library.

The ladies pulled out knitting and embroidery and talked among themselves, while their hands moved about their work. To Tamara, their hands looked like birds flitting along a fence row.

By ignoring the women's gossip, Tamara was able to overhear snatches of conversation from the men. Putnam's voice was the loudest, and she could hear him clearly. ". . . And the county clerk told me himself that Miss Tamara approached him on the very day her daddy died, and told him of her fool idea for setting all her niggers free. If she sets her niggers free, what do you think is going to happen? Why, all the other niggers is goin' to want to be free too, and the next thing you know, there won't be a workin' nigger or a safe white woman anywhere in the county. I'm tellin' you, we've got to do something about it."

Tamara got up from her chair and went into the library. It was full of smoke and the men stood clustered together chewing their cigars and waving their glasses. Tamara stood in the doorway watching them.

"Why, Miss Tamara," Putnam said as he saw her. "You shouldn't come in here. This is just men-talk."

"It's men-talk about me, Mr. Putnam," Tamara said. "I have every right to be here."

"Let her stay, Mr. Putnam," one of the others called. "Tamara, I'm going to be honest with you. Your papa would spin in his grave if he knew you were planning on setting all the niggers free."

"I'm doing more than planning," Tamara said resolutely. "I'm going to do it."

"But think about what you are doing, girl! If you set your niggers free, they'll be wanting to be free on the other plantations too. The next thing you know, they'll start revolting, and we'll have a war on our hands against the niggers."

"If you would free your people we wouldn't have any problem," Tamara said.

There was a rush of protesting voices, some of them raised in anger, until Putnam raised his hand to silence them. "It's isn't as simple as all that," he said. "There are questions here far too complex for you to understand."

"I understand the cruelty of keeping another human being in perpetual bondage," Tamara replied evenly. "And I understand the Christian brotherhood that would set them free."

Tamara walked over to the window. It was still raining, and the two little black boys who sat minding the visitor's horses were huddled beneath a piece of canvas, trying unsuccessfully to keep dry. Tamara looked up the long driveway and saw a rig approaching. Whoever it was, she thought, he was too late for the funeral, and if he was just going to agree with the others, she'd just as soon he did not come at all.

Tamara started to look away when she noticed something familiar about the driver that made her heart skip a beat with joy. She let out a little whoop of excitement.

"It's Marcus!" she said, shouting at the others. She turned to look at them with a smile of victory on her face. "Last month Papa gave Marcus permission to marry me. So what I do now is no one's business, as Marcus and I are about to be wed!"

Tamara ran from the library and out the front door, down the front steps, through the rain, and out into the driveway. She had written to Marcus that week when her father's condition had taken a turn for the worse. She was disappointed that he hadn't arrived before her father died, and more hurt than she was willing to admit that he hadn't made it for the funeral. But little did all that matter. He was here now, and he would clear up all this unpleasantness being stirred up by Mr. Putnam.

"Oh, Marcus, you've come!" she said excitedly, as his buggy stopped in front of her. "Oh, darling, I am so happy to see you. Those awful men in here, they . . ."

"Is Putnam in there?" Marcus asked, cutting her off.

"Yes," Tamara said. "He's the worst of the lot, Marcus. He keeps saying they must come to some sort of agreement about me."

Marcus stepped down from the rig and started toward the house without so much as a perfunctory kiss for Tamara. Considering that he had been away for some time Tamara found his indifference perplexing. She was hurt by it.

Tamara hurried after him, thinking that perhaps he was so intent upon righting the wrong that had been done her that he had let the greeting slip by for the moment. Such thoughts poured balm on her hurt feelings. But then, with a quick fear, she thought that he might be angry enough to do something unwise.

"Marcus, you won't do anything that might be dangerous?" she asked.

"What do you mean?"

"Like challenge Putnam to a duel or anything like that."

"Don't be foolish, Tamara," Marcus said. "I have no intention of fighting a duel."

"That's good," Tamara said with relief. "For a moment, I thought . . ."

"Don't think," Marcus interrupted.

Marcus stepped into the library, and when the others saw him, they greeted him warmly.

"How was Memphis?" one of them asked him.

"Anxious to handle as much cotton as we can produce," Marcus said.

"Ah," Putnam said, smiling. "Gentlemen, I propose a toast to the almighty bale of cotton." The others laughed, and tipped their glasses with him.

"Tell me, Marcus," Putnam said. "Did you manage to check on that matter we spoke of yesterday?"

"Yesterday?" Tamara asked quickly. She looked at Marcus in confusion. "You were back yesterday, and you didn't come to see me? You didn't even come to my father's funeral this morning?"

"I had business to attend to," Marcus said. He looked at Putnam with a set expression on his face. "You were right, sir. You have my undying gratitude for informing me of the situation before I made a fool of myself."

"It was the honorable thing to do," Putnam said. "That's why I informed you as soon as I discovered it." Putnam looked at Tamara, and Tamara saw the same strange look in his eyes as she had seen in the wagon. It was a frighteningly hungry look, with a dull, red glow.

"Marcus, Mr. Putnam, what are you talking

about?" Tamara asked, a nervousness rising in her. She looked from one to the other.

Marcus didn't answer. Instead, he looked at the other men gathered there in the library.

"Gentlemen," he said. "There will be no niggers freed from Magnolia Hills, I can promise you that."

"What?" Tamara asked, stunnned. "Marcus, how can you make such a promise? Magnolia Hills belongs to me and I can do with it as I wish."

"That's just it," Marcus said easily. "Magnolia Hills doesn't belong to you, it belongs to me. So do you, by the way."

"So do I? What are you talking about? What do you mean, Magnolia Hills belongs to you? We aren't married yet, Marcus, and if this is to be your attitude, we never shall be."

Marcus smiled. "On that point, my dear, you are one hundred percent correct. I will never marry you."

"What?" Tamara asked in a small voice. She felt her head spinning and a quick nausea in her stomach. "Marcus, what are you saying?"

"I have no desire to marry you, Tamara, and, according to the laws of this state, I couldn't marry you if I wished!"

"But . . . but we are engaged!" Tamara said. "Only last month you wrote a letter to my father asking for my hand, and he said yes. He even made you executor of his will."

"I remember," Marcus said flatly. "And I am grateful to him for that, for in the same act he made me the ultimate heir, should you be unable to inherit Magnolia Hills. By a codicil of the will, Magnolia Hills now belongs to me, land and chattel.

144

And, as part of the chattel, you, too, belong to me."

Tamara couldn't believe her ears.

"What do you mean I'm part of the chattel?"

Marcus removed an envelope from his inside jacket pocket, pulled a paper from the envelope and began reading.

"I, Amon Gilbert, do hereby attest and affirm that the following property, herein listed as collateral for a loan . . . and so on and so forth," Marcus said. "Ah, here's the interesting part. Magnolia Hills, located north of Natchez where the Mississippi River makes the first large bend to the west, said land to encompass all ground within such bend. In addition to the land there is the main house, stable and outbuildings, a row of ten slaves, as of this date, this date being August 10th, 1856. The slaves are here below listed by name: Tamara Gilbert, my issue by the slave Tricia, now deceased; Alva Morris, housemaid; Troy Parnell, overseer." Marcus looked up at Tamara. "Do I need to go on?"

"I don't understand," Tamara said in a weak voice.

"There's nothing to understand," Marcus said. "Your father needed money, so he borrowed against what he owned. He had to list all his assets and he listed you among them. Once he made his crop he paid the money back, but the statement he made was still in the bank vault. You are a nigger, Tamara."

As Lucy spoke those words, she looked up at Jaylene to measure the shock the words would have on her. Jaylene reached out and took Lucy's hand in her own.

145

"Oh, to have him treat you so cruelly," Jaylene said.

"There is more to the story," Lucy said. "More cruelty than you can imagine. May I continue, or have you heard enough?"

"Do you wish to continue?" Jaylene asked.

"Yes."

"Then do so," Jaylene said. "For you will find in me a true friend."

Lucy went on with her story.

Alva explained the circumstances to Tamara. It seemed that her father had visited a sporting house in New Orleans. All the women there were half Negro, and one of the women caught Amon Gilbert's fancy. He was so taken with her, in fact, that he bought her and took her home with him, and lived with her as if she were his wife until the day she died. That woman was Tamara's mother.

Putnam stepped into the kitchen just as Alva finished the story she was telling Tamara, and Alva and Troy both grew quiet and reserved. Tamara had noticed this subtle but ever present reaction of blacks to the presence of whites before. But now, for the first time she understood, and realized with sudden insight, that *she had reacted just as Alva and Troy had*.

"Tamara," Putnam said, looking at her with that strange, almost frightening expression she had seen in his eyes earlier. "Under the circumstances, Marcus felt it would be best if you didn't stay at Magnolia Hills. Therefore he offered you for sale and I have bought you. Get some of your things together. I'll be taking you home with me."

146

Tamara stood woodenly and walked up the stairs to her bedroom. She took a suitcase from the closet and began packing her clothes, moving mechanically, still too numbed by all that was happening to show any reaction.

The door opened.

"Alva, would you help me . . ."

"It's me," Putnam said.

"Mr. Putnam, you have no right to come into a young lady's room without knocking," Tamara said.

Putnam smiled, an evil smile, and now Tamara recognized the expression in his eyes for what it was—lust. She realized that he wanted her, and she was frightened by the realization.

"You are no longer a young lady," Putnam said. "You are a slave girl. *My* slave girl, Tamara, and I can do anything with you I wish."

"What?" Tamara asked, putting her hand up to her mouth. She stepped back, her fear growing to panic.

Putnam slipped his tunic off, then began unbuckling his belt. "Don't be frightened, Tamara," he said. "This is something all the nigger girls go through. Especially the pretty ones."

"What are you doing?" Tamara asked angrily. "Get away from me!"

Putnam reached out to grab Tamara, but she jumped back. His hand caught the front of her dress and he ripped it down the middle, revealing her small, perfect breasts. The nipples, reacting to the sudden exposure of air, tightened.

"Look at that," Putnam. His eyes grew glassy and he opened his trousers, exposing himself to her. He reached out again and grabbed her, and threw her on the bed. She tried to fight against him, but he was too strong for her, and she was unable to ward him off.

Putnam made no effort to remove her dress. He just tore it from her, ripping it all the way down the front. She tried to hold her legs together, but the effort was futile, and he loomed over her, looking like an apparition from hell.

When she felt his full weight on her, Tamara wanted to scream, but knew to do so would be useless. He entered her brutally, and she felt a searing pain. It was so acute that she cried out with the agony of it, and wondered how such a thing could happen to her in her own home. That it occurred in her own bed was the final degradation.

Finally Putnam let a grunt escape from his lips, and shuddered once as he finished. He withdrew from her then and, turning his back to her, began dressing quietly.

As Tamara lay on the bed, used, degraded, and injured, she saw a pair of scissors on the bedside table. When she looked up, Putnam was still standing with his back to her, pulling on his pants. He was talking to her.

"I know you didn't like it much that time," Putnam said. "It's always painful the first time. But you'll get used to it, like all the others, I reckon, and then . . ."

Putnam never finished his sentence, for Tamara brought the scissors down right in the side of his neck. The scissors severed an artery, and a thick, gushing spurt of blood squirted out. Putnam turned to face her with a look of surprise on his face. He made one or two futile efforts to withdraw the scissors. That failed and he collapsed to the floor. He lay there, jerking convulsively, until he died, never uttering another sound.

Alva stepped into the room a few moments later and saw at once what had happened. She gasped quietly, but she didn't scream.

"Tamara, get dressed and get out of here, quick," she said. "You mustn't be here when the white folks find out."

"Alva, I—I had no choice," Tamara said. "He *raped* me."

"No'm, honey, he didn't rape you. Nigger men rapes white women, but white men pleasures nigger women. Leastwise, that's the way they'll tell it, and you'll hang, girl, sure as Nat Turner. You've got to get out of here."

Jaylene reached over to squeeze Lucy's hand.

"I left that very night," Lucy said. "I took the name Lucy Wade. It was the name I had given an imaginary girlfriend when I was a little girl. I needed a safe way to travel and when I was in Greenville one day, your uncle gave a show there. I asked him for a job, and to my surprise, he took me on. I've been with him ever since."

"Does he know about everything?" Jaylene asked.

"No," Lucy said. "No one knows, except you."

"Your secret is safe with me," Jaylene assured her.

"I knew it would be," Lucy said.

Outside the wagon the cold rain continued to fall, but the girls were oblivious to it now. They were dry and snug, basking in the warm glow of their friendship.

CHAPTER THIRTEEN

Under a cluster of trees near the stage pike a group of horsemen waited. They wore oil slickers and wide-brimmed hats to keep out the rain.

"I don't think he'll be acomin' out in this kind of weather," one of the men said. He squirted a stream of tobacco juice toward a mudpuddle, where it swirled brown for a moment, then was quickly washed away.

"He'll come," Todd said. "When I left Winona yesterday afternoon, General Grant said he wanted him there by noon today. Grant's not the kind of person you disobey."

"Yeah, but see here, Major, ain't this Chauncey Anders fella a civilian?"

"That doesn't matter," Todd said. "Civilian or military, when they work for Grant they obey."

"Sounds like he might be a purty good Gen'rul after all," the man said. "I didn't think the Yankees had any good soldiers at all."

"The Yankees have plenty of good soldiers, and don't you forget that," Todd warned. "Remembering it just might keep you alive."

"Yeah? Well, you sure fooled 'em. You snuck in and out of Winona as if you owned the place."

"I was lucky," Todd said. "But I believe Holt was beginning to get suspicious. I asked him for the construction plans and he put me off."

"Major, I hear them coming," Sam Shelton said, and Todd held up his arm to call for silence. Then, through the rain, he could hear the driver whistling and shouting at his team to urge them on.

"Sam, keep the men here," Todd said. "I'm going to ride out into the road and stop the driver. I'll tell him I want to buy passage. When he stops, the rest of you ride out and surround the stage. That way we can pull Mr. Anders off without any gunplay."

"Hell, let's just shoot the driver," one of the men suggested. "He's a Yankee sonofabitch anyhow."

"We'll try it my way," Todd insisted.

The rest of the men melted back into the woods. Todd rode out into the road and stood there with his hand raised.

The plan might have worked but, inexplicably, there was a gunshot from the woods behind him.

"I'm sorry, Todd—the damned thing went off!" Shelton shouted.

Todd looked toward the woods in alarm, and at that very moment the man who was riding guard for the stage driver raised his rifle and shot him.

Todd felt a searing pain tearing into his shoulder, and his breath left him as the bullet knocked him off his horse. Almost as soon as he fell into the mud, he heard the guns of the others open up. He saw the driver pitch off the high seat and land spreadeagled in a puddle of water, his blood turning the water

153

red. The riders reined up alongside the stage, their horses prancing about in excitement.

"You folks in the stage, climb down out of there," Sam shouted. While they were climbing down, Sam rode over to where Todd lay and looked down at him.

"Is he dead?" one of the others called. "If he is, tell me, and I'll kill ever' one o' these sons-of-bitches."

"I'm not dead," Todd said, forcing a calmness into his voice to prevent his men from doing anything irrational.

"Are you badly hit?" Sam asked, swinging down to help his fallen chief.

"It's just a flesh wound, I think," Todd said. "Help me onto my horse."

The bullet was in fact buried deep in his shoulder. He could feel the weight of it and the heat of it, as if someone were holding a hot poker to his flesh.

"Bill—you?" one of the passengers on the stage said, and Todd, to his amazement, saw Captain Tony Holt.

"What are you doing on this stage, Tony?" Todd asked. "I thought we were coming after Chauncey Anders."

"Anders has the dysentery," Tony said. "I'm going to explain his absence to General Grant—but what are you doing here?"

"Major Todd Kirk at your service, sir," Todd said. He smiled and tried to salute, but the pain overtook him and he had to grab the saddle pommel to keep from falling.

"You are a damned spy!" Tony said.

"I was," Todd said. "At this moment I am a soldier again." He grimaced in pain. "A wounded soldier."

"Would that the ball were placed eight more inches to the right, sir! Then it would have been fatal," Tony said angrily.

"I'm sorry to disappoint you," Todd said. "Sam, let 'em go. They won't be doing us any good."

"You, guard! Can you drive this thing?" Sam asked the soldier who was sitting on the seat with both arms high in the air.

"Yes," the guard said.

"Put the driver in the coach and get on out of here."

"Major," the man who had wanted to shoot them all said. Major, we are more'n thirty miles behind Yankee lines. Iffen we let these fellas go, they're gonna tell about us, sure'n all hell."

"I imagine they will," Tod said.

"Then let's shoot 'em."

"No," Todd said.

"I think you're makin' a big mistake. They're gonna turn out the whole Yankee cavalry after us."

"Your soldier is right, Kirk," Tony said. "I intend to ride with the cavalry if they will let me."

"I didn't imagine otherwise," Todd said. "Sam, let's get out of here," he said, and he slapped his legs against the side of his horse and started down the road.

After they had ridden out of sight of the stage, Sam called out to Todd.

"Todd, we're going north. Don't you think we'd better head around, toward our own lines?"

"No," Todd said. He fought at the pain. "Don't you see, Sam? They'll block all the roads south, knowing we'll be going that way. Our best bet is to head north. We'll go into Grenada . . . there are people who can hide us out there."

"All right," Sam said. "Whatever you say."

The terrible pain finally stopped and a warming numbness set in. It was that numbness which allowed Todd to keep up with the others as they rode. But with the numbness came also a weakness from loss of blood, and by the time they rode into Grenada, just after dark, Todd was staying in his saddle only by supreme effort of will.

"Hey, Cap'n Shelton, the Major's about to keel over," one of the men called. The one who had called had taken it on himself to ride beside Todd, and for the last three hours it had been he who held the reins of Todd's horse, while Todd clutched the pommel with both hands just to stay up.

"I know a doctor in Grenada who'll fix him up," Sam said.

"Sam," Todd said. The effort of speaking made the pain excruciating. "Sam, you've got to lead the others out of here."

"You aren't in condition to travel yet," Sam said.

"Just leave me."

"Todd, I can't do that. The Yankees control Grenada. What if they discover you are here?"

"Better they get only one man instead of all of us," Todd said. "Now, you do what I say. You drop me off here, then you and the others circle around and get back."

"All right," Sam said. "But I'm going to come back in a week and get you."

"Where's the doctor?" the one with Todd asked. "He's got to get there fast."

"He's right in the middle of town," Sam said. "Marty, you come with me. You others ride down to that farmhouse down there." He pointed to a small house in a clump of trees, about three hundred yards from the road. "Tell him who you are. He'll have his woman fix you some hot grub for supper. We'll eat at the doc's house."

"When will you be back?"

"Soon as we make arrangements to leave Major Kirk," Sam said. "Now go on."

As the others left, Sam, Marty, and Todd headed for the doctor's house. It was totally dark now, and as the three rode through the street they could see small squares of golden light on the ground, cast through the windows of the houses. Sam halted them when they reached the end of the street.

"What is it, Cap'n?" Marty asked.

"That's the house down there," Sam said, pointing to a low, single-story building which sat nearly half a block away from the others. A wisp of wood smoke rose from the chimney, carrying with it the aroma of chicken frying. "I just want to make sure there's no danger."

The saddle squeaked as Sam twisted in it to look around. Todd held on, telling himself that there was only a short time left and then he could lie down.

"It looks clear," Sam said calmly.

The three of them slowly crossed the distance. They stopped just in front of the doctor's house.

B. D. WAUD, M.D., the sign by the door read. Sam didn't bother to knock, he just pushed it open. Then he and Marty half-carried Todd inside.

"What the—? What is this?" the surprised doctor asked, looking up from his supper table. His wife was standing at the stove frying chicken, and she looked around in alarm as well.

"Don't be alarmed, Doc," Sam said quietly. "It's Major Kirk. He's been hit."

The doctor moved quickly to the door and looked nervously around before he shut it. "Did anyone see you bring him here?" he asked anxiously.

"No," Sam said. "The place is crawling with Yankees, so we didn't take any chances."

Sam lay Todd on the bed, and Dr. Waud sat beside him and opened Todd's coat, then his shirt.

"He's lucky," he said. "The rain has washed the wound so there is no festering. But the bullet is going to have to come out, and he's lost so much blood I don't know if he'll survive."

"Cut it out, Doc," Todd said gamely. "I'll hold on."

"Do you men want something to eat?" Mrs. Waud asked. "Not too much chicken, but I can make lots more gravy."

Sam looked at Todd. "Todd, are you sure you want him to do this?"

"I don't have any choice," Todd said. "Go on, Sam, you and Marty get something to eat, then get out of here."

"Here's a little laudanum," Dr. Waud said, handing Todd a small bottle. "You'd better take some. You'll need it when I start probing for the bullet."

Dr. Waud's wife assisted him. They removed Todd's shirt and then the doctor began digging into the wound for the bullet. A few minutes later Waud announced that he had the bullet, and he dropped it with a clink into the pan of warm water.

"How soon before he'll be on his feet, Doc?" Sam

asked. He sat at the table eating biscuits and gravy, and looking anxiously toward his friend.

"It'll be twelve hours before he can even sit up, I'd say," Waud said. "Unless he has an awfully strong constitution."

"He's strong, Doc, I'll attest to that," Sam said. He reached into his pocket and pulled out a gold coin, then laid it on the table by his plate. "Here, Doc, this is for fixin' him up, and for keeping him around a while."

"Now, listen, I can't keep him too long," Waud said, turning and pointing a warning finger at Sam. "If the Yankees found him here they could hang me for treason."

"Tell them he's your cousin," Sam said. "He has to stay somewhere. Don't worry, I'll be back in a couple of days to get him."

"He'll be lucky if he can ride even then," Waud said.

"He'll ride," Sam said. "Come on, Marty, we have to go."

Sam and Marty left the small house and Waud and his wife stood there, looking at the door. They waited for a moment, and when they heard the horses leave, Waud walked over to look through the door.

"B.D., you knew those people?" Waud's wife said. She brushed a wisp of errant brown hair out of her eyes and looked at the young man who lay on their bed, bare from the waist up and now sleeping peacefully.

"That fellow is Todd Kirk," Waud said.

"You mean of Kirk's Raiders?"

"Sarah," Dr. Waud said from the window. "If anyone comes by, you tell them I was called to Winona. Do you have that? I'm going to Winona."

"What for?"

" 'Cause that's where General Hovey is, and he's the only one who can pay the reward for turning Kirk in."

"B.D., you're going to leave me with him, alone?" Sarah asked, surprised by his statement and frightened by the prospect.

"Don't worry. He'll be out of it for the whole night, and I figure to be back by dawn. Just in case anyone sees him, you tell him he is your nephew, wounded in the war."

"B.D., what will they do to him?" Sarah asked, looking at Todd.

"Hang him, most likely."

"Hang him? But he's a soldier, isn't he? Won't they just take him prisoner and let him go after the war is over?"

"He's a guerrilla," B.D. said. "You know what the Yankees think about guerrillas. They say they are just outlaws." He smiled. "Anyway, the reward will likely be a pretty good one, so I'm goin' for it. You just do like I told you."

Sarah put the "doctor out of town" sign on the front door after Waud left, then cleaned up the supper dishes. But all the while her eyes kept wandering over to the man on the bed. His chest, though only lightly adorned with hair, was full and muscular. The skin was clear and smooth.

Whenever Sarah caught herself looking at him, she would scold herself mentally and look away. After all, he couldn't be over thirty, and she was nearly forty . . . a married woman who had no

160

right to think about how handsome a man was. But she couldn't keep disturbing thoughts of him from creeping into her mind, and before she knew it, she would be looking at him again.

Sarah rearranged her kitchen cabinet, not because it needed it, but just to keep herself occupied so that she wouldn't look at him. But it didn't work. Once more she turned to see him, and this time she could feel a warmth in her body which wasn't brought on by the heat of the late spring night.

Sarah took off the sweater she had been wearing, and she felt some respite, but no relief from the heat that was building within. That drove her to unbutton the top six buttons of her dress, and she folded the collar back, almost all the way down to the swell of her breasts. She knew it was a scandalous move, but as she was alone she didn't care.

No, she thought. She wasn't alone. The man on the bed was with her. *But he's sleeping*, she decided, justifying her scandalous action.

Sarah walked over to the stove and poured a kettle of hot water into a basin, then carried the basin over to the bed and sat on it. She began giving the young man a bath. She was doing no more than administering to a patient, she told herself. But her breathing began to be more labored, and she felt such a churning within that it could scarcely be contained.

Then Todd's eyes opened. He started to sit up, but so abrupt was his movement that it sent a searing stab of pain into his shoulder, and he fell back down on the bed.

"Lie still, sir, and you will be more comfortable," Sarah instructed.

"Who are you?" Todd asked. He looked around. "What is this place?"

"Don't you remember coming here earlier?"

Todd looked into the face of the woman who was bathing him. It was a pleasantly attractive face, he decided, and it eased somewhat the fear that shot through him.

"No," he finally said. "I remember only the rain. The rain and the riding. Where am I?"

"This is the house of Dr. Waud, in Grenada."

"Where are the others?"

"Your friends have gone," Sarah said. "They left you here to mend."

"I'm glad they've gone," Todd said. "It would be too dangerous for them to stay."

"You insisted that they go," Sarah informed him.

Todd turned his head on the pillow and looked around the room. He saw the stove, and heard the soft hiss of steam from the pot of water. On the wall a clock ticked loudly.

"Where is the doctor?" Todd asked.

"He's . . . gone on business," Sarah said. "There are just the two of us here."

As Sarah talked, she continued to bathe Todd, and now the cloth was on his stomach. Sarah bent over and as she did her unbuttoned dress fell forward slightly, exposing the curve of her breast. She felt heat there, and looked up to see that Todd was staring at her.

"I . . . I'm sorry," she mumbled, and reached up to close the buttons.

"No," Todd said, putting his hand on hers gently. "You don't have to close the buttons if you don't want to."

162

"I'm a silly old woman," she said. She turned her head away from him, closing her eyes tightly and biting her lower lip.

"You are a lovely woman, without age," Todd said easily. He reached down and unfastened his breeches, then pushed them down and guided her hand, the hand which was now mindlessly bathing a circle on his stomach, down further, until she felt his bulging manhood.

"No," she said. "Please, no." She was trembling now, like a frightened bird. Tears streamed down her face. "Help me to fight this evil want that's come over me."

Todd put his hand behind her neck, then gently pulled her head down to his, pressing her lips to his.

Sarah let out a small whimper, and returned his kiss with surprising ardor. Her skin was incredibly warm, and he could feel the pulse in her neck beating rapidly. Finally, with a gasp, she sat up. "I beg of you," she said. "Don't you know what you are doing to me?"

Todd smiled, and pulled her back to him for another kiss. This time he began unbuttoning the remaining buttons. Without mind or will of her own, Sarah helped him, so that within a moment she lay beside him on the bed as naked as he.

Sarah tried to fight against the terrible need that was consuming her body, but she was too weak with desire. The warmth spread through her with dizzying speed, and she surrendered herself to it, no longer putting up the pretense of fighting.

Todd attempted to change positions, to move over her, but the pain in his shoulder stabbed at him again. When Sarah saw that, she smiled gently, put

163

her fingers gently on his shoulders to indicate that he should stay where he was, and moved over him, taking him into her, orchestrating the unfolding events on her own.

Sarah felt Todd beneath her, thrusting up against her, helping her as she continued to make love to him. Then, finally, she felt the jolts of rapture that racked her body and caused her to fall across him with a groan of ecstasy, even as he was spending himself in her in final, convulsive shudders.

They lay that way for several moments, with Sarah on top, allowing the pleasure to drain from her body slowly, like the heat leaving an iron. Finally she got up and looked down at him.

Todd smiled at her. "Your husband is a lucky man, madam," he said.

"My husband has not slept with me in five years," Sarah said.

"What? Why?"

"He is a man of medicine," Sarah said. "He feels abstinence will prolong his life."

"If so, who would want to live such a long life?" Todd asked. "I was wrong, he isn't a lucky man—he is a foolish man. A very, very foolish man. Is this the first time for you in five years?"

"Yes," Sarah said. She hung her head and tears of shame began to slide down her cheek. "I'm sorry," she said. "You must think I am a very evil woman."

"No," Todd said. "I think you are a lovely woman. Your husband is not only foolish, he is cruel for putting you through such a thing. And if he were here now I would tell him so."

"Oh!" Sarah said, suddenly remembering. "You

can't stay here. My husband has gone to Winona to turn you in for the reward."

Todd sat up, and felt a wave of dizziness and nausea overtake him. He sat on the edge of the bed for several moments until the feeling passed. "How much time do I have?" he asked.

"He said he wouldn't be back until morning, but if he finds soldiers between here and Winona he'll be back much sooner than that. I really don't know when he'll be back."

Todd reached for his pants. "Help me get dressed," he said, and Sarah, still naked herself, bent down beside him to help him into his clothes. Not until he was dressed did she think to pull a cotton nightgown over her nakedness.

"Now, help me to my feet," Todd said.

"Oh . . . you'll never make it," Sarah said.

"I don't have any choice," Todd said. "If I stay here I'll hang. If I leave, there's at least a chance I won't bleed to death."

Sarah put his arm around her shoulder and, supporting most of his weight, helped him to his feet.

"Here," he said. "Let me hold on to the foot of the bed for a moment, just to get my balance, then we can go."

Todd held on, breathing heavily from the exertion. His face and body broke out with sweat.

"Are you all right?" Sarah asked.

"Yeah," Todd said. "Yeah, I'm all right." He took a deep breath and looked toward the door.

"Are you ready?"

"Yeah," Todd said. "Is my horse still here?"

"Yes, the doctor took him to the barn."

"Still saddled?"

"I'm sure he is. B.D. didn't stay out there long enough to unsaddle it."

"That's bad for Diablo," Todd said. "But good for me. I don't know if I could get him saddled myself."

Leaning heavily on Sarah's shoulder, Todd made it to the back door. Then, when he reached it, he opened it himself, and with a supreme effort, stepped outside. He looked back toward Sarah and smiled bravely. "Well, here goes," he said. "Thanks for everything."

Sarah kissed him goodbye, then watched him walk through the dark to the small lean-to that served as a barn. When Todd swung onto his horse and rode away, his last sight was of Sarah standing in the doorway, watching him.

CHAPTER FOURTEEN

gerly pitched in to unload the wagons and move the material into the theater.

"Mr. Fox," an officer said approaching them

It was mid-morning, and though the streets were still muddy from the previous night's rain, everything else about Yazoo City seemed to have a freshwashed quality about it.

The two wagons of the Edward Fox Players rolled slowly down the street until they reached the theater. There, several soldiers and townspeople had gathered to greet them.

"Are you coming back to give us another show so soon?" one of the soldiers asked.

"Of course," Edward answered easily. "In fact, we are going to do a totally new show, and this will be the first place we perform."

As Jaylene and Lucy started to step down from the wagon in which they had been riding, more than a dozen men offered their assistance.

"Can we get free passes for helpin' out, like the last time?" one of the soldiers asked.

"I promise you, when we put on our show, you will be admitted free," Edward said. "But first we must have rehearsals. So give us a few days, won't you?"

The soldiers agreed to Edward's terms, and eagerly pitched in to unload the wagons and move the material into the theater.

"Mr. Fox," an officer said, approaching them.

"Yes," Edward replied, looking toward the officer. "I hope I'm not causing any trouble by utlizing these nice volunteers."

"Not at all, sir," the officer said. "I have just come to extend Colonel Culpepper's invitation to join him again, for lunch."

"Tell the colonel we accept his kind invitation with pleasure," Edward said, though Jaylene made a face that showed that she was anything but pleased at the invitation.

"I know you don't care for him," Edward said a little later. "But as we must stay here until we have learned a new play, we should do nothing to antagonize him."

"I suppose you are right," Jaylene said, agreeing reluctantly.

"And you must admit that with the wartime shortage affecting everyone else, he sets the finest table in the South."

"I know," Jaylene said. "I think that may be one of the things I have against him. It should be criminal to enjoy this war so."

"I agree," Lucy said. "But I am ashamed to say that I am actually looking forward to it. Your description of the meal he served you the last time was so marvelous that I have scolded myself often for not going. This time, I assure you, I won't miss the opportunity."

"Mr. Hardenburgh?"

"Indeed, count me in," Hardenburgh said.

Hardenburgh joined the others, and they started

to leave the theater. But before they did, Edward stopped and looked back toward the stage.

"Well, what do you think?" he asked. "Can we do it?"

"Of course we can," Hardenburgh said.

"Yes," Jaylene added. "We'll get along quite nicely without Mr. Booth."

"And be the better for his absence," Lucy added.

"You make me proud," Edward said, beaming at all of them. "Now, let us go help ourselves to the finest Colonel Culpepper can offer."

Fresh boards had been laid across the roads, so that by holding up the hems of their dresses the two ladies were able to arrive at Culpepper's private dining establishment in a relatively unsoiled state.

"Oh, Jaylene," Lucy said as they stepped inside. "It is everything you said it was."

"And wait until you taste the food," Edward said. "It is even better than this setting would suggest."

A door in the back of the room opened, and a smiling Colonel Culpepper came to greet his guests.

"Ah, what an honor to have you back in Yazoo City," he said. "And to have you share a meal with me again. It is most kind of you."

"No, Colonel, it is we who are honored," Edward replied graciously. "And we thank you for inviting us."

"I have also invited another," Culpepper said. "He is a member of General Pemberton's staff from Vicksburg, and is here to solicit my support for the defense of that city. I hope you don't mind that I've invited him to join us."

"Of course we don't mind," Edward said.

"Colonel, come join us," Culpepper called, and a

tall, blond officer came into the dining room to meet Culpepper's new guests.

"Colonel Hodding, I'd like you to meet the members of the Edward Fox Troupe," Culpepper said. "This is Edward Fox, Frank Hardenburgh, Jaylene Cooper, and Lucy Wade."

Colonel Hodding smiled as each person was introduced, until he saw Lucy. Then the smile left his face, and his features twisted into a mask of cold hate.

"Tell me, Colonel," he said in a quiet, almost metallic voice. "Are you in the habit of letting niggers dine here?"

Jaylene gasped, and looked at Lucy, only to see an ashen expression on the girl's face. Lucy had reached for Jaylene's hand the moment the colonel had come into the room, and now she was squeezing it so hard that it was painful. Jaylene knew that Lucy had no idea she was squeezing so hard.

"Niggers?" Culpepper said, looking around. "Where do you see a nigger?"

"This girl is a nigger," Colonel Hodding said, looking at Lucy. "Her name is Tamara Gilbert, and she is wanted for murdering her master."

"What are you talking about?" Edward asked, clearly confused by Hodding's strange statement. "This is Lucy Wade. She has been with me for a long time."

"Tell them who you are, Tamara," Hodding said.

Lucy's eyes were tightly shut, and tears were flowing down her cheeks. This sad event was proof enough of Hodding's accusation.

"Lucy, tell him he's wrong," Jaylene pleaded. "Tell him he has made a mistake."

171

"Jaylene," Lucy said quietly. "This is Marcus."

"Colonel Culpepper, I ask that you place this Negress under arrest," Marcus said.

"No!" Jaylene said. "Please, you can't mean it!"

"I can understand your being taken in by her," Marcus said to Jaylene. "We all were. Including Mr. Putnam, the man she murdered."

"Murdered?" Jaylene said. "How can you call it murder? It was self-defense. He raped her!"

Everyone looked at Jaylene in surprise including her uncle.

"Jaylene, you knew about this?" Edward asked in confusion.

"Yes."

"And you didn't say anything?"

"No. Uncle Edward, Lucy is my friend. She has been wronged, and now this man would wrong her again. Can't you do something?"

"Colonel," Edward pleaded. "Since she has been with me her behavior has been exemplary. Couldn't you parole her to my custody?"

"No," Marcus said. "She has committed murder—she must hang."

"Hang? Oh, my God, no!" Jaylene cried. She put her arms around Lucy, as if by that action to protect her. "I won't let you hang her!"

"Colonel Hodding," Culpepper said, "perhaps we can work something out."

"What do you mean?" Marcus asked.

Culpepper looked at Lucy and Jaylene as they stood with their arms around each other, a pitiable sight of distress. "You knew Putnam, I did not. Was he the type who would attempt to force himself upon someone?"

"This Negress belonged to him," Marcus said. "He didn't force himself on her, because as she was his property, he could do anything with her he wished."

"I wasn't his property!" Lucy said. "I wasn't anyone's property!"

"You were his because I sold you to him," Marcus said. Quickly, Marcus explained the situation to Colonel Culpepper. As Edward and Hardenburgh heard the story they gasped at the incredible cruelty which had befallen Lucy. Only Culpepper seemed unmoved by the tale, but then he said something that gave Jaylene a ray of hope.

"It was obviously a tragic turn of circumstances which forced this girl into such a rash act," Culpepper said. "Surely some consideration should be given for that?"

"I ask for no quarter," Marcus said, "and I offer none."

"Then perhaps we can work out some sort of compromise," Culpepper suggested.

"How can you compromise with the hangman's rope?" Marcus asked.

"I propose that we not hang her."

"Oh, yes, please, Colonel Hodding," Jaylene said. "Listen to what Colonel Culpepper is proposing. Let her go free."

"Well, I'm not quite proposing that she go free," Culpepper said quickly.

"If not free, then what?" Jaylene asked.

"Yes, Colonel Culpepper," Marcus replied. "I would be interested in knowing just what you are proposing."

Culpepper looked at Lucy, fixing her with a long,

attentive gaze. "I propose that you turn her over to me," he said.

"To what end?" Marcus asked.

"As you know, I am currently rounding up all the niggers I can find to aid in the construction of the defenses of Vicksburg. You are, yourself, here on a mission to return the niggers to the labor battalion, are you not?"

"Yes," Marcus said. He looked at Lucy. "Surely you don't expect this girl to be of any value in such work?"

"Perhaps not," Culpepper said. "But I believe I will be able to utilize her in some capacity here if you would parole her to me. In return, I could let you have two nigger men I had planned on keeping."

"I don't know," Marcus said, hedging a bit.

"Of course, I wouldn't expect you to agree to such an arrangement without adequate recompense," Culpepper added.

"Recompense, sir? I don't understand."

"After all, you did sell the girl to Putnam, did you not? And as Putnam is dead, then it would seem only natural that ownership of the girl would return to you."

"Yes," Marcus said, conveniently accepting that illogical statement. "Yes, I suppose you are right. Ownership of the girl would return to me, wouldn't it?"

"And, as you would not put to death a beautiful horse because of some unfortunate accident, then I would not think it logical to put to death a beautiful slave. Surely she has as much right to live as a horse?"

Marcus looked at Lucy for a long, cold moment, then something seemed to flicker in his eyes, perhaps a painful memory of a past love, perhaps even a sense of long overdue compassion.

"I will accept your offer," Marcus said.

"Good, good," Culpepper said. "Now, tell me, what would you consider adequate compensation?"

"How about thirty pieces of silver?" Jaylene suggested coldly.

Marcus looked at Jaylene with a start, then back at Culpepper. "Colonel," he said. "I consider it my duty to our government to trade you the girl for the two men you mentioned. I shall not ask for additional compensation. The knowledge that I have done right will be compensation enough."

"You are a true patriot, sir," Culpepper said. "And now, shall we have our meal?"

"I'll just wait out here," Lucy said quietly. She started for the door.

"And I shall wait with you," Jaylene put in quickly.

"No, that won't be necessary," Culpepper said. He pulled out a chair. "Lucy, my dear, you are most welcome to dine with us. You belong to me now."

"Please," Lucy said. "I don't want to cause any more trouble, I just—"

"Nonsense, my dear," Culpepper said. "I want you to join me. In fact, I insist upon it." And though Culpepper smiled as he made the statement, there was a resoluteness to the smile which indicated that he fully intended to exercise his rights of ownership.

"I shall make it easy for all concerned," Marcus said. "As I have a long trip before me, I will take the slaves I have collected, including the two new

175

ones, and return to Vicksburg to assist General Pemberton."

"Yes, Colonel Hodding," Culpepper said. "Perhaps you should at that. General Pemberton will be quite pleased to see you, I imagine. Your trip has been most successful."

"Yes," Marcus said, looking at Lucy. Again there was an expression on his face that Jaylene could not fathom. And then she realized what it was. Marcus felt betrayed! But why? Certainly it had not been Lucy who betrayed Marcus, but rather Marcus who had betrayed Lucy. Perhaps Jaylene thought, Marcus felt betrayed by the system that had forced this upon him.

Marcus saluted; then, with military crispness, turned and left the restaurant.

"Well," Culpepper said, rubbing his hands together. "It is good to be rid of that unpleasantness, don't you agree?"

"Colonel, you don't know how grateful we are to you for what you have done," Edward said. "Why, to think of Lucy being hanged!" Edward put his hand to his throat almost unconsciously and was unable to go on.

"Yes, it is most distressing, I agree," Culpepper said. "No, I couldn't stand by and watch a beautiful woman be hanged. I had to act."

"Colonel," Jaylene said cautiously. She had not yet given herself over to joy. She was grateful that Lucy's hanging was no longer imminent, but there was something about the events that had just taken place which was unsettling. She was anxious for Lucy's immediate future. "Is there some way we can compensate you for what you have done?"

176

"Oh, no," Culpepper said. "Compensation won't be necessary."

"Then you intend to allow Lucy to stay with us?" Jaylene asked.

"Stay with you? Well, no, I'm afraid not," Culpepper said.

Edward gasped in surprise, though Culpepper's statement didn't surprise Jaylene at all.

"I see," Jaylene said. "Then you intend to go through with this charade? You are going to keep Lucy, as if she were a slave?"

"She *is* a slave, my dear," Culpepper said. "She is *my* slave. But I assure you, she has nothing to fear from me."

"Colonel, I don't understand," Edward said. "I thought you bought her to spare her life."

"Oh, but I did," Culpepper said. "I did. And that is precisely why I can't understand why you are now expressing displeasure."

"We are—"

"Grateful," Lucy suddenly said. It was the first thing she had said in several moments.

"Lucy, you don't mean it?"

"Please," Lucy said, putting her hand on Jaylene's arm. "I don't wish to be a burden to anyone any more, and I don't want to carry this around with me any more. I shall go with Colonel Culpepper and serve him in whatever way he wishes."

"But, Lucy!"

"Please, Jaylene. Try to understand," Lucy said.

Culpepper smiled broadly and looked at Lucy with flashing eyes. "Lucy, my dear, I can see now that we are going to get along splendidly."

CHAPTER FIFTEEN

Clear and sweet, Jaylene's voice rolled over the campsite, and the words she sang touched every heart. Many were the soldiers who turned their faces in the dark, so that their companions would not see the tears that brimmed in their eyes.

"We marched across the stormy land
with strong and fearless tread,
Though worn with toils and scantily
supplied with wartime bread.
No stimulant but blood that burned
our suffering race to save—
Following with joy our youthful chief
to victory or the grave.
Sulphurous flames from countless guns
illumed the grim night air—
No fitful flash, but blazing on
with one continuous glare!
We staggered not—we halted not
for wounded friend or dead—
Through surging shell and hissing shot
fast toward the foe we sped.
'Onward, my boys!' our leader's voice

rings cheerily o'er the storm;
'We'll gain the parapet, and there
your shattered ranks reform;
Onward my friends, my heroes, come,
for every human right—
For kindred, country, hearth and home,
honor and freedom fight.' "

Jaylene left the stage to thundering applause, and was replaced by her Uncle Edward who, with a dramatic reading, soon had the soldiers as attentive to his words as they had been to Jaylene's song.

Hardenburgh was standing behind the makeshift curtain, awaiting his time on the stage. He looked at Jaylene and saw her wiping tears from her eyes. The tears, he knew, were not entirely caused by the poignancy of the song she had just completed.

"You are still thinking about this morning, when we left Lucy, aren't you?" Hardenburgh asked quietly.

"Yes," Jaylene said. "I'm thinking of her. But it's more than that. I . . . I feel guilty somehow, as if I let her down."

"How could you have let her down?" Hardenburgh asked. "There was nothing you could do for her. Be glad, dear, that she wasn't summarily hanged."

"Yes," Jaylene said sadly. "I suppose there is that to be thankful for."

"Of course there is," Hardenburgh assured her. "And when this war is over, we will be able to petition for her freedom."

"I hope you are right," Jaylene said. "But I feel

181

so helpless now. Perhaps we shouldn't have left Yazoo City."

"What could we have done by staying there?" Hardenburgh asked. "You said it yourself, we are helpless to do anything."

"I could have provided her with the comfort of my company," Jaylene said.

"No," Hardenburgh suggested quietly. "Dear, don't you realize that seeing you with your freedom would have, by contrast, greatly intensified poor Lucy's suffering?"

"Yes," Jaylene said. "Yes, you are right, I know you are. Still . . . it was a difficult thing for me to leave her back there."

Jaylene thought back on the decision her uncle had made this morning. The loss of Lucy had reduced their acting company to three people, and there were few plays which could be done with a cast of three. Therefore, Edward abandoned the idea of doing plays, and instead decided to feature the special talents of the three who remained. Jaylene and Hardenburgh would sing solos and duets while Edward provided dramatic and inspirational readings. Edward also worked out a series of *tableaux vivants* which, though featuring only three people, were guaranteed audience pleasers. He also decided he would utilize some of the soldiers from the audience, and that would enhance their popularity even more.

Edward finished his dramatic reading, and Hardenburgh went on stage. Now it was time for something lighter, and Hardenburgh could supply it to them. He was dressed somewhat like a dandy, and his very proper English accent added to the humor of the song he sang.

At first, Jaylene had thought Hardenburgh's song—a song of a wife's infidelity—would not be appreciated by the soldiers. After all, they were away from home, and such an idea might be an unpleasant one. But she learned what observers of soldiers have learned from every war since Caesar's legions were entertained by traveling showmen: a soldier laughs best when he laughs at himself.

Hardenburgh tipped his hat forward, leaned upon his cane like a dandy, and began his song:

"I came home the other night,
as drunk as I could be.
And what do you think my wondering eyes should
    see?
A horse, where my horse should be.
So I said to my wife, my pretty little wife,
'Explain this thing to me.
What's a horse doing,
where my horse should be?'
And she said, 'You old fool, you drunken old fool,
can't you plainly see?
That's nothing but a milk cow
my mama gave to me.'"

The audience roared with appreciative laughter, and Hardenburgh went on:

"Well, I've been around this country,
maybe ten times or more,
but a saddle

and a bridle on a milk cow,
I never saw before."

More laughter.

"I came home the other night,
as drunk as I could be,
and what do you think my wondering eyes should
    see?
A hat, hanging on the hatrack,
where my hat ought to be.
So I said to my wife, my pretty little wife,
'Explain this thing to me.
What's this hat doing on the hatrack,
where my hat ought to be?'
And she said, 'You old fool, you drunken fool,
can't you plainly see?
That's nothing but a chamberpot
my mama gave to me.'
Well, I've been around this country,
maybe ten times or more.
But a feather on a chamber pot,
I never saw before."

"What happened next?" one of the soldiers
yelled.
"You didn't believe that, did you?" another
asked.
Hardenburgh, playing the injured and innocent
husband, tipped his hat back, stepped forward as if
taking the soldiers in on his story, and continued.

"I came home the other night,
as drunk as I could be.

And what do you think my wondering eyes should
    see?"

"There's no tellin'!" one of the soldiers shouted,
and all guffawed with laughter. Hardenburgh, playing the crowd beautifully, merely raised one eyebrow as if totally taken in by it all, then continued.

"I saw pants, on a chair,
where my pants ought to be."

"Mister, you had better wake up," one of the soldiers called.

"So I said to my wife, my pretty little wife,
'Explain this thing to me.
What are these pants doing here,
where my pants ought to be?' "

"I'd like to hear her get out of that," someone
shouted.

"And she said, 'You old fool, you drunken fool,
can't you plainly see?
That's nothing but a dishrag
my mama sent to me.'
Now, I've been around this country,
maybe ten times or more.
But belt and buttons on a dishrag,
I never saw before."

"Why, you old fool, don't you know what she's
doing to you?" someone in the front row yelled.

* * *

"I came home the other night,
as drunk as I could be.
And what do you think my wondering eyes should
    see?
A head, on the pillow,
where my head should be."

"I told you!" one of the soldiers shouted. "You
should've figured it out the moment you saw that
strange horse."

Hardenburgh raised his hand and pointed his finger. He made a face like an irate husband challenging his wife with irrefutable evidence.

"So I said to my wife, my pretty little wife,
'Explain this thing to me.
What is this head doing on my pillow,
where my head ought to be?' "
"And she said, 'You old fool, you drunken fool,
can't you plainly see?
That's nothing but a mushmelon
my mama sent to me.' "

"A mushmelon?" one of the soldiers yelled. "And
you believed her?"

"Well, I've been around this country,
maybe ten times or more.
But, a moustache on a mushmelon, I never saw be-
    fore.
Yes, a moustache on a mushmelon, I never saw be-
    fore."

* * *

Hardenburgh finished his song with a sweeping bow, and then left the stage to the howls of laughter from an appreciative audience.

After the show, Jaylene, Edward, and Hardenburgh moved through the audience, talking to the soldiers and visiting with them. One of the soldiers asked Jaylene if she could write.

"Yes," she answered, puzzled by the strange inquiry. "Why do you ask?" She looked at the man. He was about forty, with a long black beard and close-set, coal-black eyes. He was holding a piece of paper and a pencil out toward her. "I got me these writin' implements, 'n I ain't all that good at my letterin'. I was hopin' you'd write a letter for me. That is, iffen it ain't gonna put you out none."

Jaylene smiled at him. "Certainly I'll help you," she said.

"Why, I thankee, ma'am," the soldier said, smiling broadly. "These here other fellers helps me sometimes, but they got their own letters to write, 'n it ain't fittin' of me to be abeggin' of them all the time."

The soldier folded his poncho double, then put it on a log, making an elaborate show of preparing for Jaylene a place to sit. She accepted the seat and the pencil and paper, and prepared to take his dictation. She looked around and saw that several other soldiers had drawn close to listen to the letter as well.

"Would you rather go someplace where you can dictate more privately?" Jaylene inquired of the soldier.

"Oh, no, ma'am," the soldier said. "All the boys, they like to listen to the letters I write to Marthy, 'n then they like to listen to the letters Marthy writes me back, 'cause the truth is I got to have them read to me, same as I got to have them writ for me. I ain't only no good at makin' letters, I can't make 'em out when someone else makes 'em. Marthy, she's good at that 'n she used to do it for me whenever I was to home."

"Very well," Jaylene said. She smoothed the paper. "I'm ready when you are."

"Dear wife," the soldier began. "I take this opportunity to write you again, having as my pen this time a lovely fair young belle of the South. But don't you be jealous none, as my love is only for you, as you know. I am well, and I hope these few lines may come safe to hand and find you enjoying the same blessing.

"We are going to fight a big battle tomorrow, and with God's blessing, whip them Yankees good. Maybe that will make them think again before they come down here to raid us in our own homes."

Jaylene looked up in surprise. "You . . . you are going into battle tomorrow?"

"Why, yes'm," the soldier said. "We'uns is gonna attack the Yankees at Millikin's Bend, and try 'n drive 'em back. Didn't you know that?"

"No," Jaylene said. "No, I'm afraid I didn't."

"Didn't you see the pork at suppertime?"

"I didn't notice," Jaylene said.

The soldier smiled. "Whenever we get meat like that, we kin allus tell that somethin' is up. Then our cap'n, he had a meetin' with the colonel, 'n when he come back, he tole us what we already know'd. They's gonna be a battle tommora'."

"I'm sorry I interrupted," Jaylene said. She looked back at the letter. "Do you want to go on?"

The soldier began dictating again.

"Tell Mother I am well and I would like to see her very soon. Tell her to write to me as soon as you get my letter, dear wife. Tell our son Johnny that it is up to him to make the crops now, and you tell him I don't want to hear any more about his signing up to fight. I'm doing the fighting for both of us, 'n he has to do all the farmin'. But he's fourteen now, 'n I reckon that's big enough to walk behind a plow.

"Kiss little Anne and tell her that her daddy loves her very much. Martha, if you could get into Jackson and have your likeness made at that place that takes the likenesses and send it to me, I would carry it next to my heart forever.

"I must close now, and remain your husband until death. Direct your letters to Hosea's Infantry, D Company. Signed, T.J. Cole."

"Here it is," Jaylene said as she finished the letter and handed it back to Cole.

"Thankee, ma'am. I thankee kindly," Cole said, taking the precious missive from her.

"Miss, would you do one for me too, please?" another soldier asked, and Jaylene took a pen and paper from him to write his letter. After his there was another, and then another, and Jaylene wrote letters until the failing light made it impossible to write any longer. Finally she begged off, explaining that she couldn't see, and saying that she had to get back to the show wagons.

When she returned, her uncle and Mr. Hardenburgh were sitting near the fire, drinking coffee. A blue coffeepot hung over the fire, and Jaylene could smell the rich aroma of the brew.

"Would you like some coffee, niece?" Edward asked.

"Yes, please," Jaylene said, settling down beside the fire. She stared into the flames for a moment, thinking of nothing save the small line of blue where the flames first leap from the wood before they turn orange and yellow.

"Here," Edward said, handing her the cup.

Jaylene sipped the bracing coffee.

"Did you know these men are going into battle tomorrow?" she asked.

"Yes," Edward said. "The colonel told me."

Jaylene looked out over the camp, and at the winking campfires. She was very pensive for a long moment.

"Tomorrow, so many of them will be dead," she said.

"And as many Yanks," Edward put in.

Jaylene had a pained look on her face. "Uncle Edward, we have played for them too. Is there any difference in human life?"

"No, dear, there isn't," Edward said quietly.

"What a waste," Jaylene said. "What a foolish, foolish waste. How can God let such a thing happen?"

"There have always been wars, darlin'," Edward said.

"I wonder if there has ever been another for as foolish a reason."

"That I couldn't tell you," Edward said.

"All wars are for foolish reasons," Hardenburgh said. He drained the last of his coffee, then stood up and stretched. "Edward, I am going to bed now." He looked over at Jaylene. "You will be without your wagonmate tonight," he said gently. "Wherever she sleeps tonight, I hope she is comfortable, and well."

Jaylene gasped. She had not thought of Lucy for several hours! It made her feel guilty.

CHAPTER SIXTEEN

The distance between Jaylene and Lucy that night was less than ten miles. But Lucy could have been on the other side of the world, so far apart were they actually. For while Jaylene was still following the life of the traveling actress, Lucy had completely left that life. And, whereas Jaylene was white, Lucy was black.

At this moment, Lucy was lying in bed with her hands folded behind her head, staring up at the ceiling without thought. It was the only way she could keep from crying, for otherwise she would think of her fate, and the cruel twist it had taken.

Jaylene did not want to leave with the others when they left at noon, but Lucy was glad she did. For if Jaylene were still here, Lucy would not be able to suspend all thought, and if she couldn't suspend thought, she couldn't bear what she must bear in order to survive.

Culpepper had been kind enough to her during the day. He had not made her work, nor had he mistreated her in any way. And yet she knew that she could take little comfort in that, for to do so would be an exercise in false security.

Culpepper pleaded the press of business to excuse himself in mid-afternoon, but before he left he showed Lucy where she would sleep that night. It was an exceptionally nice room, large, clean, and airy. But Lucy would have traded it in an instant for the cramped quarters of the wagon, and the company of Jaylene and the others.

She lay in the big bed, listening to the sounds of the town drift in through her open window. She kept her mind free of painful thoughts by watching the shadow patterns which were projected onto the ceiling by the trees that waved gently in the evening breeze. As the limbs of the trees moved, they interrupted the silver splash of moonlight, creating the lacy images in which she could lose herself.

Then the silence she had willed to her mind was interrupted by the sound of footfalls in the hallway outside. Despite all efforts to blot out the sound, Lucy was unsuccessful, and she lay in trembling fear as the footsteps grew louder and louder. For one quick moment she hoped they would pass by, but then they stopped right outside her door. She felt a cold fear in her heart.

The door opened and Culpepper stepped inside. He pushed it closed behind him, and she heard the bolt being thrown.

"Well," Culpepper said. "You didn't have the bolt thrown to keep me out, did you? I can see right now, my dear, that you and I are going to get along quite well."

Lucy had not thrown the bolt specifically to insure a good mood in Culpepper when he came to her room. For she knew he would come, and she knew she would be unable to prevent it. Her only hope lay in pleasing him so that he would treat her gently.

Culpepeper lit a lantern, then turned the flame down very low so that the light cast from the globe was little brighter than that which the moon had already provided, though where the moonglow was silver, the lantern gleam was gold, and a subtle mix of the colors suffused the room.

"Now," Culpepper said, turning to look at Lucy. She was staring back at him with black eyes, which for all their darkness glowed nearly as brightly as the lantern, and seemed almost to light the room by themselves. "I just want you to understand the way things are around here. You belong to me. Have you got that?"

"Yes," Lucy said.

Culpepper's hand lashed out, striking as quickly as a snake. He slapped Lucy in the face, not a brusing blow, but one that stung sharply, the more so because of its unexpectedness. Lucy gasped and put her hand to her face. Already her cheek was glowing red from the slap.

"We'll get a long much better if you remember to say yes, master," Culpepper said. He didn't raise his voice, and he didn't change his tone, and the words slid out as smoothly silken as they had all day. Somehow Lucy found that even more frightening than if he had yelled at her.

"Y-yes, master," Lucy stammered.

"There now, that's better," Culpepper said. He folded his arms across his chest and looked at her for a long moment. Lucy longed to avoid his gaze, but some sense of survival told her to meet it head on, not defiantly, but directly.

196

"Who do you belong to?"

"I belong to you, master," Lucy said quietly.

"That's a good girl," Culpepper said. "Now, what will you do for me?"

Lucy hesitated for a moment too long before she answered, and Culpepper lashed out again.

"I'll ask you again," Culpepper said. "What will you do for me?"

"Any—anything you want," Lucy said. Then she saw the twitch of Culpepper's shoulder as he started to reach out and slap her again, so she added, quickly, "Master."

Culpepper smiled broadly. "There now," he said. "You seem to be learning after all, don't you? I've always maintained that it is no more difficult to train a nigger than it is a horse or a dog. Though niggers do seem to have a little more spirit." He reached his hand up to Lucy's face and rubbed her cheek with the backs of his fingers. "You are a most beautiful girl, my dear," he said.

Lucy looked down. "Thank you, master," she ssaid, speaking so quietly he could barely hear her.

"Strip for me, my dear," Culpepper said. "And do it very slowly, please. I want to enjoy it."

Lucy stood up and began removing the nightgown, unbuttoning it slowly as Culpepper had ordered. Culpepper watched with pleasure, feeling his pulse quicken and the heat in his body flame up. She wore nothing under the nightgown, and soon she was naked to his gaze. Her golden skin was shining as if lit from within, catching the subtle reflections of the lantern.

"There, on the dresser," Culpepper said. "There is a bottle of whiskey there. Pour me a glass."

197

"Yes, master," Lucy said. She moved over to the dresser and picked up the bottle and the glass. As she moved the lights played upon her body, brightening her breasts, making dark and mysterious the triangular shadow at the junction of her legs. She poured the drink, then handed it to Culpepper. He tossed the drink down, feeling the controlled fire on his tongue, then pointed to the bed.

"Get in it," he ordered, getting out of his own clothes.

Lucy settled herself down on the bed and lay on her back, her dark eyes watching Culpepper's every move. Her eyes seemed to burn holes into Culpepper, and he felt both highly aroused and slightly uncomfortable.

Naked, Culpepper stepped to the bed and slid in beside her. He pulled her close to him, and Lucy felt his hairy body and angular hardness against her. Culpepper pressed his cheek against hers, and began to massage her breasts.

Lucy didn't resist him, for she knew that to do so would only make things worse. She closed her eyes and tried to pretend it wasn't Culpepper but Sam Shelton who was in bed with her. Such a ruse, she knew, had worked for Jaylene, when Booth raped her.

Lucy wasn't able to substitute Sam for Culpepper, but such a tactic did make what was happening to her bearable. She didn't respond to Culpepper's lovemaking, but she did move her body where he wanted it. But she did it mechanically, and she took no initiative.

Culpepper moved his hand down between her legs, and Lucy moved again, opening herself to his exploring fingers. When he showed signs that he wanted to enter her, she helped him.

With a snarling sound, Culpepper thrust into her roughly. Lucy did not cry out, even though the brutal invasion of her body was painful. Instead, she thrust back against him, tangling her hair with his, providing him with some pleasure, though deriving none for herself.

Culpepper continued his thrashing, thrusting, grunting activity until, much more quickly than he wanted, he spent himself into her, groaning with a mixture of pleasure for the moment, and disappointment at the shortness of it.

After he was totally spent, he rolled to one side of Lucy and lay there for a few moments, breathing heavily. Lucy moved away a little to avoid all skin contact with him.

"Did you enjoy that?" Culpepper finally asked.

"It was for you to be pleasured," Lucy answered. "You are my master. That is my purpose, isn't it?"

"Yes," Culpepper said. "Yes, I guess it is at that, but most nigger girls seem to like it when they are pleasured. It didn't seem to me that you enjoyed it that much."

"No, master," Lucy said. "I didn't enjoy it all that much."

"I suppose it is because you have so much white blood, that being the part which doesn't enjoy bedding with a man. Oh, well, it makes no difference to me, I get my pleasure just the same." Culpepper yawned. "I'm going to go to sleep now."

"Where?"

Culpepper laughed. "Where? Why, right here, of course."

"You mean . . . this is your room?"

"Yes," Culpepper said. He laughed again. "Do you see what a nice fella I am? I'm letting you sleep in here with me."

Lucy turned over on her side so that her back was to him. She had thought she would have a room by herself, and was bitterly disappointed. With him in the room with her, she could never escape, for he would no doubt wake up as soon as she got out of bed.

Lucy bit her bottom lip to silence the sob of frustration and despair that had welled up in her throat. Now there was no hope of escape.

For one instant she thought of killing him. It had been so easy with Putnam. She had felt no remorse at all. She could do it again.

But no. Killing Putnam had been a spontaneous thing done in the heat of fear and anger. If she killed Culpepper it would have to be slow and measured. And that kind of killing, Lucy felt, was murder.

She couldn't do murder.

CHAPTER SEVENTEEN

The slanting bars of the early morning sun fell across the field which, just the night before, had been alive with campfires and soldiers. Now it was nearly deserted. Here and there a wisp of smoke curled up from a nearly dead fire, and in a small ravine near the wagons a fly tent was pitched, and half a dozen men were working feverishly, tearing strips of cloth and forming the cloth into rolls.

"They're gone," Jaylene heard Edward say. It was Edward's voice that awakened her, and she lay for just a moment until she realized where she was. Then she got up and looked through the canvas flap of the wagon.

"Good morning, Uncle Edward," she said. She looked over the empty field. "I didn't even hear them leave."

"I've started a fire for our breakfast," Edward said. "Before the army left, the quartermaster provided us with a goodly portion of provisions. He claimed that they could travel lighter without being so encumbered. We have bacon, flour, and even fresh eggs."

"How generous of them," Jaylene said. "I'll start

our breakfast right away." She climbed down from the wagon and opened the trunk on the side to remove the utensils she would need to prepare the meal. She saw the soldiers who were in the nearby tent.

"Uncle, may I invite those men to take breakfast with us?" she asked.

Edward looked toward them. "I don't see why not," he said. "It's actually their food you'll be cooking."

"I'll go ask them," she said, and holding her skirt up to avoid the early morning dew on the high grass, she walked the fifty yards to issue the invitation.

"Good morning, ma'am," an officer said as she approached the tent. Jaylene looked around and saw three tables, sitting side by side. At the head of each table was a knife and a saw, and the soldiers who had been busily making rolls from the cloth were placing the rolls by the tools.

"Good morning," Jaylene replied.

"Is there something we can do for you?" the officer asked.

"I've come to invite you all to breakfast," Jaylene said.

"Thank you, ma'am," one of the other soldiers said, smiling broadly. "We'd be proud to come."

"Baker, I'll speak for us," the officer said sharply.

"Well, Doc, ain't you gonna say yes?" Baker asked.

The officer smiled and looked back at Jaylene. "Yes," he said. "But I wanted the opportunity to say it myself."

"Good," Jaylene said. "I'm so glad." She looked again at the tables and at the men. "Captain, what is going on here?"

"Here? Why, we're rollin' bandages, ma'am," the captain said. "I'm the surgeon, and we are getting ready to treat the wounded."

"The wounded?" Jaylene said, looking around. "I don't see any wounded."

"No ma'am," the doctor said. "There aren't any. At least, not yet. But by nightfall there will be several of them, and we have to be ready."

"You mean you are going to . . . to *operate* on them, right here, in the field?"

"Yes, ma'am," the doctor replied. He looked at Jaylene in surprise. "What did you expect us to do, ma'am?"

"Why, I thought . . . I mean, surely we have hospitals for the wounded."

"Yes, ma'am, we do. But the nearest one we have right now that isn't in Yankee hands is in Jackson. And by the time we'd get the men there, most of them would die, if we didn't take care of them out here first."

"Oh, I . . . I see," Jaylene said. An involuntary chill passed over her.

"We do the best we can, ma'am," the doctor explained. "And we save a good share of them. That's something, isn't it?"

"Yes, doctor," Jaylene said. "Yes, it is." She pulled herself up, as if putting such unpleasant thoughts behind her. "I suppose I had better get back if I am going to fix breakfast for all of you. It'll be ready in a short while."

"Again, ma'am, we thank you," the doctor said,

and as Jaylene started back to prepare the meal, the soldiers returned to their task of rolling bandages.

"Major Kirk! Major Kirk!" the rider cried, arriving in camp at a full gallop. He swung off the horse before it came to a halt, and ran up to Todd to salute and render his report.

Todd started to return the salute but he winced with pain and dropped his arm back to his side. He smiled laconically.

"I'm going to have to teach you men to quit saluting me, at least until this wound gets better."

"I'm sorry, sir," the rider said.

"It's not your fault," Todd said easily. "You didn't put that ball in my shoulder. Now, what has you so excited?"

"We weren't supported, sir," the rider said. "Cap'n Shelton's had to retire, sir."

"Sam didn't get through? I don't understand, didn't Sherman take the bait?"

"That's just it, Major. Colonel Hardacre didn't make his demonstration against Gen'rul Sherman like he was supposed to, and we was purt' near cut to pieces."

"Casualties?"

"Fifteen killed, sir, 'n maybe twenty wounded."

"Damn," Todd said, and he made a fist and drove it into his palm so hard that he felt a sharp spasm of pain in his shoulder. "I don't understand. Why didn't Hardacre attack Sherman's flank? How could anyone expect Sam to slip through the lines if Sherman wasn't diverted? What the hell was Hardacre doing?"

"He was attacking the coloreds, sir."

205

"He was what? You mean he used an entire regiment to track down runaway slaves?"

"No, sir, they ain't slaves, sir," the rider said. "They might have been at one time, but now they are soldiers, sir, 'n the Third Mississippi attacked them at Millikin's Bend."

"But why? Why would he leave Sam so totally exposed?"

"Colonel Culpepper changed Hardacre's orders, sir. He said it was important that the colored soldiers get whipped."

"Yes, he would think that," Todd said. "What about Sam? Was he hurt?"

"No sir. There was balls whizzin' all about him, but he wasn't even scratched. He tried to get through anyway, Major. You should'a seen him," the rider said proudly.

"Well, it's no disgrace that he was unable to," Todd said. "Pemberton's entire army can't get through. I scarcely think one troop of cavalry could."

It was nearly noon before Captain Shelton and his ragged bunch of men returned. Sam had intended to slip through the lines into Vicksburg, which was the city under siege, to carry them the information Todd had gathered with regard to the channel which the Yankees intended to dig around the city. But without a diversionary attack by Colonel Hardacre on Sherman's flank, there was no way Sam could get through.

"I intend to face Culpepper with this," Todd explained. "And I would like you with me."

"Yes, sir, I'll be glad to go," Sam said. He looked

at his limping, wounded men, waiting for their wounds to be treated. "I blame him for this."

"I'm ready as soon as you are rested," Todd said.

"Todd, I'm ready to go now," Sam replied. "But I don't think you are. A ride that long could be too much for you."

"Nonsense," Todd said. "I'm healing nicely."

But Todd didn't realize how bad his wound was, and by the time he and Sam reached the outskirts of Yazoo City, it was all he could do to stay in the saddle. Despite the pain and weakness, he had not made one complaint during the trip, and Sam, talking angrily about Culpepper, didn't notice his comrade's difficulty.

"Well, we're here," Sam said as they arrived. "Let's go find the sonofabitch and dress him down for the incompetent that he is."

"All right," Todd said. They guided their horses over to a hitching rail, then swung down. As Todd stepped down he became very dizzy, and had to hold onto the saddle pommel for a moment for support.

"Todd, what is it?" Sam asked, noticing his friend's problem for the first time.

"Nothing," Todd replied. "I guess I just got a little dizzy for a moment, that's all."

"Here, let me help you," Sam said. He tied his horse off, then came around to take the reins of Todd's horse. "My God, Todd, look at you," he said, gasping in surprise. "Your shirt is all bloody."

Todd's wound had broken open again, and his shirt was soaked in blood.

"I didn't realize I was bleeding again," Todd said groggily. "I guess I'd better get a little rest."

"Get a little rest? What you need is to go to a doctor and get yourself fixed up right," Sam said. "Here, come along with me. Can you walk?"

"Of course I can walk," Todd said. He let go of his horse and took a few uncertain steps.

"It's not far," Sam said reassuringly. "Just a couple of doors down the street." Sam took Todd's good arm around his shoulder, and half supported, half dragged him until they reached the doctor's office. He kicked the door open with his foot and barged in.

"Hey, Doc!" he called. "Doc, up front."

The doctor stepped out of a back room and saw the two soldiers. When he saw the blood on Todd's shirt he reached for him quickly.

"What's wrong, was he shot?"

"Yeah," Sam said. "About one week ago," he added.

"One week ago? He was shot one week ago and we are just now discovering it? What has he been doing all this time?"

"Nothing, Doc," Todd managed to say. "I got treated the same day it happened."

"It looks as fresh as the day it happened," the doctor said. "Here, you sit down here."

Todd settled gratefully onto a couch, then leaned back and promptly passed out.

"Is he going to be all right, Doc?" Sam asked.

"I think so," the doctor said. "But he's lost a lot of blood. He needs rest."

Sam sighed. "Yeah. Well, we all need rest, I guess. You take care of him, will you? I've got to see Colonel Culpepper. When he comes to, tell him I'm taking care of our business."

208

"All right," the doctor said, almost absentmindedly, already busy cutting away the blood-soaked bandage around Todd's shoulder.

Sam walked down to the Lexington House, where he hoped to find Colonel Culpepper. He intended to give Culpepper a good, stout piece of his mind.

A private stood in front of the door, and he stepped in front of Sam, barring his entrance.

"What the hell are you doing?" Sam asked.

"I'm sorry, sir," the private answered. "But the colonel, he don't let nobody go in till after they've been announced, 'n he says it's all right."

"Oh, is that so?" Sam said. He stared at the soldier for a moment, contemplating shoving him forcefully to one side. He knew that if he did it there would be others on the scene in no time, though, so he just sighed.

"You tell him Captain Sam Shelton of Kirk's Raiders is here," Sam said.

"Can I tell the colonel what this is about, sir?" the soldier asked.

"What it's about? I'll tell you what it's about. It's about cowardice and incompetence."

"Come in, Captain Shelton," a voice suddenly said from the door, and Sam looked up to see Culpepper standing there.

"Thank you," Sam said. He pushed the private out of his way, gently, then stepped through the door to follow Colonel Culpepper into the dining room.

"Now, what's this I hear about cowardice and incompetence? Those are pretty harsh words, aren't they?" Culpepper asked.

"Harsh enough, I reckon," Sam replied.

209

"I see. And who do you apply them to?"

"I apply them to . . ." Sam was about to say that he thought those words fit Culpepper himself. But just before he finished the sentence, he saw a vision so lovely that it took his breath away. For across the room, Lucy had just stepped through the door. She was wearing a golden silk dress and flashing gold earbobs, and she looked at Sam with an expression that he could only attribute to joy—and then with a strange, intense sadness.

Sam felt a quick thrill, for her reflected joy could only be in seeing him.

"Lucy!" he said. "Lucy, what are you doing here?"

"Oh, do you know my nigger girl?" Culpepper asked calmly.

"What?" Sam asked, confused by the question.

"The girl you just called Lucy," Culpepper said. "Her real name is Tamara Gilbert. She's a runaway nigger."

"What are you talking about?" Sam asked. "That is Lucy Wade."

"Yes, she had many people believing that story. I'm sorry that you, too, fell for it."

"Lucy, has he gone mad? What is all this about?"

"Tell him, girl. Tell him who you are," Culpepper said.

Lucy lowered her eyes to the floor.

"I'm your slave, master, sir," she said.

"You see, Captain, she admits it handily enough," Culpepper said. "She has been passing herself off as a white girl, and I must admit that her skin is light enough, fair enough, that she could easily fool someone."

"What are you doing with her?" Sam asked.

Culpepper chuckled and looked at Lucy. "Well, now, Captain, you are a man of the world, are you not? What would you do if you suddenly came into the ownership of such a delightful morsel?"

Lucy's face flushed red in shame and embarrassment, and Sam felt a sudden rush of blood to his temples. For one quick moment he believed he was going to be sick; then he feared he was going to let out a bellow of rage. Finally he managed to restrain himself, and he forced a weak smile on his face. Then a plan, born on the moment, came to him, and he looked at Culpepper cunningly.

"I get your meanin', Colonel. Uh . . . you wouldn't be selling her services to others, would you?"

"Sell her services?" Culpepper asked, with a look of interest on his face. "I'm not sure what you mean."

"I mean I'm willing to pay you one hundred dollars in gold for the privilege of spending one night with this girl."

"Captain, are you crazy? One hundred dollars? You can have the finest octoroons in New Orleans for ten dollars."

"I'm not in New Orleans, Colonel, and it's likely to be a long time before I do get there. And I must confess to having fancied this girl when I first saw her on the stage."

"Yes, she was in show business," Culpepper said. He cupped his chin in his hand and stared at Lucy for a long moment. "Captain, I fear I must confess something to you. This girl . . . well, for a hundred dollars you have the right to know."

"Know? Know what?" Sam asked.

"She's not like other nigger girls. She doesn't particularly like being pleasured."

For some reason Sam took heart from that statement, and though he knew that Culpepper had to have bedded Lucy in order to know the truth of it, he also knew that it was obviously against Lucy's will. He smiled.

"Maybe you just don't know how to be nice to her," Sam said.

Culpepper laughed. "Maybe you are right at that," he said. "Well, a hundred dollars, eh? Let's see . . . if I could do that ten times, I'd have a thousand dollars." He looked at Lucy. "Girl, you may just be the golden goose every man looks for. All right, Captain, if you are willing to pay one hundred dollars for her services, you may have her."

"For the whole night, now," Sam said. "Not just for an hour or so."

"For the whole night," Culpepper agreed. "Uh . . . after I see the money."

"It's in my saddlebag," Sam said.

"Now, what is this other business?" Culpepper asked.

"Other business?"

"Yes. You burst in here complaining about someone who was incompetent and cowardly, I believe. Who would that be?"

Sam had intended to tell Culpepper to his face that *he* was the incompetent coward. But that was before he saw Lucy. Seeing her changed everything.

"Uh, it is Colonel Hardacre, sir," Sam said.

"Did Hardacre fail to carry out my orders?" Cul-

212

pepper asked sharply. "Did he not attack the nigger troops at Millikin's Bend?"

"I don't know," Sam said. "That's not what I was talking about. I was referring to the fact that he was supposed to make a demonstration against General Sherman, so that I might slip through the lines into Vicksburg, and he failed to do so."

"Oh, I see. Well, Captain, he failed to do so because I ordered him to change his plans."

"But why, Colonel? It was vitally important that I get through to Vicksburg."

"Your mission to Vicksburg had only a short-term importance," Culpepper said. "That being in the defense of the city itself. But the defeat of the niggers at Millikin's Bend might well be the most important battle of the entire war. Don't you understand, Captain? If the niggers think they can take up arms against us, then there is likely to be hell to pay. If, on the other hand, we defeat them soundly at the first opportunity, then we will never have to worry about them again."

Sam Shelton didn't see it at all. But he had no wish to antagonize Colonel Culpepper because he didn't want Culpepper to change his mind about allowing him to spend the night with Lucy. He had a plan, and it was important that he have some time alone with Lucy in order to carry out that plan.

He told himself that that was the only reason he offered to buy her services. He told himself that, and he tried very hard to believe it.

CHAPTER EIGHTEEN

By nightfall Jaylene knew the purpose of the rolled bandages and the tables and the saws and the knives. More than four hundred wounded returned from the fight at Millikin's Bend, some walking, some who were carried by their comrades, and many who were riding in wagons, thrown in like so much cordwood, stuck in to suffer the bumps and bruises and pain of the long trek back.

The wounded kept coming, and the surgeons operated far into the night, sawing off arms and legs to save the bodies from the gangrenous wounds. The sounds of the soldiers screaming under the saw and the piteous moans and groans of the wounded were unnerving even to the most hardened of men. Jaylene wished they had left before the wounded returned, but Edward thought they should offer their services in whatever way they could.

"Somehow, being a fool upon the stage doesn't seem enough at this point," he told the others that afternoon, and they all agreed to stay.

Jaylene had been doing her part by carrying water to the wounded and otherwise comforting them in whatever way she could. She was giving water to a group of soldiers when another wagon arrived. Two blood-soaked aides walked to the back of the wagon and started to unload it.

"Wait a minute, Jim," one of the aides said. He peered more closely at the forms on the wagon. "Hey, you, driver, did you think this was the morgue? What did you come here for?"

"What do you mean?" the driver asked. "I've got a load of wounded." He turned in his seat and looked back at his load.

"You've got a load of bodies," the aide said. "Not one of them is alive."

"Damn," the driver swore. "They were all alive when I left the river."

Jaylene felt an involuntary chill, then went back to administering to the wounded. They were lying shoulder to shoulder, stretched out in rows of twenty to thirty men. Some lay stiff and quiet, but many were writhing in pain, moaning and groaning, occasionally screaming out a curse or a prayer.

Everywhere there was blood, dirty bandages, the smell of unwashed bodies, purged bowels, and emptied bladders. Added to this was a vicious swarm of mosquitoes, gorging themselves upon the pitiful victims.

"Miss," one of the soldiers called.

Jaylene pasted on a smile and moved quickly to the soldier. "Yes?"

"Miss, would you see to Tim? He's been sufferin' somethin' fierce. Me'n him was talkin', you see, but he's quiet now, 'n I'm worried about him."

"Which one is Tim?" Jaylene ased.

'He's the feller over to the fence there," the soldier said, raising himself with effort and pointing to a prostrate figure.

"I see him," Jaylene said. "I'll see how he is for you."

"Thankee, ma'am," the soldier said, lying back down.

Jaylene picked her way through the men, passing those who lay dull-eyed, with hands clutched to wounds, glued there now by coagulated blood, until she reached the soldier named Tim.

Jaylene gasped. It was T. J. Cole, the soldier whose letter she had written earlier in the day. She bent down to look at him, but even as she did, she knew that T. J. Cole would never need another letter written, or get back to his farm, or kiss his little Anne, or see the likeness of his wife, Martha. For T. J. Cole was dead.

"How is he, miss?" the soldier called.

Jaylene swallowed hard.

"Tell me, miss, me 'n Tim, we're good friends. How is he?"

"He's—he's—" Jaylene couldn't say it.

"He's dead, ain't he, miss?"

"Yes," Jaylene said.

"Poor ole Tim."

"Are you all right?" Jaylene asked. "Can I do something for you?"

"No'm, they ain't nothin' you can do," the soldier said. "I'm shot through the arm. Like as not the doc's gonna take it off. I guess I'll just lay here 'n enjoy it while I got it. It hurts somethin' fierce, but they's some comfort in havin' an arm to hurt, I reckon. I tell you, them niggers was some good fighters. Who'd a thought niggers would fight like that?"

"What? What are you talking about?"

"The battle we just fought," the soldier said. "They was all niggers in the Yankee army. We didn't know we was goin' after niggers, but that's what they was. And don't let nobody fool you none, miss. They was some good fighters. We give about as good as we took, I reckon, but it was some fight."

"A good fight? Who can call it a good fight?" Jaylene asked. She looked around and took in all the dead and wounded with a sweep of her hand. "Look at this, all the suffering. There's nothing good about it. There's nothing good at all."

"Yes'm, you may be right," the soldier said. "Still, they was nobody what was a coward, 'n that includes the niggers on the other side. You know? I think I might have changed my mind about niggers today."

"What do you mean?"

"Well, I never figured they was as good as a white man, you know? I mean, I just figured niggers was different sort of creatures. But anyone who will stand and fight like those men did today, why, they could hold their heads up in anyone's army. Did you ever know a nigger, ma'am?"

"Well, of course," Jaylene said.

"No'm. I don't mean know 'em like they was just property or somethin'. I mean know one real. Know what he thinks and what he feels."

Suddenly Jaylene thought of Lucy. "Yes," she said. "Yes, I have."

"I never have," the soldier said. "But now I think I'd like to."

Another soldier called for water, and Jaylene left the one she was talking with. His conversation had

219

started her thinking, though. She had felt a degree of self-righteousness in having accepted Lucy as her friend, even though she was black. But now she realized how hollow and condescending that was. Was she ready to accept all other blacks as well? And if so, why did she not do anything to help them? And why didn't she start with Lucy?

Jaylene made the decision then and there that she would help Lucy escape from Colonel Culpepper, even if it meant that she had to return to Winona and do business with Captain Tony Holt.

"Hang on, Lucy," she said softly. "I'm going to get you out of there."

Jaylene wasn't the only person with plans to help Lucy escape. Sam had those same intentions.

Sam wasn't certain exactly what he was going to do, but he felt that by telling Culpepper he wanted to spend the night with Lucy, it would give him time to work something out. And if he couldn't work anything out, Todd could. Todd was the best person Sam ever knew about coming up with plans to do the impossible.

But Todd was of no help. When Sam returned to the doctor's office, he was informed that Todd had a fever, brought on by his weakened state.

"How long will the fever last?" Sam asked. He was standing in the doctor's front office, by the little glass case of instruments, bandages, pills and potions. The windows were open to let in a breeze, and the muslin curtains waved at the interior of the room, but it was still stifling hot.

"I don't know," the doctor said. The doctor's glasses slid down his nose, and he pushed them back up, then walked over and opened the door to peek into the other room. In there, on a high bed, Todd lay sleeping, though it was not a restful sleep but a feverish period of unconsciousness. "I'd say it will be a good twenty-four to thirty-six hours before his fever breaks. Then he will have to stay right here for another week, or the same thing will happen again."

"I see," Sam said. He ran his hand through his hair. What should he do now? He had to make his move tonight.

"Uh, Doc, can I go in and wake him up? I have to talk to him. I have to ask him something."

"I don't think you can wake him up," the doctor said. "And if you could, what he said would make no sense. The fever has him out of his mind right now."

"But you don't understand," Sam said. "He's my commander, I have to—"

"*You* have to be the commander now," the doctor said. "Whatever it is, it will have to wait."

"It can't wait."

"Then you'll have to make the decision yourself."

"Yeah," Sam said. "Yeah, I suppose I will at that, won't I?"

Sam picked up his hat and left the doctor's office, then started down to the Lexington House. But halfway there he stopped. It would be dangerous, but he knew what he was going to do. But he would have to hurry if he expected to be back by nightfall. He returned to his horse, swung up on to the animal's back, and rode out of town at a full gallop.

It was just after dusk when Sam returned to Yazoo City. The first place he went upon his return was the doctor's office, hoping that Todd was conscious, so he could discuss the plan with his chief. But Todd wasn't awake, and that left Sam on his own. Whether he succeeded or failed now was entirely up to him.

Next Sam went to the Lexington House. He was carrying a small sack of gold.

"Well," Culpepper said, looking up from his dinner. "I was beginning to think you weren't going to show."

"I'm here," Sam said.

"I can see that," Culpepper replied. He dabbed his mouth with a napkin. "I must confess, I rather hoped you wouldn't return. I would have made use of the lady myself, had you not."

"But I *am* here," Sam said rather urgently, momentarily frightened that Culpepper would change his mind. "And you said—"

Culpepper chuckled. "Yes, I know what I said. My, you are anxious, aren't you?"

"Yeah," Sam said.

"Do you have the money?"

Sam handed the sack to Culpepper, and Culpepper loosened the drawstring, then poured the coins into his hand. He hefted the weight of them and held them under the chandelier to observe their soft golden sheen.

"Ah, yes," he said. "It's all here."

"Then I can have her?" "Yes, yes, of course," Culpepper said. "She's upstairs, the third door on the right."

Sam started toward the stairway, but Culpepper called to him, and Sam stopped. "Yes?" Sam asked.

"If for some reason you decide that you don't

want her for the entire night, you might send her back to me. She knows where to find me."

"I paid for the whole night. I will keep her for the whole night," Sam said.

"As you wish," Culpepper said, and he sat down again and poured himself a glass of wine as Sam climbed the stairs.

Sam knocked on the door, but no one answered. Cautiously, he pushed it open and stepped inside.

"Hello? Lucy, are you here?" He looked around, but she wasn't there. For a moment he wondered if Culpepper was playing some sort of trick on him. Then the door opened and Lucy came in. She moved into the room in an effortless glide.

"I am here, Captain," she said quietly. Her voice fell on Sam's ears like the tinkling of wind chimes stirred by a breeze. Sam was thunderstruck. He didn't believe he had ever seen anyone so beautiful, or heard a voice so soft. The plan he had in his mind slipped away, and he could think of nothing except the fact that he was here, in this room, with this girl.

Lucy walked over to the bed and stood quietly by it. "This is what you wanted, isn't it?"

Sam wanted to tell her no, not unless she wanted it. He wanted to tell her that he was here to save her, not to take advantage of her. But when he opened his mouth, only one word came out.

"Yes."

Lucy turned her back to him and began undressing. Sam watched, spellbound, as the girl's shoulders, then the smooth expanse of her back, and finally her whole body was exposed. Within moments Lucy stood nude.

Sam felt rude, uncouth, and clumsy. He felt inadequate for the task of rescuing Lucy, and inferior to her. He was caught up in her spell.

Lucy slipped under the sheet. "Captain," she said quietly, "if you will pull out the top drawer of that dresser you will find a robe. Please step into the dressing room and remove your clothes."

Sam wanted to tell her that she didn't have to go through with all this. He wanted to tell her that he wasn't in alliance with Culpepper. But his tongue grew thick and his mouth felt dry. So he took the robe and left without a word.

Lucy lay in bed, waiting patiently for Sam to return. At first, when she heard him offer Culpepper one hundred dollars for the right to spend the night with her, she was hurt and angry. Did Sam, too, think she was someone who could be bought?

She didn't expect Sam to love her. After all, Sam was white—all white. She wasn't. There could be nothing between them.

And yet, one hundred dollars was a great deal of money. Perhaps Sam did this to show her that he really did care. Perhaps he was sending her a message. But he had said nothing to her yet. Surely if he cared for her, really cared for her, he would tell her.

Perhaps all he wanted was her body. Perhaps he merely wanted to use her. Perhaps she merely wanted to use him.

That thought sprung suddenly and surprisingly into Lucy's mind. Did she just want to use him? She didn't know the answer to that. But did she want him?

Yes, oh, yes, she thought. She wanted him more than she had ever wanted anything in her life. She would be his slave willingly. How wonderful it will be to give herself to him in sweet surrender.

Sam came back into the room and stood by the bed. He was wearing the robe, but after a moment he took it off. His chest was broad and covered with dark hair, and as his arms moved Lucy could see the knots of muscles bulge in the soft moonlight.

"Lucy," he said quietly. "Lucy, I love you."

Lucy's heart thrilled to his pronouncement, and she tried to sit up, but he pushed her back down gently, then pulled the sheet down.

He caught his breath at what he saw. Her beauty overwhelmed him, and slowly he reached out to her. One of his hands covered a breast and gently caressed it and then moved further down. His hand was so hot to Lucy that she looked down, fully expecting to see a red mark on her breast. She saw only the hard little buttons of her nipples.

Sam's hands moved across her smooth golden skin, spreading fire wherever they went. Then Lucy felt him move over her and thrust deeply into her. With a small cry of joy she gave herself to him. How unlike this was to anything she had experienced before. Before there had been pain and humiliation. Now there was the most intense pleasure she had ever known. She felt a consuming hunger to be satisfied, a need that was being completely fulfilled. She cried when it was over, but only because it was over.

Sam lay beside her, and for several moments the only sound in the room was the sound of their breathing.

"Sam," Lucy finally said.

"I like that," Sam said.

"You like what?"

"I like it when you call me Sam, instead of Captain."

Lucy laughed again. "Sam," she said again. "Did you mean it?"

"Yes," Sam said.

"You didn't ask what I'm talking about."

"I don't have to," Sam said. He raised himself up on one elbow and looked down into her face. It glowed softly in the moonlight. Her hair was fanned out on the pillow around her. He reached down and touched his finger to her lips, then let it trail softly across her chin, down her neck, onto her chest, and then across her breast. It rested on one of the nipples, incredibly hard against the silken-smooth softness of her breast. "You want to know if I meant it when I said I love you."

"I love you too," Lucy said. For a moment her eyes reflected a tremendous joy; then they were quickly clouded with intense sadness. It was the same expression he had seen on her face when he first saw her in the dining room earlier.

"He will never let you buy me," she said.

"Buy you?" Sam said. He laughed. "Who's going to buy you? I'm going to marry you, you silly goose."

"But you can't marry me," Lucy said. "Even if I weren't in bondage, you couldn't marry me. The laws of this state forbid it."

"We won't be in this state," Sam said.

"What are you talking about?"

Sam got up, walked over to the window, and looked toward the street. He was still naked. Lucy

226

looked at his lean, hard body, and for a second could feel again the thrilling experience they had just shared.

Sam turned back toward her.

"We're getting out of here tonight," he said.

"What? How? Sam, no matter where I go, I'll be discovered and brought back. I've already found that out."

"No," Sam said. "Not if you take the underground railroad north."

"I'd never make it."

"Yes, you will," Sam said. "I've set it up."

"How?"

"This afternoon," Sam said. "I rode into a Yankee camp and met with the commander. I told him who I was and what I wanted to do."

"You made a deal with the Yankees?"

"Yes," Sam said. "At midnight, a Yankee patrol will be waiting just outside town. I'll take you to them and they'll get you out of here. Go north, Lucy. You'll be safe there, and after this war, I'll find you."

"Oh, Sam, I don't know," she said. "It's too dangerous."

"Lucy, nothing is worth having if it isn't worth taking a risk for. Now, will you do it? Will you let me get you out of here, and will you wait for me and marry me?"

"I'll marry you, Sam Shelton. But are you sure you want to marry me? Colonel Culpepper is right. I am part colored.

Sam smiled. "You may be part colored—but you are *all* woman," he said. "And that's what I've fallen

227

in love with. Now . . ." he laughed. "I never thought I would hear myself say this, but get dressed. We've got to go."

"How are we going to get out of here without Culpepper seeing us?"

"Through this window," Sam said. "I've been looking it over. We can do it. You won't be frightened, will you?"

"No, darling," Lucy said. "I'm not afraid of anything any more."

CHAPTER NINETEEN

Sam used Todd's horse, and Lucy was on Sam's horse. Together they rode through the alleys of the town, staying in the shadows until they were on the edge of town, then moving onto the main road. By that time, however, Sam figured they were fairly safe.

"Where will the soldiers be?" Lucy asked.

"About a mile down the road," Sam said. "If they get any closer to the city, they might run across our pickets."

No sooner had Sam said the word than they were challenged by one of the pickets he had spoken of. Sam and Lucy reined in their horses, and a tall soldier stepped out from behind a honeysuckle bush. He was sucking on one of the sweet flowers, and he spit it out before he spoke.

"Who be ye, and where are ye headed?"

"I'm Captain Sam Shelton," Sam said. "I'm with Kirk's Raiders."

"Who's the lady?"

"She's my sister," Sam said.

"Your sister, Cap'n? What's she doin' out here?"

"Our farm is just down the road," Sam said. "I'm

escorting her home. You wouldn't want her out alone, would you?"

"No, sir," the picket said. "No, sir, I reckon not. But Cap'n, you'd best be careful. We ain't got no regulars anywhere north of here."

"I know," Sam said. "That's why I'm with her. May we pass now?"

"Yes, sir, go on ahead," the soldier said.

"Oh, and soldier, I'll be coming back this way shortly. Will you be on the lookout for me, and pass it on to your relief?"

"Yes, sir, Cap'n, we'll be lookin' for you," the soldier said.

"Thanks," Sam said. "Come along, Prunella."

They rode several yards in silence, until at last Lucy couldn't hold it back any longer. The laughter she had kept bottled up inside her bubbled out uncontrollably. "Prunella?" she said. "Did you call me *Prunella*?"

"Well, I couldn't think of anything else," Sam lamented.

"But Prunella?"

"What's wrong with it?" Sam said. "I rather like the name. In fact, that's what we'll name our first child if it's a girl."

"Hmmph," Lucy said. "I hope it's a boy, for his sake." But even talking about their child, was thrilling to Lucy, and she basked in the warm glow of it as they rode on.

Finally, after having ridden for about a mile, they were halted by a whispered call from the side of the road.

"Captain Shelton?"

Sam and Lucy stopped. "Yes," he said.

There was a rustle in the bushes and two soldiers rode out. They were dressed in the blue uniforms of the Union army.

"I'm Lieutenant Miller. This is Sergeant Moore. Where is the contraband?"

"Here," Sam said, pointing to Lucy.

The Yankee soldiers looked at Lucy with surprise. "I don't understand," Lieutenant Miller said. "I thought you said you wanted to send a colored north over the Underground Railroad."

"I do," Sam said. "This is her."

The saddles creaked as the two Yankees examined Lucy. Finally Miller spoke again. "Excuse me, ma'am. But you don't look like a colored to me."

"I am," Lucy said.

"Well, I'll be."

"Lieutenant, can we get on with it?" Sam asked impatiently.

"Yes," the lieutenant said. "Ma'am, if you'll just come with me, we'll—" The Yankee officer's statement was cut short by the hollow sound of a minié ball striking him in the chest. That was followed almost immediately by the sound of a musket shot. The lieutenant let out a groan and pitched out of the saddle, mortally wounded.

"Damn you!" Sergeant Moore shouted. "You set up a trap!"

"No, I didn't," Sam said. "Run for it!"

The Union sergeant wheeled his horse around and, leaning low over the horse's neck, urged it away at a full gallop. He was blessed with a fine animal, and it reached its top speed amazingly fast.

"Let's go!" Sam shouted to Lucy, but before they

232

could go, Lucy's mount was brought down by rifle fire. Sam had no recourse but to stop and try to swing her onto his horse behind him.

"Hold it right there, Captain Shelton," someone called. "Or the girl may be the next to get it."

Sam stopped.

"No, Sam, go on," Lucy urged.

"No," Sam said. "I can't take a chance on you getting hit." Sam put his hands in the air as their assailants rode up to them. In the distance the hooves of the retreating Union sergeant's horse were now growing dim. It was obvious to Sam that they really cared nothing about the Yankees. They only wanted the two of them.

"Well, well, well," Colonel Culpepper said, approaching them. "What's the matter, Shelton? One night wasn't enough for you?"

"No," Sam said.

"That's too bad," Culpepper said. "Because this little episode tonight is going to cost you your life. Tomorrow morning, you will hang."

"Hang?" Lucy said in an agonized shout. "Why?"

"Treason, my dear. He was consorting with the enemy, was he not? Who knows what nefarious schemes he had in mind?"

"He didn't have any schemes in mind," Lucy said. "He was just trying to help me."

Culpepper laughed. "You will testify to that, my dear?"

"Testify? Yes, of course I will testify to that. He was only trying to help me escape to the north. Those men were part of the Underground Railroad."

Culpepper laughed again, then looked at the other soldiers with him. "You all heard that, didn't you?"

"Yes, sir," one of them said. "You bet, Colonel," another answered. The rest laughed.

"What is it?" Lucy asked. "What have I said?"

"Conducting slaves to the Underground Railroad is a treasonous offense, punishable by hanging," Culpepper said, laughing.

"What?" Lucy asked, gasping, and putting her hand over her mouth, as if by that action she could recall her damaging testimony. "You mean I have convicted Sam?"

"I'm afraid you have," Culpepper said. "But don't worry about it, dear. We would have hanged him with or without your testimony."

"No!" Lucy screamed, and she jumped off the back of Sam's horse and started pummelling Culpepper, who was himself mounted. Culpepper's mount reared and whinneyed and lashed out with its hooves. One of them caught Lucy in the side of the head. She saw it coming, and at the last minute managed to twist away from its full force. That action probably saved her life. But the blow was still severe enough to knock her out immediately. She fell to the ground as blackness closed over her.

By the time Jaylene had given what comfort she could to the last wounded soldier, it was nearly 4 A.M., and she staggered wearily back to the wagon, crawled in, and fell immediately into an exhausted sleep. When Edward decided that they should leave the next morning, Jaylene didn't even wake up, and she slept in the back while Edward drove her wagon and Hardenburgh drove the other. Slowly but relentlessly the wagons moved back toward Yazoo City, finally arriving at nine-thirty in the morning.

From the moment they arrived Edward knew something was going on. There was a sense of expectation in the air, and not a pleasant expectation at that. The soldiers were all wearing their dress uniforms, and down at the other end of the street they were being drawn up into ranks of company formations. One soldier hurried by the wagon, buttoning his tunic as he passed.

"You, soldier," Edward called out to him. "What is going on here?"

"A hangin', sir. They're fixin' to hang a Yankee spy."

"I wonder who it is?" Hardenburgh asked after the soldier ran off.

"I don't know," Edward replied. "Good Lord! You don't suppose it could be Lucy, do you? They were set to hang her once before!"

"My God, I hope not!" Hardenburgh replied.

As Hardenburgh was on one wagon, and Edward the other, it was necessary for them to raise their voices in order to talk to each other. Their voices awakened Jaylene, and in her groggy state, she heard them mention Lucy and hanging.

"No!" Jaylene shouted from the back of the wagon. She moved quickly to the front and pulled open the canvas. "Uncle Edward, we can't let them hang Lucy!"

"Take it easy, darlin'," Edward said, reaching over to pat her with his hand. "Nobody said they were hanging Lucy."

"But you just did."

"No I didn't," Edward said. "I was just wondering who it was they are hanging."

"Then you don't know?"

"I don't have a clue."

"Then it *could* be Lucy, couldn't it?"

"Well, I suppose it could," Edward said. "But I rather doubt it."

"Uncle, drive down to the other end of the road, quickly. I must satisfy myself as to who it is."

"Darlin', no matter *who* it is, you don't want to watch it. A hangin' is not a pleasant sight to see."

"Please, Uncle!"

Edward sighed, then clucked at his team.

"Very well," he said. "If you wish. Hardenburgh?"

"I believe I shall stay here, if you don't mind, Edward. No matter who the unfortunate victim, is, I have no wish to be present."

"But if it's Lucy, maybe we can do something," Jaylene insisted. "We'll *have* to do something!"

"Darlin', I don't think there is anything we can do," Edward said. "But we'll try."

Jaylene stood up and peered anxiously ahead as Edward maneuvered the wagon down the road. Finally she breathed a sigh of relief.

"Oh, it's *not* Lucy," she said. "It's a man standing on the cart."

"Good fortune for Lucy," Edward said. "But as a fellow human is about to die, I scarcely can feel good about it."

"Nor can I," Jaylene said. "Oh, the poor man . . . they are giving him the sacraments now."

A chaplain stood on the cart beside the unfortunate man, holding a silver chalice to the man's lips.

The chaplain's voice could clearly be heard because of the dreadful quiet that had descended over the assembled men. As the condemned man turned to take the chalice, Jaylene saw his face and gasped aloud.

"Oh! It's Sam Shelton!"

Sam heard her voice and looked toward her.

"Jaylene," he called. "They wouldn't let me see Lucy. Tell her I love her!"

"No!" Jaylene called. "No, don't hang him! Let him go! Please, let him go!"

Sam saw Edward reach for Jaylene and comfort her. Then one of the guards started to place a hood over his face.

"No," Sam said quietly. "When I meet my Maker, I want Him to see my face, so that He may judge me innocent of any wrongdoing."

The guard looked toward Colonel Culpepper, who was standing on the ground beside the cart, and Culpepper nodded. The hood was not affixed.

Oddly, Sam felt no stomach-wrenching fear. Instead, a sense of calm had come over him. Gone was the anxiousness he had felt when first caught. He was going to die now, and he knew it. He stood on the cart and accepted it as calmly as if he were waiting for the visit of a friend. *After all,* he told himself, *isn't death a friend? Death will come to everyone, and once it has arrived, what difference does it make how long one is able to hold it off? For one who has been dead but an hour differs not from one who has been dead for a thousand years.*

"Have you any last words?" one of the guards asked.

Sam looked out over the crowd. He had no idea

how many were there. Up front, near the cart, the soldiers stood in neat, orderly rows. Just behind the soldiers was the wagon with Jaylene and her uncle, and beyond the wagon were the townspeople, all the way back to the other end of the street. Men, women, even little children, all had upturned, curious faces.

From Sam's newly arrived rapprochement with death, he was able to observe them casually, objectively. Many had looks of sympathy or sorrow on their faces. Some looked horrified; others merely curious. What did surprise him, though, was the great number of expressions of eager anticipation on the faces of those who were obviously enjoying the gruesome spectacle they were about to witness.

Sam wanted to laugh at them, to tell them that they weren't actually going to see anything; that only his body would feel the hangman's noose, but he wouldn't be in his body. But he fixed a solemn expression on his face, as if playing out his role upon the stage.

"Long live the Confederacy!" Sam shouted. And his shout was met with cheering. "And may all men—black and white—be free!"

The cheers changed to boos and catcalls, and shouts of "Traitor!" and "Treason!"

"Would you take your place, Captain?" the hangman asked, courteously but firmly.

Sam moved into position as ordered, then looked down at Culpepper. Sam smiled at him, a secret smile of defiance.

"Hold your head up, please, sir," the hangman said, and as Sam did so, the hangman slipped the noose around his neck. "Now, sir, if you'll let your neck be relaxed, it'll snap like a twig and be over in a second. Tighten it up, 'n it's likely to take a little longer. I've seen 'em kick for near half an hour."

"Thank you," Sam said. "I shall heed your advice."

The hangman stepped down from the cart and Sam felt it move under the hangman's shifting weight. The hangman took a whip, walked over to the horse, drew the whip back, held it for one long moment, and looked at Sam.

The moment the hangman held the whip was the only thing left between Sam and eternity. It was a brief moment in the lives of those who stood on the ground watching, but it was a lifetime for Sam. And he used it to fix Lucy's face upon his mind, so that if any impression survived this transition, it would be of her.

The whip snapped sharply against the animal's back, and the horse leaped forward. Sam felt himself dropping off into space.

"Culpepper! You sonofabitch! I'll kill you for this!"

The agonized scream jerked everyone's attention away from the man who dangled, lifeless at the end of the rope. The man who had screamed stood on the boardwalk, dressed only in trousers, naked from the waist up except for the large bandage that wrapped several turns around his waist and shoulder. It was Todd Kirk, and he was carrying a pistol. He raised the pistol and pointed it at Culpepper.

"Don't be a fool, Kirk," Culpepper said calmly.

"If you pull that trigger, one hundred men will shoot you." And even as Culpepper spoke, several soldiers pointed their rifles at him.

Kirk stood there, holding the pistol aimed at Culpepper.

"I don't care," he said. "What right did you have to do this?"

"I had the right of military commander," Culpepper said. "I was merely carrying out the law. Your friend was a traitor."

"He was no more of a traitor than I am," Kirk said.

"Perhaps we should look into that too," Culpepper suggested.

"Someone else can look into it, Culpepper, after you and I are both dead." Todd cocked the hammer on his pistol.

"Todd, no!" Jaylene called, and she jumped from the wagon and ran toward him.

"Jaylene, what are you—" but Todd was unable to get the words out, for when his attention was diverted by Jaylene, two soldiers who had been sneaking up behind him jumped him and wrestled him to the ground.

Todd tried to fight back, but there were two of them, they had the advantage of surprise, and he was still weak from his wound. He was quickly disarmed.

"What do you want to do with him, Colonel?" one of the two men asked.

Culpepper looked at Todd for a moment, then dismissed him with a shrug. "Put him on his horse," he finally said. "Let him get back to his troops. Major Kirk, I want your word as a gentlemen that you won't try something like this again."

Todd didn't answer Culpepper.

"Your word, Major," Culpepper said again.

"You have it," Jaylene said. "Colonel, please let him go. He won't try this again, I promise you."

The men laughed, and so did Culpepper.

"Well, Kirk, shall I take this lady's word on your behalf? You say nothing? Then I shall take it. You, Major Kirk, are bound by a lady's word. Now, get on your horse and get out of my town. And, Major, never come back. Not for any reason, do you understand?"

Todd's horse was led up to him. Ironically it was the same horse that had jerked the cart out from under Sam, and the mark of the whip was still on the animal's flank.

Todd climbed onto the horse's back, and looked toward Culpepper with hatred.

"Todd," Jaylene said. "Todd, please, go on before he changes his mind."

Todd looked at Jaylene then, and she saw, to her shock and dismay, that the expression he wore as he looked at her was little different.

"Todd, what is it?" Jaylene asked. "What's wrong?"

Todd turned his horse and started out of town. As he rode slowly through the streets, a few started hurling catcalls at him. The catcalls were joined with laughter, and by the time he was at the end of the street, the whole town was laughing at him. He slapped his legs against the side of his horse and it sprang forward in a gallop. Behind him were the jeering and laughing soldiers of Culpepper's command, a hurt and confused Jaylene, and the body of his friend, twisting slowly on the rope as he dangled from the scaffold.

CHAPTER TWENTY

"Miss Cooper, how glad I am to see you again," Tony said. He stood to greet Jaylene as she stepped into his office.

"Captain Holt, I need your help," Jaylene said, getting right to the point.

"How can I help you?"

"I want you to help me rescue Lucy."

"Sit down," Tony invited, and when Jaylene was seated he sat back in his own chair and crossed his arms across his chest. "Now, why don't you tell me about it?"

"You remember Lucy Wade, who was with our company?"

"Yes, indeed I do," Tony said. "She is a most lovely girl. But you said *rescue* her. What danger is she in?"

"Lucy is a black woman," Jaylene said. "Colonel Culpepper is holding her in bondage to him."

"So . . . *that* is who Sergeant Moore was talking about," Tony mused.

"Who? Who is Sergeant Moore?"

"Miss Cooper, one week ago two of my men undertook a rescue mission," Tony said. "They were

244

Lieutenant Miller and Sergeant Moore. They had been contacted by a man who identified himself as Captain Sam Shelton. Captain Shelton made arrangements to meet them at midnight outside Yazoo City, at which time he said he was going to turn over a runaway slave for them to conduct north. But it was a trap, Miss Cooper. Lieutenant Miller was killed, and Seargeant Moore just barely managed to get away. Seargeant Moore said that the contraband was a very beautiful white woman, whom Captain Shelton introduced as a black. I hope you aren't dealing with Captain Shelton in this, Miss Cooper, for he obviously isn't to be trusted."

"Captain Shelton is dead," Jaylene said.

"Dead?"

"You are right," Jaylene said. "It was a trap. But the trap was for captain Shelton and Lucy, and not your two men. I think even the killing of Lieutenant Miller was an accident. They wanted Captain Shelton, so they could hang him."

"I see," Tony said. He pursed his lips and tapped against them with his finger. "I'm very sorry. Captain Shelton was obviously a very brave man, and we badly misjudged him."

"He was a brave man," Jaylene said. "But it's too late to worry about him now. Lucy, on the other hand, can still be saved, if you will help me."

"Why would Culpepper think Lucy Wade is a black woman?" Tony asked.

"Because she is," Jaylene said. "Her real name is Tamara Gilbert." Quickly, Jaylene told the story of Lucy's background, omitting nothing, even the killing of Putnam.

245

"Hmm," Tony said. "I agree with you then, she is in great danger."

"Then you will help me?"

"I'll do what I can," Tony said. "But as she is in Yazoo City and I am in Winona, I don't know what I can do."

"You can go to Yazoo City with me," Jaylene said.

"Oh, of course, I can just walk in."

"You could go in disguise," Jaylene suggested.

"Do you know what that would mean if I were caught?"

"Yes. It would mean you would hang. Like Sam Shelton," she added.

"Yes, like Sam Shelton." Tony got up and walked over to the window and stared through it for a long moment. "Miss Cooper, it is extremely dangerous for the soldier of one nation to masquerade as someone else and pass freely through the lines of another nation, if those two nations are at war. I don't think you fully comprehend what you are asking of me."

"Captain, you told me your mission in conducting an underground railroad was motivated by your own personal beliefs. Are your convictions not strong enough for you to bear an element of risk?"

"Yes, my convictions are very strong," Tony said.

"As strong as Major Kirk's belief in what he is doing?"

"Kirk? What about Kirk?"

"Did Major Kirk not disguise himself and move in your camp?" Jaylene asked.

"Yes. But how did you know?"

"I recognized him the moment I saw him," Jaylene said.

"You . . . you *recognized* him, yet you said nothing?"

"What was I supposed to do?" Jaylene asked. "Turn him in, perhaps?"

"Yes," Tony said. "If, as you say, you believe in the same things I do."

"I believe in the principle of freedom for every man and woman," Jaylene said. "But I am, by birth, a Southerner, and I will not consciously play a role in placing any Southern soldier in jeopardy."

"He wasn't a soldier, he was a *spy*," Tony said. "I have no use for spies."

"Despite our differences now, Captain, I do believe we share a common national heritage," Jaylene said. "And isn't one of our national heroes Nathan Hale?"

Tony looked at Jaylene with a quick expression of surprise; then his face broke into a broad, easy smile.

"So he is, Miss Cooper, so he is. And, he was a spy. But surely you aren't comparing Todd Kirk to Nathan Hale?"

"Yes, I am," Jaylene said. "And I should compare you as well, if you really have the strength of your convictions."

"Well now," Tony said, "let us just test the strength of our convictions, shall we?"

"What do you mean?"

"I mean, Miss Cooper, that if I am to risk my life by venturing into a Southern camp, then it is my intention to gather as much information as I can to pass on to Generals Grant and Hovey. If I am to take the same chances as a spy, then I intend to garner the same rewards."

247

"I . . . I could expect you to do no differently," Jaylene said.

"And if you help me, Miss Cooper, then *you* are also to be considered a spy against your fellow countrymen."

"But no," Jaylene said. "I do this only for Lucy."

"You must make up your mind," Tony said. "Is your loyalty to your friend greater than your loyalty to a people who would do this sort of thing to your friend?"

"Yes," Jaylene finally said. "Yes, you are right. My loyalty to Lucy *is* greater."

"You will help me gather information?"

"I will protect your identity," Jaylene said. "And I will do this in full knowledge of your espionage activity. That makes me guilty as well."

"Good, good," Tony said. "Now, I suppose I could pass myself off as an Inspector General from Pemberton's forces, and . . ."

"No," Jaylene said quickly. "Most of the senior officers in this district are Mississippians. That means that Culpepper knows every one of them. He'd spot you as a phony in a minute."

"Perhaps I could be a liaison officer from Beauregard's army," Tony suggested.

"No," Jaylene said. "That wouldn't work either."

"Well, what, then?"

"An actor."

"What? Are you serious?"

"I'm very serious," Jaylene said, now growing excited by the idea. "Yes, I think that is just perfect."

"I don't know anything about acting," Tony protested.

"Don't worry about it. Uncle Edward, Hardenburgh, and I will teach you everything you need to know."

"I don't think that will work," Tony said. "What's he going to think when your troupe turns up with a new actor?"

"He'll think we finally found one," Jaylene explained. "Look, first we lost Booth, then we lost Lucy. With both of them gone, we were no longer an acting troupe. We were just a repertoire company, making do as best we could. Now, with you, we can be an acting company again. And, as we had returned to Yazoo City the last time to learn a new play, it is only natural that we go back there."

"I don't know," Tony said, hedging a bit.

"Besides, you are a very handsome man," Jaylene said. "You will be wonderful on the stage."

"Really?" Tony replied, obviously flattered.

"Really," Jaylene said. She laughed. "Who knows, this may be the start of a new career for you. You could become an actor."

"To be or not to be . . ." Tony said, rolling the lines sonorously.

Jaylene grimaced in jest. "I don't know, though," she said. "We are going to have to do a lot of work with you."

"Oh, I thought I did that rather well," Tony said with mock hurt.

"I was teasing. You did do it well. Tony, I know this will work."

Tony smiled brightly and, emboldened by her use of his first name, tried it himself. "All right, Jaylene, I will do it," he said.

"Oh, thank you," Jaylene said and, spontaneously, she kissed him.

Tony was surprised by Jaylene's action, but he responded quickly, taking her into his arms and returning her kiss with fervor. Jaylene had intended only a short, uninvolved kiss, but Tony had other plans, and now, feeling his lips on hers and her body pliant against his, she let herself be swept up into the passion of the moment as quickly as he.

Tony broke off the kiss before Jaylene did. He turned away from her and took a couple of steps back toward his desk. He leaned on his desk for a moment, trying to regain his breath.

"I . . . I'm sorry," he said. "I don't know what got into me. You must forgive me."

Jaylene had felt a quickening heat in her own body, a rush of blood and a dizzying of senses. She too, was out of breath from the experience, but now she was puzzled. Why was Tony apologizing?

"There's nothing to forgive," she said easily.

"Yes," Tony said. "I fear that there is. You . . . you don't know what I was thinking."

Jaylene smiled suggestively. "I think maybe I do," she said.

"You must be mortified," Tony said. "That is so unlike me. Please tell me you forgive me."

"Well, of course," Jaylene said. "Though in truth, Tony, there is nothing you need forgiveness for."

"I . . . uh . . . had better make some arrangements if we are going to go through with our plan," Tony said. "Why don't I meet you and the others tonight, in the building where you gave your play before. Perhaps the three of you can work with me, and make somewhat of a silk purse from a sow's ear."

"Perhaps," Jaylene said, still puzzled by Tony's odd behavior.

"I'll see you tonight," Tony said, walking toward the door; and that, Jaylene knew, was her dismissal.

Jaylene thought about the strange episode as she walked back down the boardwalk to the warehouse where Hardenburgh and her uncle were waiting for her. Why had Tony been so apologetic for what seemed so natural? Or was it really natural? Perhaps those people who suggested that there was something different about theater people were right. Perhaps decent ladies and gentlemen didn't enjoy bedding together. But Todd had obviously enjoyed it.

Ah, but Todd, by his own admission, was no gentleman. And she, by her own reasoning, was no lady.

So what? If Todd Kirk could accept his condition, even revel in it, then so could she. She had chosen her life; she wasn't forced into it. She liked the theater. She loved the feeling of swaying an audience with the power of her performances or the beauty of her songs. She loved it, and she accepted it, no matter what the others thought.

If she could accept that about herself, why couldn't she accept the fact that she was no lady, and admit that she liked bedding with a man, if the man appealed to her? And Tony Holt was just such a man.

Uncle Edward and Hardenburgh were sitting in front of the warehouse when she returned.

"Well, Jaylene, will he do it?"

"Yes," Jaylene said. "Uncle Edward, he is going in with us."

251

"Going in with us? You mean we are going to smuggle him in?"

"Yes. I mean no, not exactly," Jaylene said. "He's going in with us, but in plain sight. He is going to be disguised as an actor."

"Jaylene, do you know what they will do to us if they discover him? It won't be only the Yankee captain who is in danger."

"I know," Jaylene said. "So I guess what I'm asking is for you and Mr. Hardenburgh to take a chance on saving Lucy."

Edward looked at Hardenburgh. "I can't ask you to do this, old friend," he said.

"You don't have to ask," Hardenburgh replied. "I'll do it without your asking."

Edward smiled, then took Hardenburgh's hand and shook it warmly. "Thank you," he said. He looked back at Jaylene. "All right, we're in," he said. "What do we do?"

"First, we must teach Tony to act to make him believable."

"Why must we do that?" Hardenburgh asked. "Booth couldn't act, and he got away with it."

Edward and Jaylene both laughed.

"What about his experience?" Edward asked.

"Experience? I told you, he doesn't have any. We have to teach him."

"Teach him, all right," Edward replied. "But we have to give him some experience. Otherwise, Culpepper might be suspicious as to why we would just hire someone out of the blue."

"Oh, I see what you mean," Jaylene said.

"How about another touring theater?"

"Are you kidding?" Jaylene said. "There are fewer

than half a dozen, and Culpepper has the names of all the players."

"The legitimate stage then?"

"No," Jaylene said. "That's no good, either. It would be too easy to check up on. A telegraph here and another there, and Culpepper would know he was a fake."

"How about the *Delta Mist*?" Edward asked.

"The *Delta Mist*? What about it?"

"Why don't we say he was one of the stars of the *Delta Mist* stage? There is no one left to check on that story, except you." Edward laughed. "And if they ask you, you can verify it."

"Yes," Jaylene said. "Yes, that might work."

"Can he sing or dance, do you suppose?"

"I doubt it, uncle."

"Then we'll have to work out a dramatic reading for him. All right, I'll choose one. When is he coming?"

"He's coming tonight," Jaylene said. "And we'd better work quickly, for tomorrow I think we must go back to Yazoo City. I'm afraid to leave Lucy with Culpepper for too much longer. She may be in great danger."

Lucy had not witnessed the hanging. She regained consciousness sometime during the night, and discovered that she was being confined to her room under guard. Upon questioning, she learned that Sam was going to be hanged the next morning.

Lucy cried and pleaded with the guards to allow her to see Culpepper, so that she might petition for Sam's life, but Culpepper had left word that he didn't wish to see her, and her entreaties fell on deaf ears. Then she pleaded for a chance to see Sam, to at least tell him goodbye, but that too, was denied her.

The next morning, she lay in bed aware only that the hanging was going to take place that day, but not knowing any of the details. Her room overlooked an alley, so she couldn't see the street from her window, nor could she see the gallows. She had no idea of the size of the crowd that had gathered to watch the execution. Had she known that Sam's hanging was turning into such a show, that would have made it even worse for her.

At the moment the cart was jerked from under Sam, Lucy felt a searing pain in her heart, as if she had been stabbed by a dagger of fire, and she sat bolt upright in bed screaming Sam's name. She knew, without being told, that he was dead.

After that, something inside of her died as well. The pain that had seared her insides left them numb and unfeeling. She didn't cry over Sam's death, nor did she lament her own fate. She was now ready to accept whatever fate might deal her.

Fate, as it turned out, dealt Lucy a new and particularly cruel blow. Ironically, it was Sam who set the stage for Lucy's new treatment, for his offer of one hundred dollars to spend the night with Lucy had emboldened Culpepper to try this with others, and to his delighted surprise he found that there were others who were willing to pay the same price. In the first week after Sam had been hanged, Lucy was forced to accomodate eleven men. Like Sam, they paid one hundred dollars for the privilege, and Culpepper now realized that he had stumbled onto a gold mine. Lucy, and the money she was bringing him, suddenly became more important to Culpepper than the prosecution of the war.

Culpepper protected his interest in Lucy. He kept one guard posted outside her door and one outside her window at all times. He justified it by saying that she was contraband. There had been one previous attempt to spirit her away to the North, and he intended to see that the Yankees would be no more successful on subsequent attempts.

On her part, Lucy played her new role with a singular lack of enthusiasm. She no longer had to sleep with Culpepper, and that might have been considered an improvement. Though Lucy didn't care, one way or the other. She was only a shell now. She didn't resist anyone's demands, and she never complained, no matter what was asked of her. But neither did she cooperate, or show the slightest response.

Ironically, it was this that most intrigued the men who paid for her services. Her cool and aloof sexual response matched her cool and aloof appearance. The men fantasized that they were bedding with a princess, beautiful beyond description, but obviously far above such things as sex. They were able to use her for their own gratification.

And they did use her, one after another, while in his room down the hall, Culpepper counted his money and laughed.

CHAPTER TWENTY-ONE

"No, no, no, no," Edward was saying. "You have to put some *feeling* into it!" Edward climbed up onto the boxes that had been put together to form a castle wall. He held a wooden sword aloft and looked up as he spoke to Tony. "You are a king," he said softly, "a king who has just been defeated because of the betrayal of those you thought were loyal to you. Now, you descend from the walls of Flint Castle to meet the victorious Bolingbroke in the courtyard below. As you descend, you are speaking, and by descending as you speak, you symbolize the depths to which your nobles descended in their treachery. And when you speak, say the words with feeling. You have been beaten, but not defeated. You can never be defeated."

Edward crooked his left arm in front of him and spoke the lines as if pulling them from his heart.

"I can never do *that* well," Tony said.

"Of course not, but neither can anyone else," Hardenburgh said. "Edward Fox may well be the greatest Shakespearean actor alive today."

"Then how can I hope to match him?" Tony asked dispiritedly.

"You cannot, nor should you expect to," Harden-burgh said. "But you should strive to do so, for in so trying you are sure to improve your performance."

"Uncle Edward, you are being too hard on him," Jaylene defended. "I think he did quite well, considering."

"Considering?" Edward said, handing the sword to Tony. "Considering that if he is exposed we will all be hanged as spies and traitors? A poor performance upon the stage will, at worst, elicit boos and groans of displeasure from the audience. But a poor performance in this play, my dear, and we shall pay for our bad acting by dancing."

"By dancing?"

"From the end of a rope."

"Maybe I shouldn't try it," Tony said.

"No!" Jaylene put in quickly. "Tony, you can do it, I know you can. Uncle, why did you choose King Richard?"

"It is a good play."

"Choose *Romeo and Juliet* instead. Tony, I will be Juliet. You respond to me. Forget that it is a play, forget that there is an audience. Respond only to me. We have spent the night together, and the dawn is breaking. You must flee before my family finds you in my bedroom. I don't want the night to end, and I speak."

Edward thumbed quickly through a book to find the place Jaylene was speaking of, and he handed the book to Tony just as Jaylene began to speak her lines.

Tony answered, and as he read, the halting, stumbling voice he had used for King Richard fell away to be replaced by the voice of one who didn't merely read the part, but *became* the part.

Jaylene touched her fingers to the side of Tony's cheeks as she spoke, and so convincingly was she that the old-fashioned language seemed natural.

Tony's cheek jumped once under Jaylene's cool fingers, and for a long moment he looked into her eyes. Then, slowly, he raised the book and continued to read his lines.

"There, now," Jaylene said. She looked at her uncle and Hardenburgh, who had watched the impromptu performance in fascination. "Didn't he do better that time?"

"Yes," Edward said with an expression of awe in his voice. "My boy . . . I can't begin to tell you how well you *did* do. It was marvelous."

"I . . . I was inspired to perform beyond my ability," Tony said modestly.

"Nonsense," Jaylene said. "You merely performed up to your potential. But all this makes me hungry. I'm tired of working. Tony, have you no interest in taking a girl to dinner?"

"Ah, dinner, now that's a good idea," Edward said. "Perhaps we could all—"

"Perhaps you could fare better with just Hardenburgh," Jaylene interrupted. "I want to work with Tony some more, and I think I can work best without the two of you."

"What?" Edward asked, surprised by Jaylene's bold proposal. But he smiled and accepted it readily enough, and took Hardenburgh with him as he left, joking that "Romeo and Juliet wish to be alone."

"I'm sorry I didn't think to ask you to dinner earlier," Tony apologized. "I guess I was concentrating too hard on learning to act."

"You don't have to concentrate so hard," Jaylene said. "Acting comes naturally to some people."

"Like you?"

"Yes," Jaylene said. "Like me." She took her shawl from where it had been carelessly thrown across the back of a chair and handed it to Tony. Tony draped it around her shoulders, and then they left the building and walked down the dark street toward the restaurant. Music spilled out of a saloon, and a drunken soldier lurched along the boardwalk, grabbing onto a lamp post to keep from falling.

"I'm sorry," Tony said.

"About what?"

"About all this," Tony said, taking in the town with a sweep of his arm. "We have drunken soldiers on the streets of your towns, we have taken over your restaurants, your hotels, your places of business."

"It is no different in the towns occupied by Southern troops," Jaylene said. "You have nothing to apologize for."

They reached the restaurant, and Tony held the door open for Jaylene, then followed her inside. The hour was late for dinner and the restaurant was uncrowded, so they quickly found a table and ordered.

"Why did someone as lovely as you get into the business of acting?" Tony asked.

"By the tone of your question, I take it that you don't approve of the business of acting," Jaylene said.

"It isn't my place to approve or disapprove. But

261

you must admit that such a profession does bear a certain degree of disrepute."

"Unjustly so," Jaylene answered. Their meal arrived then, and she paused long enough for it to be served, then went on. "But regardless of what others may think, I am proud of my profession and make no apology for it."

"Nor would I request you to do so," Tony said. "Please don't think I am finding fault. I was merely inquisitive, that's all."

Jaylene softened, then smiled. "Besides," she went on, "are you not a member of this same profession?"

"Well, I suppose I am," Tony said.

The conversation turned to other things during dinner, and they went beyond pleasantries into each other's backgrounds. As they talked, Jaylene felt herself becoming more and more attracted to Tony. She tried to fight the attraction off. After all, he was a Yankee officer, so he was her enemy. And yet, even as she thought that, she also realized that in one very important aspect he wasn't her enemy, he was her ally. He was going to help her free Lucy.

But what of Todd Kirk? Wasn't she being untrue to him?

What was there to be true to? Hadn't Todd fixed a look of hate upon her as he rode out of Yazoo City? Wasn't he angered and hurt by the death of his friend, and didn't he feel that she had just heaped more humiliation upon him?

No, she had no reason to be true to Todd Kirk.

"Jaylene," she heard Tony saying, "if it isn't too presumptuous of me, could I invite you to my room for a quiet drink?"

"To your room?"

"I'm sorry," Tony said. "That was presumptuous of me, I'm sure. But it would be unseemly to go to your room, as you might be embarrassed before your neighbors. In my hotel, however, such things are frequently done, and done in innocence, so you need have no fear for your reputation. And I very much want to spend some time with you."

Jaylene smiled. "It's sweet of you to concern yourself with my reputation, Tony. But in truth, as you yourself have noted, my reputation has long been stained by my profession. So without fear of doing it further damage, yes, I will join you in your room. Though I don't wish to drink."

Jaylene's voice had been throaty, almost husky, as she accepted the invitation, and she smiled as she saw a small shiver coursing through Tony's body. She was having an effect on him.

Jaylene clung tightly to Tony's arm as they walked from the restaurant to his hotel. The lobby was dark and quiet and as the desk clerk had his back to them as they came in, they moved across the carpeted floor unseen, then started up the staircase to the second floor.

The hallway was dimly lit by one gas lantern that flickered at the head of the stairs. As Tony's room was the last one off the hall, it was very dark outside his door, and he had to fumble for the keyring.

Tony was aware of Jaylene's perfume. It was subtle, though effective enough to titillate his senses. As if unable to control his own actions, he moved a step closer to Jaylene, and when he did, she looked at him and smiled. Her face was only two inches from his, and her lips were open and glowing. Her

263

golden brown eyes were deep and they pulled him to her, and then they were kissing. It wasn't a tentative, exploratory kiss, but a full-born lover's kiss, open-mouthed and hungry.

Jaylene wasn't quite sure how it had reached this point, but it was here, and she felt her insides growing white with the heat of quick building passion. Tony interrupted the kiss once, and looked at her with his face mirroring confusion. For a moment Jaylene was afraid he was going to apologize to her again, and that would ruin everything. To forestall an apology, she spoke.

"Don't you think you should open the door?"

"Oh, uh, yes, of course," Tony said. He opened the door and they went inside. Jaylene didn't move into the room; instead, she stopped just inside, and when Tony closed the door and turned around, she was there before him.

The overpowering urge to kiss her came over Tony again, and again Jaylene sensed it, and sensed also that he was trying to fight it.

"Tony?" she said softly, looking deep into his eyes and reading his thoughts.

Tony put his arms around her and pulled her to him to kiss her again. It was a deep kiss, with even more fervor than Jaylene had thought he would show. Tony's hands began to move across the folds of her dress, bunching up the material of the skirt until he felt her bare leg. He put his hand on her warm flesh.

"Oh, Tony," she said, speaking into his throat, and she felt strong arms lift her and carry her gently to the bed.

"Jaylene, I can't help myself," he said. "I want

264

you more than I have ever wanted anything. I know it is wrong, but I can't help it."

As Tony was talking to her, he was smothering her face with kisses. Meantime, his hands were busy opening the fastenings and catches of the dress, awkwardly but effectively, until Jaylene began to help and within a moment had slipped out of her clothes and lay on the bed naked before him, feeling the silken caress of the air against her skin.

Tony stood over her, removing his own clothes as quickly as he could, looking down at her with a face set in an expression of wonder and want. Then he moved down onto the bed with her, touching her nude body for the first time, scorching her skin with the heat of passion. She felt his weight come down on her, and she breathed his maleness as he came to her. Her legs were downy soft and creamy white beneath his muscle-hard, swarthy ones. When she felt him enter her, she thrust against him, feeling a pleasure so intense that she cried out from the joy of it.

Their movements established an easy rhythm, and they matched each other move for move as she gave him freely all that was hers to give. Then it began: a tiny, tingling sensation that started deep in her womb, exploding out in rapidly widening circles until her entire body was caught up in the maelstrom bursting over her. There were a million tiny pins pricking her skin and involuntary sounds of pleasure came from her throat. She lost consciousness for just an instant as her body gave its final, convulsive shudders.

They lay together for a few moments while Jaylene experienced secondary peaks of pleasure, less explosive, but greatly satisfying. Finally Tony withdrew, then got up and began gathering up his clothes.

"You needn't get up so quickly," Jaylene said. "I was enjoying it."

"We shouldn't have done this," Tony said.

Jaylene sat up on the bed and drew her legs up to her chest. She wrapped her arms around her legs and leaned her chin on her knees. Her long, tawny hair cascaded down around her shapely legs.

"Why not?"

"It isn't right," Tony said. He looked at her, struck with her beauty, then turned his face away. "You should get dressed," he said.

"All right, Tony," Jaylene said. She was puzzled and hurt by his strange behavior, but she didn't say anything. She began dressing.

"I'm sorry," Tony said. "I shouldn't have forced myself on you like that."

"Tony, do you actually believe you *forced* yourself on me?" Jaylene asked. She had slipped the dress over her head and was buttoning the buttons.

"Yes."

"What makes you think that?"

"Because you are a decent girl, and you . . ."

"And a decent girl would only do this if she was forced to do it?"

"Yes," Tony said.

"Tony, you didn't force me," Jaylene said.

"Yes, I did. I mean . . ."

"You didn't force me," Jaylene said again. Tony looked away from her. "Look at me," she said.

Tony looked at her. "Jaylene, please, don't—" he started.

"Don't what? Don't force you to look at me?

Why not, Tony? Are you afraid that you will see the real me?"

Tony looked at the floor.

"No, Tony," Jaylene said rather sharply. "Look at me. Look in my face. What do you see?"

"I see a beautiful, desirable, decent girl."

"No," Jaylene said. "You see a beautiful, desirable, decent *woman*. And women have feelings, Tony, just as men do. I wanted it, Tony."

"No . . ."

"I *wanted* it," Jaylene said. "And what's more, I feel no guilt about wanting it."

Tony looked at Jaylene for a moment longer, then stepped toward her and threw his arms around her.

"Jaylene, I don't know," he said. "I should feel shocked, or indignant, or something, but I feel only one thing."

"What do you feel?"

"Love, Jaylene. Despite all reason and propriety, I feel love. I want you, and I love you, and despite what you are, I love you. I love you, and I want you."

Jaylene lost herself in his embrace and his kisses, and for a moment the words "despite what you are" were entirely lost upon her. She felt she had won a moral victory, not only over Tony, but over herself as well. For from this moment, she would never again lie to herself, or to anyone else, about her feelings.

CHAPTER TWENTY-TWO

Todd stood at the window of the cabin and looked toward the eastern horizon. There, a bright band of rose preceded the rising sun, and the fingers of darkness had already been pushed back from the hills. Over the small grassy meadow a blanket of mist arose, then hung, seemingly held pinned to the earth by the tips of the tall pine tree. Drifting up to join the mist were a dozen wisps of smoke, curling out from under pots of coffee and pans of bacon. Out in the valley, soldiers stirred reluctantly from their night's sleep.

"Umm," a woman's voice said, and the springs creaked as she turned in the bed. Todd turned to look toward the woman with whom he had spent the night. She was small and pretty, with deep blue eyes, and she had come into the camp unabashedly the night before with five other girls, offering her services for a price. Todd had taken her and a bottle of whiskey into his cabin. He had made love objectively, dispassionately, feeling no more emotional relief from it than he would from a sneeze.

Strangely the more detached he held himself, the more the girl seemed to enjoy it. She was a woman

270

who made a living at sex, and had been with so many men that she had learned the trick of detachment long ago. But to have that same trick worked on her aroused passions she thought were long dead, or at least dormant, and she responded eagerly to his lovemaking.

Now she lay in bed and looked back at this strange, brooding man, and she felt a stirring within.

"Do you want to do it again?" she asked. She stretched, and arched her back proudly, causing the covers to slip off so that her nude body was bridged into the air. The nipples on her small, firm breasts were drawn tight, and her skin grew chillbumps as she thought of it.

"Why not?" Todd asked with a smile, and he came to her and with no preliminaries made love again, again as dispassionately as the night before, but again bringing the girl to rapturous release.

When they were finished Todd began dressing. By now the entire camp was awake, and the sounds of the morning were drifting in through the window. A soldier shouted, and one began to sing. A peal of laughter came from one of the distant campfires. Todd said nothing.

"Are you the strong, silent type?" the girl asked.

"I suppose so."

"You are a strange one," the girl said. "I'll give you that. She looked at the scar on Todd's shoulder, now beginning to heal, and she touched it lightly. "Does it still hurt?"

"Not much," Todd said. He pulled a shirt over his head and tucked the tail into his pants, then washed his face and hands in the basin and dried his hands in his hair. "You are going to have to leave the camp pretty soon," he said.

"I know. I'll bet if I was your sweetheart I wouldn't have to go. Do you have a sweetheart?"

Todd thought of Jaylene, and of the fool she had made of him in Yazoo City. "No," he said firmly.

"But you did have one, huh? I can tell by the tone of your voice."

"No," Todd said. "I don't think I ever had one."

The girl sat up and smiled brightly. "Then maybe I could be your sweetheart. I could quit this business," she said. "I have enough money set back now to last me for quite a while. I could quit whorin'."

Todd smiled for the first time. "You would do that?"

"Sure," she said, encouraged by his smile. "Would it bother you that I was a whore?"

"No," Todd said. "No, that wouldn't bother me."

"Then do you want me to quit?"

Todd walked over and kissed the girl lightly on the lips, then reached down and patted her backside. "No," he said. "I've discovered that a man in my profession has no right to have a sweetheart. But I thank you for your offer. I truly do."

There was a knock at the door, and Todd walked over to pull it open. It was Lieutenant Pearson, his new executive officer. Todd had promoted Pearson to take Sam's place.

"Yeah, Pearson, what is it?" Todd asked.

Behind Todd, the girl got out of bed and, unconcerned over the fact that her nakedness was clearly visible to Pearson, she began getting dressed, as slowly and leisurely as if she were in the privacy of her own bedroom.

"Uh, Major," Pearson started, then he stopped and stared around Todd at the girl.

"She's getting dressed," Todd said.

"Uh, yes, sir, I can see that," Pearson said. He continued to stare at the girl.

"Well, what is it?"

"Oh, uh, the scouts came back a few moments ago," he said.

"And?"

"We can hit McClernand's flank, sir. They've pulled out maybe three regiments to reinforce Sherman."

"Good," Todd said. "If you can keep McClernand tied up, I can get into Vicksburg and complete the mission Sam started."

"There's only one thing, Major," Pearson said.

"What's that?"

"We've only got enough men to make a demonstration. If McClernand gets reinforced, we are going to have to pull back."

"I know that," Todd said.

"Major, if we pull back, like as not we'd wind up leavin' you in Vicksburg. You'll be trapped there, with the others."

"I'll get out," Todd promised. "The thing now is just to get in."

"Yes, sir," Pearson said. "When do you want to do it?"

"Now."

"Now, sir?"

"Yes, Lieutenant," Todd replied. "As soon as we can get there."

Pearson smiled broadly. "Yes, sir," he said. "I

imagine the men are about ready for a little action. I'll tell them."

Todd reached up and took his gunbelt from a nail, then strapped it on. "We'll move out in one hour."

"Yes, sir," Pearson said, snapping Todd a salute, then leaving to pass along the order.

"Are you really going into Vicksburg?" the girl asked. She was buttoning the last of her buttons.

"Yes," Todd said, reaching for his hat.

"You're crazy."

"There are those who would agree with you."

"You are really crazy," the girl said. "Don't you know that Vicksburg is under siege? No one can get in or out."

"I'll get in," Todd said easily.

"Well, suppose you do get in," the girl said, combing her hair. "You won't have anything to eat. They are starving in Vicksburg. Why, I even heard they are eating horses and mules."

"I won't stay long enough to take any of their food."

"You're crazy. How do you expect to get out?"

Todd smiled and held up a finger. "As quickly as I can," he said.

It was common knowledge to everyone, even the beleaguered defenders of Vicksburg, that General Grant was going to have Sherman launch a major assault on the Confederate defenses. To aid him in accomplishing his mission, he had taken on additional units from other elements of the Union army that surrounded Vicksburg, and was building up a major force.

274

The Confederate army, under Pemberton, knew Sherman was building up, and they knew he had increased his strength at the expense of the other units arrayed before the city. But such knowledge did them no good. They might be able to mount a counterattack through the weakened part of the Federal lines, but if they did, they lacked the strength to turn Sherman's flank, and therefore they would be unable to follow up on it. Pemberton's army could escape through the thin lines, and there were those who felt that it should, so that it would remain intact to fight another day.

But others believed Vicksburg to be of such vital importance to the South, because of its strategic position on the river, that there would be no "other day" if the bastion fell. Besides, many in the army felt constrained to stay and defend the city, feeling that to abandon it would be a crime against the valiant townspeople.

What the Confederate soldiers didn't stop to realize was that the townspeople would have been far better off if Pemberton had taken his army through the lines and led them in an escape. For if he had done that, there would no longer be the need to hold the city under siege. If the city weren't under siege, they wouldn't have the daily rainfall of cannon balls and shells, and food could get in and out. Some of the townspeople said to Pemberton, "Please surrender the town, or take your soldiers and go. We are civilians, and shouldn't be exposed to this."

Of course, the people who said such things said them quietly, for it wouldn't take too much to be accused of treasonous behavior in a time of frayed nerves. News traveled fast, even through a blockade, and most had heard of the recent execution of Captain Sam Shelton. Most of the people knew Sam Shelton, or at least knew of him. He was second in command of Kirk's Raiders, and at a time when much of the river and many Mississippi towns were in Yankee hands, the exploits of Kirk's Raiders were among the few things the South had to cheer about. And now they learned that even this was denied them, for Sam Shelton was a spy.

Not so, others said. He was guilty only of falling in love with a beautiful woman, and she was a Yankee spy. It had been the woman who had led Sam Shelton astray. Sam Shelton could be forgiven an affair of the heart, in fact, even admired, for it was said that he went to his death without incriminating the woman.

She was an actress, some said; a nurse, others insisted. There was even a story that she was Abe Lincoln's illegitimate daughter. One rumor, quickly discounted, was that she was a black woman.

CHAPTER TWENTY-THREE

Todd stood on a rock at the top of a hill, looking north toward the city of Vicksburg, holding a pair of field glasses to his eyes. The Mississippi River made a wide, sweeping bend at the city, and from here it looked deceptively peaceful. Shortly downriver though, the illusion was shattered by a flotilla of Union gunboats that was firing into the southern tip of the Confederate defensive line.

The boats had formed a circle, and as each boat came into position, it would loose a fusilade against South Fort, then steam on around the circle, allowing the next boat in line to take its place and fire its guns.

From here, Todd could see the white puffs of smoke issuing from the sides of the gunboats, but as he was nearly a mile away, it was fully five seconds before the low thumping sound of the explosions reached his ears. So consistent was the cannonading, though, that soon it became a low, almost sustained roar, like distant thunder. A sizeable cloud of white smoke drifted lazily over the city. Finally the gunboats broke out of the circle and steamed away.

As the smoke drifted off, the city and the line of

battle came into clear vision. There, nestled against the side of the river, was the city, with the Warren County Court House dominating the skyline. A large semicircle of fortifications, square redoubts, triangular redans, and crescent-shaped lunettes formed the Confederate defensive works. The line began at the north with Fort Hill, an extremely heavily fortified hill just off the bank of the river, and it stretched all the way around the eastern part of the city until it was anchored on the south by South Fort, another strongly defended position. About a hundred yards away, and generally conforming in shape to the Confederate defensive lines, were the Union siege lines, a series of trenches, gun positions, and sharpshooter stations. Vicksburg was, as General Grant once stated, "in a sack. All we have to do is squeeze the top shut."

"What do you think?" Pearson asked.

Todd lowered the glasses and ran his hand through his hair, then sighed. "It's just a matter of time," he said. "And I doubt that it will be very much time."

"You mean Vicksburg is going to fall?"

"Of course it's going to fall."

"But you are still going to try to get in, aren't you?"

"Yes," Todd replied. "General Pemberton deserves every bit of assistance he can get, and if information as to Grant's plans on digging a canal will help him defend the city, then he deserves that information."

"How are you going to do it?"

Todd handed the glasses to Pearson, then

pointed. "Look there," he said. "Do you see that bayou running alongside the road?"

"Warrenton Road?"

"Yes," Todd said. "That is Stout's Bayou." Todd laughed. "I used to fish that bayou a lot when I was a kid. It has some of the best catfish in the state."

"And some of the biggest cottonmouth snakes, too," Pearson said.

"I know," Todd replied. "The Yankees know too, and because of that they've given it a pretty wide berth. So my plan is, you hit McClernand about a thousand yards east of that bayou. That will draw his men away from the bayou and I'll sneak in."

"What about the snakes?"

Todd laughed. "What about them? I told you, I used to fish there when I was a kid. I know where all the snakes are. Hell, I even know their names. I'll get in all right. You just make a lot of noise with your demonstration."

Pearson smiled broadly. "If noise is all you want, we'll make enough to wake up General Grant."

"Good," Todd said. He turned and looked back down the hill at his men. They had dismounted and were holding their horses quiet, waiting for the word to attack. They knew they were going to be attacking a heavily fortified position, and they knew they were going to be outnumbered by the defenders at a rate of ten to one. And yet they would attack without hesitation and without question. Todd was very proud of them, but he couldn't help but feel a nagging sense of guilt and futility. Why should the blood of such fine young men be spent so foolishly? These young men were the cream of a nation. Not only his men, but the men in blue as well, were representative of the best America had to offer. If they were all killed in the war, what then? Who would be left to harvest the "fruits of victory"?

But Todd didn't put his doubts into words. Instead he smiled at Pearson. "All right, Lieutenant," he said, "make the attack."

"Yes, sir!" Pearson said, returning Todd's smile with an even broader one of his own. He saluted, then turned and ran quickly down the hill, holding onto his sword and pistol so that those weapons wouldn't be dislodged as he ran.

"Mount up!" he called. "Mount up, men. The attack is on!"

Todd waited for a few minutes until after the others had left, then rode down to the bayou, dismounted, tied his horse, and started down the bank toward the muddy, murky water. Just before he got there, though, he stopped, then returned, untied his horse, and slapped him on the flank, sending him on his way. If a Yankee patrol discovered his horse, they might figure out what he was doing, and if they didn't catch him in the bayou, they could catch him merely by waiting by the horse until Todd came back. Also, though he didn't like to think about it, if something happened to him he didn't want his horse left unattended.

Todd turned to go back down the bank, slipping and sliding down until he slipped into the water. The bayou was shallow, and the water didn't come above his knees. He stayed close to the bank, shielded by the low, overhanging boughs of the bankside trees. It was slow and arduous to push through the bayou, stepping over logs, picking his way around brambles, ducking under limbs, and always to be on the lookout for snakes. He saw several water moccasins slithering down the muddy bank and into the bayou, then arrowing through the water gracefully, leaving a small, silent wake behind them.

Todd carried a forked stick with him, and if the snakes got close, he would ensnare them in the fork of his stick, pick them out of the water, and fling them up onto the bank. When caught they would invariably display their fangs, opening wide to show their white mouths that gave them their name, and hissing angrily as he flipped them away.

Once he was startled by a voice, just after he had flipped a snake up onto the bank.

"What was thet?" the voice said.

"What? What are you talkin' about?" he was answered.

"Did you see thet?"

"She what?"

"A snake."

The other voice laughed, "Jim, you been seein' snakes ever since Sergeant Law put you over here."

"Thet's the truth, I have," Jim said. "But this here snake come flyin' toward me!"

The other voice laughed again, this time more boisterously than before. "You say he come flyin' at you, did he? The fellers'll enjoy thet tale, I reckon."

"I'm tellin' you, this here snake come *flyin'* at me now," Jim said. "Why would I make such a thang up?"

" 'Cause you don't want to be here guardin' this here bayou, thet's why," the other voice said.

"Lissen, I'm tellin' you the truth."

"Well, what do you expect?" the other man

asked, laughing again. "It be a rebel snake, don't it? Maybe they've trained their snakes to attack Union soldiers."

"You can joke about it if you want to, but I'm keepin' my eyes open from now on," Jim said.

The sound of gunfire reached Todd's ears. The two Union soldiers heard it as well, and Jim commented on it. "Listen, the fellas over there is gettin' some action."

"Maybe they've been attacked by a battalion of rebel snakes," the other man said.

"I'm going to climb up on that hill yonder 'n have a look see at what's agoin' on," Jim said.

"Yeah," the other replied. "I think I'll go along with you."

Todd waited until the sound of their conversation and the snapping of twigs died away, and he knew they were safely out of range, before he continued his trek. From then on, he vowed to be more careful about flipping the snakes onto the bank.

Half an hour later, Todd climbed up out of the bayou and, bending low, ran toward a ridge line. He scrambled up over it, then dropped on the other side, surprising a dozen or so soldiers who were there.

"What the—? How did you get here?" one of the men asked.

Another grabbed his rifle and pointed it at him. "Never mind that," he said. "Who are you? Are you a Yank?"

"I'm a Confederate, same as yourself," Todd said. "My name is Major Todd Kirk. I've slipped through the Yankee lines."

"Mister, Confederate or not, you are *crazy*," the

first soldier said. "Why the hell would anyone slip through the lines to get in to a city under siege? We'uns is tryin' to figure out a way to get *out* of here."

"What did you come here for?" the one with the rifle asked.

"I came to see General Pemberton," Todd said. "Look, who is your commanding officer? Take me to see him."

"It's Colonel Garrott," the one with the rifle said.

"Isham Garrott? I know him," Todd said. "Take me to see him. He will vouch for me."

Colonel Isham W. Garrott, tall and thin, commanding officer of the 20th Alabama, the unit manning Fort Garrott, as the redoubt was called, greeted Todd with a smile.

"Well, Todd, still as crazy as ever, huh? What on earth made you sneak into here?"

"Isham, do you remember the canal Grant had dug up in Missouri early last year, when the Yankees captured Island Number Ten?"

"Yes," Garrott said. "They slipped their gunboats through and invested the island from both sides. Once they did that, the island fell."

"He's trying the same thing here," Todd said.

"Where?"

"Where the river makes the horseshoe bend," Todd said. "It is Grant's intention to cut a channel through there. That way the gunboats can be slipped through, the city can come under fire from both sides, and the boats won't have the danger of running the shore batteries."

"I see," Garrott said. He scratched his chin, then called to a nearby officer. "Captain Nelson, escort

Major Kirk to General Pemberton's headquarters."

"Yes, sir," Nelson replied, and Todd, with a salute and a handshake, left Garrott.

"Yes, yes," Pemberton was saying to one of his officers. He seemed agitated, but Todd knew that he had every reason to be. His position was a desperate one, and under the circumstances he was doing as well as could be down. Now the situation was rapidly deteriorating, and Pemberton knew it.

Pemberton was not a Southerner by birth, and it showed in his brusque manner of speaking. No slow drawl for him. He had been born in Philadelphia, educated at West Point, and spent a lifetime serving in the United States army. But he was married to a Virginia woman, and it was his ties through marriage that led him into service for the South.

Pemberton was faced with conflicting orders now. Jefferson Davis had ordered him to hold Vicksburg at all costs. General Joseph Johnston had ordered him to evacuate. Now it was impossible to do one and too late to do the other, and all he could do was hang on.

Pemberton was tall and thin, and wore a moustache and chin whiskers, though the sides of his face were clean-shaven. He had a dark complexion and flashing dark eyes. He looked up when Captain Nelson brought Todd to him.

"General, this man says he is—"

"Todd," Pemberton greeted him warmly. "Todd Kirk, how nice to see you again."

"Hello, General. It's good to see you again too. Though in truth I would have chosen better circumstances." Todd looked around Pemberton's headquarters and saw the signs of a commander under siege. A map on the wall told the whole painful story at one glance.

"Yes, I dare say I would as well," Pemberton said. "Major Kirk, I want you to know what an inspiration you and your men have been for the rest of the South. Your exploits have been about all we've had to cheer about of late."

"Thank you, General. But your fierce resistance here has stiffened the resolve of the South, and you are to be congratulated as well."

"Yes," Pemberton said. He scratched at his beard. "Well, we shall see how kindly history treats me for submitting the population of an entire city to a siege. Do you realize that no American city has ever been under siege before?"

"No, sir."

"Well, that is a fact, Major. And now I shall go down in history as being the commander who was stubborn enough to subject his people to such terrible deprivation."

"But Grant will go down in history as the general who prosecuted the siege," Todd reminded him.

"Yes, yes, maybe you are right," Pemberton said. "I can only hope so, anyway. I tell you, Major Kirk, I wouldn't even attempt to hold out, were it not for the fact that General Lee is thrusting into the North."

"He is? I didn't know that," Todd said.

"No one knows it yet," Pemberton said. "I just received it by secret message from the last courier to get through the Yankee lines. The last one before you, that is. Tell me, how did you get in?"

"I walked in through Stout's Bayou, General."

"What? But isn't that ditch filled with snakes?" Pemberton asked, his eyes wide with disbelief.

"Yes, sir," Todd said, smiling. "They were my allies, for they kept the Yankees out of my way."

"I dare say they would," Pemberton replied. "After all, who would want to share a ditch with a cottonmouth?"

"They aren't dangerous, sir, if you know what you are doing."

"I guess not," Pemberton said. "But I shouldn't want to put it to a test." Suddenly Pemberton's mood grew somber. "Todd, I heard about Sam Shelton, and I want to apologize. Had I received word of Culpepper's plans before he carried them out, he would never have hanged your friend."

"Culpepper hanged an innocent man, General," Todd said.

"If you vouch for him, that's all I need," Pemberton said. "It's too late to do anything about your friend now, but I promise you, I shall clear his good name."

"Thank you, General."

"Now, tell me. Why did you risk the danger of coming into Vicksburg?"

"General, I have a map in my tunic pocket," Todd said, "which I copied directly from a Yankee map. It shows where, when, and how the Yankees plan to cut a canal."

"A canal?"

"Yes, sir," Todd said. He took the map from his pocket and spread it out on the table before Pemberton, holding the corners of the map down with a paperweight, an inkwell, a book, and his pistol.

"They'll cut right across here," he said. "And

then Vicksburg will be subject to bombardment from both ends of the river."

"I see," Pemberton said. "Yes, that would be most uncomfortable for us, should General Grant decide to increase the number of calling cards he leaves for us each day."

"Calling cards, sir?"

Pemberton smiled. "That's what we call the shot and shell he sends to us each day."

"That's a good name for them, I suppose, sir," Todd said, laughing at the general's macabre sense of humor.

Pemberton looked at the map a bit longer. "Todd, you know this land. Can they dig it with manpower alone?"

"No, sir," Todd said. "Not soon enough to do them any good, that is. They'll have to have steamshovels."

"I see," Pemberton said. He looked up at Captain Nelson, who had stood by quietly for the entire conversation. "Captain Nelson, find Colonel Higgins for me."

"Yes, sir," Nelson said.

"Higgins is my river battery commander," Pemberton explained. "I want you to tell him everything you just told me. If the Yankees are brining in a steamshovel, it will have to come down the river, and when it does, we will be ready for it."

"Yes, sir," Todd said.

There was a sudden explosion outside, then a rush of air, followed by another explosion. Pemberton pulled his pocket watch out and looked at it.

"Well, I see it is about dinnertime. You can always tell, because we get shelled at about this same time every day."

As Pemberton spoke, two more explosions occured outside, and then Colonel Higgins came into the room.

"Ed, you have those Yankees mad at you again," Pemberton teased.

"They must be, sir," Higgins replied.

"Then what did you come in here for? You know they'll just keep shooting at you."

"I thought there would be a good place to hide over here," Higgins said. He looked at Todd and smiled. "Is this the brave man who ran the siege line?"

"Yes, Colonel Higgins, this is Major Kirk."

"I've heard of Kirk's Raiders," Higgins said, shaking Todd's hand. "It is an honor to meet you."

"Todd has brought us some important news," Pemberton said. "I'll have him explain everything to you. Afterward we can have supper and make plans about what we are going to do about this tomorrow."

"Tomorrow?" Todd asked.

"Surely you didn't plan to do anything tonight?" Pemberton replied.

"Well, no, sir, I guess not," Todd said. "But I did rather hope to leave here tonight."

"Don't we all, Major," Pemberton said. "Don't we all?"

Pemberton was neither challenging nor sarcastic in his remark. He was resigned. And it was that sense of resignation, more than anything else, which convinced Todd that he should stay in Vicksburg, rather than try to get out again, at least, for a short time.

It was not a prospect he relished.

CHAPTER TWENTY-FOUR

While we write, the fate of Vicksburg is un-decided. But whatever that fate may be, the sturdy and splendid prowess of the gallant defenders, who have fought for a month against overwhelming odds, will be one of the most glorious traditions of the war.

They stand beside the river that is their river. They fight not only for the great and general cause of our government, but for the rights of men to be free. To the wiles of dema-gogues and desperate invaders, they present a glistening front of silent steel. Throughout the loyal South, and throughout our history, the praise of these men rings, and shall ring for-ever.

"I see you are reading my article," a sparsely be-whiskered man said. Tony looked up from his news-paper. He was sitting on a box at the Yazoo City theater.

"Yes," Tony said.

The man smiled broadly. "What do you think of

it? Isn't it a piece designed to inspire men to give their last full measure of devotion and duty?"

"He had just made that very comment," Jaylene said quickly. She got up from the trunk where she had been unpacking costumes and offered her hand to the intruder. "I am Jaylene Cooper."

"Yes," the man said. "I recognize you from before. I am Theodore Biggs, publisher of the Southern Defender and author of the piece this gentleman was reading. You are, I believe, the new actor we heard about?"

"Yes," Tony said. He stood and offered Biggs his hand, then bowed formally. "Jeremy Tremont at your service, sir."

"Mr. Tremont, I should like to do a story on you," Biggs said, pulling a pencil and pad from his pocket. "I am most certain my readers would be interested in you."

"Oh, I really have nothing in my background of note," Tony said.

"Mr. Tremont is being too modest," Jaylene put in quickly. "He was for several months the star attraction on my father's boat, the *Delta Mist*. When we heard he was available, I urged Uncle Edward to contact him and see if he would join us."

"Then you know Mr. Tremont?" Biggs asked.

Jaylene put her hand on Tony's arm. "I have known him for a long time," she said. "And I will vouch for his talent and for his ability to thrill an audience. The people of Yazoo City and the gallant soldiers we shall visit will be the beneficiaries of his luminous presence."

"Thank you," Biggs said writing down everything

Jaylene said. "This will make a fine story. Yes sir, a fine story."

"We appreciate the publicity," Jaylene said.

"My dear, I can assure you, everyone in town will be anxious to see your new play," Biggs promised. "Oh, I almost forgot. Colonel Culpepper sends his regards, and issues an invitation for you to join him for dinner, as you have before."

"I'm sorry, no," Jaylene said.

Biggs was surprised by Jaylene's refusal, and he stammered in confusion, "But . . . do you realize what you are doing? Colonel Culpepper is the military governor of the district."

"Yes I understand what I am doing," Jaylene said. "And I think Colonel Culpepper understands why I am doing it. But, just in case he doesn't, tell him it is because of Lucy Wade."

"Oh, yes, I know the story," Biggs said. "But you might be interested to know that Colonel Culpepper asked me not to print what I knew, in order that no one be embarrassed."

"I'm sure he wasn't concerned for Lucy's feelings," Jaylene said. "He had other feelings in mind when he issued such a directive. No, Mr. Biggs, we will not come to dinner with the colonel, and you may tell him that for me."

"Yes, Miss Cooper," Biggs said. He cleared his throat. "If you will excuse me now, I have a newspaper to get out." He held up his pencil and pad as if using it to verify his statement; then, giving a hesitant bow, he excused himself again and backed out of the theater.

"Are you certain that was wise?" Edward asked.

"Perhaps we should have accpeted his invitation."

"No," Tony said. "Jaylene is right. The fewer times I am exposed to direct examination, the fewer chances I have of being discovered. It is good that we avoid people as much as we can." He sighed. "For that reason, I would have preferred saying nothing to the newspaper man."

"You didn't," Jaylene said. "I had to do all the talking for you."

"Nevertheless, it is just one more story that can be checked on," Tony said.

"How will they check?" Jaylene asked. "My father is dead, the other crewmen have long since gone their own ways, and I am the only one available to authenticate your story. No, we are quite safe with that story."

"I suppose so," Tony said. "At least for a short while. But I can't stay in Yazoo City for too long a period of time. I must get Lucy and get out of here. Do you have any idea where she might be?"

"My guess is that she is staying in the Lexington House," Jaylene said. "That has been completely taken over by Colonel Culpepper."

"Then I need to get a look at it. How would I do that?"

"You could have seen it, had we accepted Culpepper's dinner invitation," Edward said.

"Not really," Jaylene replied. "For when one dines with Colonel Culpepper, one sees only the dining room."

"That wouldn't do me much good," Tony said. "I need to know the layout of the entire building. How does one get upstairs, and where exactly is Lucy kept?

Also, what does the building look like from the sides, and rear? What other buildings are around it?"

"I can do nothing about getting you inside the building," Jaylene said. "But if you wish, we can take a walk around town and I can show you the building from the outside."

"That is an excellent idea," Tony agreed. "Also, I would like to get an overview of the city and the roads into and out of town."

"Then shall we go?" Jaylene invited.

Jaylene gave Tony her arm, and they walked along the boardwalks of the city. When they passed the place where Sam had been hanged, Jaylene felt an involuntary chill, and she shivered slightly.

"Are you cold?" Tony asked.

"Perhaps a little," Jaylene said. She had no wish to explain what had really made her shiver, for she didn't want to relive the incident, even in words.

They talked as they walked, reviewing things Tony would have to know in order to carry off his deception, and, as Tony was responding with the correct answers to every question posed, Jaylene began to have more confidence in the success of their mission.

When they reached the Lexington House they walked around it and observed it from every possible angle. It wasn't difficult to ascertain the room where Lucy was being kept, for posted outside in the alley below were two armed guards.

"What do you think?" Jaylene asked.

"I think we are going to have a difficult task before us," Tony replied.

"Will we succeed?"

"Of course," Tony said easily. He looked at Jaylene and smiled at her. "The first one-third of success is believing in it," he said. "And the second third is believing in yourself."

"Then we are two-thirds there," Jaylene said. "For I believe we will do it, and I believe in you."

They were standing just behind a building, looking down the alley toward the rear of Lexington House. For that reason they were unobserved by anyone on the street, and Tony took the opportunity to lean down and kiss Jaylene.

"Well?" Jaylene asked a moment later, when their lips had parted.

"Well, what?"

"Aren't you going to apologize to me?"

Tony smiled again. "No," he said. "I don't think I have anything to apologize for."

"You don't feel it was wicked, or that you took advantage of a poor, defenseless girl?"

"No."

This time, Jaylene returned his smile. "Then in that case," she said, leaning over to him, "perhaps I shall return the kiss."

They kissed again, longer than before, and Jaylene felt heat flaring within her. For one wild, reckless moment she thought he was going to push her down there in the alley and take her there, with people passing by on the street just a few feet away. And for an equally wild moment she wanted him to do just that.

The kiss ended a moment later with both of them breathing heavily. They said nothing about it, but both of them knew that they would be in bed together that very night.

Any plans they may have had were delayed when

they returned to the theater, for Edward had set the stage for a rehearsal and was insisting that they go through with it. They worked for approximately two hours and were just about to quit for the evening when from the darkened cavern of the empty seats came the sound of a single person's applause.

"Bravo, bravo, my dear, players," Colonel Culpepper's voice called from the darkness. "Even in rehearsal, you are magnificent to behold."

Colonel Culpepper's voice startled the actors on the stage. Jaylene gasped, and wondered quickly if, during the time they believed themselves to be alone, they had said or done anything to compromise Tony's disguise.

"What are you doing here?" Jaylene asked.

"Sir, this was a closed rehearsal," Edward added. "No one is permitted at a closed rehearsal."

"No one," Culpepper said, coming toward the stage so that the disembodied voice finally took on shape and substance, "no one except the military governor, who can do anything he wishes."

"Perhaps so, Colonel," Jaylene said. "But you should have told us you were here."

"Oh, no," Culpepper said. "I have discovered that I see and hear so much more when people don't realize I am around. Your new actor, what is his name?"

"Jeremy Tremont," Jaylene said.

"Ah, yes, Jeremy Tremont," Culpepper said. "And he was with your father?"

"Yes," Jaylene said. She wondered how thorough his interrogation was going to be, and she was on her guard lest she inadvertently disclose something she didn't want him to know.

298

"Ah, now, you see, that is what has made me curious. I was once a passenger on board the *Delta Mist* and I don't recall seeing him."

"Perhaps it was one of the shows he missed," Jaylene suggested.

"Perhaps so," Culpepper replied. He turned and looked back into the darkened part of the theater. "So I brought someone with me who saw many more of the shows. Surely, if your Mr. Tremont was in the plays, as you say, this person would remember him."

"Who is it?" Jaylene asked.

Culpepper snapped his fingers in the darkness. "My dear, would you come up here, please?"

Jaylene heard the hollow sound of footsteps and the swishing of a full skirt, so that she knew the person was a woman. But who the woman was, Jaylene had no idea, until the visitor stepped into the golden bubble of light produced by the footlights of the stage.

"Hello, Jaylene," the woman said.

Jaylene gasped, and put her hand to her mouth to keep from calling out. For there, standing before her, was Emily McLean.

CHAPTER TWENTY-FIVE

"Mac—— was in town, and I was able to verify——

Mr. Tremont with his stock—mes——

There's nothing to forgive, Colonel," Tony —d

——

——ens ——— the —blic ——

——litary commission and —o ———— —e ——— ——

——nds of—matter ——

————

"It is so nice to see you again, Jaylene," Emily said, smiling sweetly. She looked at Tony, and her eyes flashed brilliantly. "And dear, dear Jeremy, how good it is to see you as well. You've lost none of your ability to project, I see. Though I do believe you have added a touch of gray to your temples since I last saw you. Or is that merely stage makeup?"

"You mean you two *know* each other?" Culpepper asked, a little surprised.

"Know each other, Colonel?" Emily said, raising one eyebrow. "We were once lovers. In fact, it was because of a lover's quarrel we had that Jeremy left the *Delta Mist*. Perhaps that was why no one you spoke with had ever heard of him."

"Perhaps so," Culpepper said. He tugged at his chin for a moment, then smiled, though the smile appeared to be one he had pasted on his face. He presented a half-bow to Tony, Jaylene, and the others. "I do hope you will forgive the suspicions of a cautious man," he said. "But as I had never heard of Mr. Tremont, nor could I find anyone else who had, I felt it necessary to check further. Fortunately,

302

Miss McLean was in town, and I was able to verify Mr. Tremont with her expert witness."

"There is nothing to forgive, Colonel," Tony said. "I admire and respect the efficiency of a prudent man."

"I was certain you would," Culpepper said. "As military commander and governor here, I cannot err on the side of caution. Why, only a short time ago I had to hang a traitor right here in town."

Jaylene looked quickly away.

"Oh, I'm sorry, my dear, you knew the man, didn't you?"

"Yes," Jaylene said.

"He was quite a hero to some," Culpepper said. "Why, even I had praised his exploits. But that was before I knew his treacherous qualities."

"Did he give secrets to the enemy?" Tony asked.

"Worse than that, sir," Culpepper said. "He tried to help a nigra escape." He sighed. "Perhaps his execution will be a warning to others who might share his treasonous feelings. In the meantime, I know you have a play to prepare for, and I've no wish to delay you any longer." He saluted. "If you will excuse me? Come along, my dear," he said, offering his arm to Emily.

"Colonel, if you don't mind, I would like to stay a while and visit," Emily said. "These are old friends whom I haven't seen in a long time."

"Yes, of course," Culpepper said. "But I shall expect you later."

Emily smiled brightly at Culpepper, and then they watched him as he disappeared into the darkness. A moment later they heard the back door slam.

303

"Jaylene, it is good to see you again," Emily said.

"I must say, seeing you gave me quite a fright," Jaylene said.

"I can well imagine that it did."

"Why did you say you recognized Jeremy Tremont?" Jaylene asked.

"Because I do recognize him," Emily answered.

"What do you mean?"

"This man is a Yankee officer. His name is Captain Tony Holt. I saw him many times in Winona."

"Can that be true?" Tony replied. "I don't remember seeing you, and truly, madam, you are not a woman a man could easily forget."

Emily laughed. "I would be if I wore a gray wig, glue to wrinkle my skin, and old clothes to bend and twist my body with age. Perhaps you remember the old woman who delivered pies to the officers' dining room?"

"Only vaguely," Tony said. "I never paid any attention to her."

"That was my intention," Emily said.

"You?"

Emily smiled. "You prefer apple pie, I believe."

"Why, yes. Yes, I do," Tony said. "But I don't understand."

"What is there to understand?" Emily asked. "I'm a spy."

Jaylene gasped. "So that's what became of you?"

"Yes," Emily said. She looked at Jaylene and her features softened. "Jaylene, I've much explaining to do to you, but you didn't give me the chance. Will you give me that chance now?"

"I . . . I don't know," Jaylene said. "Emily, if you only knew how hurt I've been!"

304

"My god, girl, do you think the hurt was reserved for you alone? Or even for you and your father? I was part of it too, you know. The pain hit all of us. And it was the more severe because I was never given the opportunity to tell my side of the story."

"Emily, in truth, it didn't appear as if you *had* a side to tell. We saw what we saw. How can that be changed?"

Emily sighed. "Perhaps it can never be changed," she said. "But it can be explained, if you will but let me."

"I must think about it for a while," Jaylene said. "In the meantime, I want to thank you for not giving Tony away."

"As do I," Tony said. "But I am puzzled, madam. By your own admission, you are a spy, and I take it you are spying for the Confederacy."

"Yes."

"Then why do you protect my identity?"

Emily smiled. "Perhaps it is a natural inclination for self-preservation. Spying can be very dangerous work, so when you see the opportunity to help a fellow spy, sometimes you will, even if he is for the other side. Besides, you were with Jaylene, and she was obviously trying to protect you. That is good enough for me."

Tony cleared his throat. "I wish I could return the favor," he said. "But in all good conscience, I cannot. I am afraid that if I see you dispensing pies again, I shall have to expose you."

"I know," Emily said. "But don't worry. My business there is finished." She looked at Jaylene, and a long, wistful expression fell across her face. "And, I suppose, my business here is finished as well," she said quietly.

Jaylene didn't meet her gaze, and after a moment Emily turned to leave.

"Jaylene," Edward said softly. "Call her back."

"I can't," Jaylene said, squeezing a tear out of her eye. "I'm sorry," she said. "But I just can't."

Todd walked the busy streets of Vicksburg the next morning, looking at the city under siege. It was in an uproar. The population was swollen with refugee civilians and wounded soldiers, and every third or fourth person had a rumor he was willing to pass on as news.

Already the day was hot, and flies flew about in swarms, fat, lazy flies that found food where the people could not. Then Sherman's artillery began its morning bombardment, a distant, sustained, rolling thunder that a few days earlier had sent thirty-six hundred shells into Vicksburg in one hour's time.

By looking toward Union lines, and the huge, white cloud that had built up like a mountain of cotton in the west, Todd could see the missiles as they screamed into the city. They were round, black, ominous-looking things, and the shells, those foul machines that exploded on the streets and in the houses of the city, trailed little plumes of hissing smoke as their fuses burned.

The first volley slammed into the city, followed by explosions and a rain of debris. One entire wall of a building collapsed into the street, right in front of Todd.

"Hey, mister, you better come in here before you gets yourself kilt," someone called laconically.

"Them's cannon balls fallin' out there, not rain-drops."

The call had come from a cave tunneled out of the side of one of the many bluffs of Vicksburg. Todd heeded the stranger's advice and ran to the welcome sound of his voice. A thin, gaunt-faced man stood just inside the mouth of the cave. One of his legs was gone at the knee, and he had a peg leg. He had a malarial complexion, pale blond hair, and washed-out blue eyes. He wore the rags of what had once been a gray uniform.

"You a soldier?" the man asked.

"Yes," Todd said.

"Light out on 'em, did you?"

"No," Todd said. "No, of course not."

"You don't need to get huffy about it," the man said. "My name's Kindig. Elias Kindig." He stuck out his hand and Todd grasped it. It was bony and clammy. "I don't mind tellin' you, I lit out. I was with the Fourth Alabama, until they deserted me."

"They deserted you?" Todd asked.

"Yep. They left me for dead on the battlefield, 'n I commenced ter get myself into Vicksburg. Some sawbones took off my leg, 'n he tole me I didn't have to go back, so damned if I didn't decide to just stay here."

"I don't think anyone will hold it against you," Todd said.

"If you ain't deserted your unit, what are you doin' here?" Kindig asked.

"I sneaked through the Yankee lines into Vicksburg to bring some information to General Pemberton," Todd said.

307

"You sneaked in? You mean you wasn't inside already?"

"No."

"Mister, you are either the bravest man I know or the biggest fool," Kindig said.

"I'm beginning to think it is the latter," Todd said.

There was another rushing sound, followed by another explosion, and even though he was in the cave, Todd could feel the stunning blow of concussion from the explosion.

"Them damned things could get dangerous," Elias said laconically.

Todd spent the next forty-five minutes with Elias, until the bombardment ceased. Then the streets filled with civilians again as the people started once more to go about their business. Todd thanked Elias for his hospitality and joined the others.

Todd walked down to the river batteries, which were in Colonel Higgin's command, and saw that a couple of guns were being disassembled. He was puzzled by it, until he saw Colonel Higgins.

"Major Kirk, I have great news!" Colonel Higgins said.

"What news, sir?"

"Thanks to your propitious warning, and the sharp eyes of a couple of my lookouts, there will be no canal built across the bend."

"Why? What has happened?"

"It is the *Cincinnati*, sir," Colonel Higgins said. "My lookouts spotted her early this morning, trying to sneak in close to the shore. And guess what she has on board?"

"What?"

"Steamshovels, sir. Two giant steamshovels, without which it will not be possible to dig a canal."

"Colonel, we've got to stop those steamshovels from being off-loaded," Todd said.

Higgins smiled and pointed to the two great batteries which were being disassembled. "In civilian life, I am an Episcopal priest, did you know that?"

"No, sir."

"I am. In fact, General Polk, who is an Episcopal bishop, was *my* bishop. The bishop suggested the names for these two guns: St. Peter and St. Paul. He has four guns of his own, Matthew, Mark, Luke and John, you know."

"Yes, I've heard," Todd said.

"I believe when Peter and Paul speak to the *Cincinnati*, there will be no steamshovels unloaded."

"Will you be able to get them into firing position soon enough?" Todd asked.

"Yes," Higgins said. "Don't worry about that, Major. My men are quite adept at moving, setting, up, and firing again. We have already done it several times." He pulled out his pocket watch and looked at it. "Come," he said. "While they are setting up, we will go down to the courthouse."

"To the courthouse? What for?"

"General Pemberton is going to make a speech," Higgins said. "Have you ever heard him speak?"

"No, sir, I can't say as I have."

"Then you are in for a treat, son. I do believe that man was born with a silver tongue in his head." Higgins laughed. "Why, I'd rather hear him speak than listen to a pretty girl sing. Come along. You are going to appreciate this, I know you are."

Todd followed Higgins, who moved in a quick-

stepped gait as if always in a hurry, from the river
battery emplacement to the courthouse lawn. There,
a group of people were waiting for General Pemberton to appear. The question on everyone's lips was
whether or not Pemberton would surrender the city.
Most of them had come to some accomodation with
the situation, and were resolute in their desire to
hold fast.

Pemberton arrived then, amid the hurrahs and
applause of the townspeople. He climbed upon the
half wall around the portico and held on to one of
the pillars as he spoke.

As Higgins had said, Pemberton was a golden-
voiced orator, and his words were inspirational. He
spoke for several minutes, telling of the bravery and
the hardships of the soldiers, and complimenting the
bravery of the citizens. Finally he got around to the
subject that everyone was there to hear.

"You have heard," he said, "that I am incompetent and a traitor, and that it was my intention to
sell Vicksburg. Follow me, and you will see the cost
at which I will sell Vicksburg. When the last pound
of beef, bacon, and flour, the last grain of corn, the
last cow and hog and horse and dog shall have been
consumed, and when the last man shall have per-
ished in the trenches, then and only then, will I sell
Vicksburg!"

Even while the people were cheering Pemberton's
speech, a lieutenant hurried up to Colonel Higgins
to tell him that the guns were in position, and the
Cincinnati was in range.

"Fine, fine," Higgins said. He turned to Todd.
"Well, Major, let us go see the fruit of your labors.
We are about to sink the *Cincinnati*."

Todd followed Higgins through the crowded streets of Vicksburg, then north out of town along Milldale Road and up a bluff until there, newly mounted, were the two ten-inch guns, St. Peter and St. Paul. Both gun crews were standing by their guns, and powder and shot were stacked alongside.

The captain who was in charge of setting up the guns reported to Colonel Higgins.

"How does it look, Captain?" Higgins asked, walking over to sight along one of the guns.

"It looks wonderful, sir," the captain said. "As you can see, we are in position for plunging shot. We should be on target within three rounds, and there is very little the *Cincinnati* can do. By the time she turns to bring her guns to bear, she'll be mortally wounded."

Higgins removed a pair of field glasses from his leather case and looked down at the boat, then handed the glasses to Todd. "What do you see?" he asked.

"I see an iron-clad gunboat," Todd said. "There are four gun holes on the portside, and three forward. What is that round thing, just forward of the flag?"

"That's an armored turret for riflemen," Higgins said. "It's covered with the same armor as the rest of the boat, two-and-a-quarter-inch iron plating."

Todd whistled. "Will your guns be able to penetrate that?"

"Peter and Paul will," Higgins said. "Especially from this angle. Now, look aft of the smokestacks. What do you see there, under the canvas?"

"I don't know," Todd said. "It's hard to . . ." Suddenly he stopped and pulled the glasses down,

311

then looked toward Higgins with a big smile on his face. "I see a steamshovel," he said.

"There are two steamshovels there, actually," Higgins said, "if you look close enough. One of them is named Champion Number Ten, and the other is named Samson. Champion Number Ten was used to excavate the canal up in New Madrid, Missouri, at Island Number Ten. That's where it gets its name."

"Colonel, they're making steam," the captain said quietly.

"Very well, Captain, you may fire as soon as your guns are laid in."

"Fire!" the captain said, and the touchholes of both guns were fired at the same time. The guns let out an earth-shaking roar.

"Two direct hits, Captain," a sergeant called out.

"Reload and fire again," the captain called.

The *Cincinnati* answered the batteries with all four guns on her port side blazing away. But the shots fell far down the bluff, not even coming close to Colonel Higgins's battery. Peter and Paul fired a second volley and, as before, the shot found its mark, both balls penetrating the iron-plating on the side of the boat.

"I can't understand why she's not coming around," Higgins said.

"There's why, sir," the captain said. "Look, her tiller ropes have been shot away!"

Water began churning behind the boat as she tried to get away, but another volley smashed into her pilothouse, and even from here Todd could see the carnage it caused.

312

"She's shipping water fast," the sergeant lookout called.

"Fire another volley of solid shot at her waterline," Higgins ordered. "Then commence firing with shell."

"Yes, sir," the gun captain said, and a moment later, Peter and Paul belched flame and smoke as two more rounds of plunging shot found their mark.

Now the *Cincinnati* was going down fast by the bow, though her guns valiantly returned fire.

"Rake her with shell," Higgins ordered. "We've got to drive the men off before they run her inshore. We can't let them save the steamshovels."

Peter and Paul were reloaded, this time with shell, which would explode into shrapnel on impact and scatter the men.

"Fire!" the captain said, and again came the stomach-jarring roar.

Todd watched the shells, trailing a wisp of smoke, as they arched across the water, then dropped right onto the boat, there to explode in two fiery roses. Officers and men leaped into the water, grabbing planks of wood, tree limbs, even the bales of cotton which had provided additional barricading for the crew, as they fought desperately to avoid drowning.

"Cease fire," Higgins called, and the captain passed the word along. "She's going down fast now. There's no need to fire into the men."

Slowly the *Cincinnati* went down. The water steamed and bubbled as the boilers went under and finally the whole boat settled into the mud, with water up to the upper deck. Both steamshovels had slipped into the water and were lying on their sides, useless.

"Well, Major Kirk," Higgins said. "There will be no canal now, thanks to you."

"And thanks to your men, Colonel. That was as prodigious an exhibition of shooting as I ever saw," Todd said.

"Peter and Paul did it, Major," one of the privates said, grinning and patting the two artillery pieces proudly. "Give the credit to them."

Todd looked at the two guns, then back toward the river. Along with the flotsam and jetsam from the sunken gunboat, he saw the bodies of nearly a dozen men, floating face down in the water. Somehow the thought of naming the two guns after Biblical saints seemed inappropriate, but he said nothing. The men would have been just as dead had the guns been named for all the demons of hell.

CHAPTER TWENTY-SIX

It had been three days since Jaylene, Tony, and
the others had come to Yazoo City to rehearse the
new play. During that time Tony had laid plans for
rescuing Lucy. He had no idea how effective the
plans would be, because he had not been able to co-
ordinate them with Lucy, or even to let her know
that such a plan was in the offing.

Culpepper had systematically avoided allowing
Jaylene or any of the troupe to see Lucy. With no
communication, they had to hope that Lucy would
be ready and would cooperate when Tony made his
move.

There was one possible way to contact Lucy,
though Jaylene was loathe to do it. Tony had suggested that Jaylene return Emily's call and enlist her
aid. Emily had left word every day that she wanted
to meet with Jaylene, but so far Jaylene had steadfastly refused.

"But she might help us," Tony said. He and Jaylene were walking through the streets of the town,
ostensibly enjoying a pleasant evening stroll, but in
reality to allow Tony to check the positions of the
guards and their schedule once again. He had come

here every evening, checking the movement of the guards, determining how long it took them to walk their posts.

"I can't trust her," Jaylene said.

"Jaylene, what is it?" Tony asked. "What happened between you and Miss McLean?"

"She killed my father," Jaylene said quietly.

"Are you serious?"

"Oh, I don't mean with a gun or a knife, or anything like that," Jaylene said. "Though she was just as effective with the weapon she did use. She broke his heart."

"I see," Tony said.

"I don't think you do," Jaylene said. "You don't understand what—"

"Jaylene, I can understand an affair of the heart," Tony interrupted. "And I know the pain one can feel if things aren't right. I feel well qualified on that subject, as I have experience in it."

"You have suffered a broken heart?" Jaylene asked, surprised by Tony's unexpected statement.

"No," Tony said. "At least, not yet. Though the conditions are right for just such a thing."

"I don't understand," Jaylene said. "What are you talking about?"

"I'm talking about us, Jaylene," Tony said. "I've been giving a great deal of thought to us, lately."

"And what have you thought about us?"

Tony cleared his throat. "I've thought about our situation, me being a Union officer, you being a Southern girl. And I've thought about—uh—you know, what we did."

"You mean about our making love?" Jaylene asked.

Tony cleared his throat again. "Yes," he said.

"And what have you thought about us making love?"

"I . . . I think you are right," Tony said. "I mean when you said there is nothing wrong with two people making love. And I want to do it again."

Jaylene laughed a bubbling, lilting laugh. "You silly goose. Do you think it is something one does as casually as taking a stroll?"

"Well, I . . . I really don't know," Tony said. "I mean you—uh, that is, you seemed so open about it."

"Perhaps it seemed that way," Jaylene said. "But there is more to it than that. The time has to be right, the place has to be right, and the people have to be right. I felt something for you, didn't you realize that? I couldn't have done it otherwise."

"Then I was right," Tony said, looking at her and smiling triumphantly. "You *did* feel something for me."

"Of course I did. You don't think I could just go to bed with anyone, do you?"

"No, of course not," Tony said. He cleared his throat again. "This makes what I want to say somewhat easier."

"Oh? And what is it you want to say?" Jaylene asked. "I must confess, Tony, you are being so mysterious that you have greatly aroused my curiosity. What is it?"

"Jaylene, my dear, I've given a great deal of thought to this. I know Mother would have a hard time accepting you, but in time she would learn to love you as much as I. I just know it."

"Your mother?" Jaylene asked.

"Yes," Tony said. "I would want her approval, and with your help I know we can bring her around."

"Her approval for what, Tony?" Jaylene asked. "Tony, I'm afraid you aren't making too much sense."

Tony laughed. "No, I suppose not. Though I would have thought you would have guessed by now. Jaylene, I want you to marry me."

Tony's proposal was such a surprise to Jaylene that it took her breath away. She had no idea he had even considered such a thing.

"Well?" Tony asked. "What do you say?"

"Tony, I . . ."

"Uh, uh," Tony cautioned. "I don't like the way you were starting that. It sounded as if you were going to say, 'Tony, I am honored, but . . .' I don't want to hear that."

"What *do* you want to hear?" Jaylene asked.

"I want to hear you say yes."

"Are you certain that is what you want me to say?" Jaylene asked.

"Yes," Tony said. "Listen, I know this has come as a surprise to you. Perhaps if I were more demonstrative I could have let you know my feelings earlier. But I thought it wise to keep my feelings to myself until I had weighed all the aspects of it. After all, there is much to consider before taking such a step, you know."

"Yes, I know," Jaylene said.

"There is the fact that you are a Southerner and I am a Northerner, and our people are at war."

"A small consideration, yes," Jaylene said ironically.

319

"And of course, our cultural differences."

"Of course."

"And my mother. She is really a wonderful, dear, sweet lady. But she is quite old and set in her ways, and the thought of me marrying you would be difficult for her."

"I see," Jaylene said.

"It's not just you, darling," Tony said, quickly. "In fact, she would feel the same way about my marrying anyone from outside our circle in Boston. I believe she has already picked out the girl she wants me to wed, but I won't do it. I won't be pushed into it."

"Are you willing to defy your mother?" Jaylene asked.

"Jaylene, darling, I am willing to defy anyone and anything, my mother, my cultural background, even my own ideas of behavior, in order to marry you."

"Why?" Jaylene asked.

"Why?"

"Yes," Jaylene said. "I want to know why you are willing to defy everyone and everything in your background?"

"Because, Jaylene," Tony said. "I thought you understood."

"I don't understand," Jaylene said. "You will have to tell me."

"Because I love you," Tony said simply.

Jaylene squeezed Tony's arm and looked up at him with a large smile. "That is what I wanted to hear you say," she said.

"I love you, Jaylene," Tony said again. "I love you, I love you, I love you! And I will say it as often, and as loud as you wish. I'll shout it like the thunder or whisper it like the breeze. But it will all come out the same. I love you."

Jaylene felt her heart soar at such thrilling words, and she wanted to laugh and sing and dance all at the same time.

"Will you marry me?" Tony asked again.

"Yes," Jaylene heard herself saying. "Yes, Tony, I will marry you."

"More claret, my dear?" Culpepper asked, holding the decanter up. The red liquid caught the soft light and glowed as if from an inner fire.

"Thank you, Hamilton, but I fear that any more would make me too sleepy," Emily McLean said. She smiled seductively. "You wouldn't want me to get too sleepy, would you?"

"No," Culpepper said. He looked at Emily, at the scandalously low-necked dress she was wearing, and at the creamy tops of her breasts. His eyes seemed to glow with a light as deep and as red as the wine in the decanter he was holding. "No," he said again. "I wouldn't want you to get too sleepy."

Emily picked up a silken napkin and tapped it lightly against her rouged lips. "Hamilton, dear, if you will excuse me, I think I shall go up to my room now. If you want me later, you know where you can find me."

Culpepper pulled a watch from his tunic pocket and looked at it. "I have a few things to take care of," he said. "But they shouldn't take over an hour. I hope that isn't too long."

"An hour?" Emily said, pouting prettily. "Hamilton, surely I shall be in bed within an hour."

"Perhaps I can hurry it up," Culpepper said.

Emily smiled broadly. "I shall be in *bed*, Hamilton, but I shan't be asleep. As I said, if you want me . . . you know where to find me."

The lights leaped back into Culpepper's eyes, and this time when he answered her he spoke thickly.

"Yes," he said. "Yes, I know where to find you."

Emily excused herself and then started up the stairs. She walked down the long, darkened corridor to her room, and as she did she shuddered as she thought of what she would have to do. She would have to sleep with Hamilton Culpepper to carry out her mission.

Emily had told Tony that she hadn't exposed him because he was a fellow spy. What Tony didn't realize was the depth of truth to that remark. Emily was a spy, but not for the Confederacy, and not even for the North. She sold her services to the highest bidder. She was loyal to her employer, and provided brilliant service, for a fee. For Emily was one of the thousands of people who was unable to become passionately involved with either side of the war. She was able to maintain her equilibrium only by being true to herself.

Jaylene had spoken to her the other day as if only Jaylene and her father had been hurt. Jaylene had no idea how deep the pain had been for Emily. And though Emily didn't die of a broken heart, it wasn't because she didn't want to. It was only because she was an exceptionally strong woman who managed to survive despite all the heartbreak and travail and injustice.

And there *was* injustice. Not once did anyone give Emily a chance to tell her side of the story. Vir-

322

gil kicked her off the *Delta Mist* and Jaylene shut her out of her heart. Wherever Emily went, she was Jezebel, the whore whose infidelity caused Virgil to die of a broken heart. Long-time friendships were broken, stage doors were closed to her, and Emily wandered in the limbo of lost souls for the next couple of years. She even had to change her name for a while, because up and down the river her name became synonymous with whore.

The ironic twist of the whole affair was that the man in Emily's bed that fateful afternoon was her husband.

Lucas Palmer had given Emily's father forty dollars and a mule, when Emily was fourteen years old. Emily was too young to realize that she could have resisted the marriage, so, tearfully, she went through with it.

Lucas was a terrible husband, a poor gambler who drank and took out his frustrations over his gambling losses by beating Emily. Then one day, while Lucas was sleeping off a long drunk, Emily ran away. Eventually, she turned up on the *Delta Mist* as an actress and a singer, and there she fell in love with Virgil Cooper.

Virgil wanted to marry her, and begged her to marry him, but Emily kept turning him down. She knew that Lucas would never give her a divorce, and she was afraid to find him to ask him for one. She was afraid that if she did find him, he would force her to go with him again, and she had already vowed that she would kill herself before she did that.

Then one day she got a message from Lucas. He

had discovered her location and was going to meet the boat when it arrived in Natchez.

Emily was terrified, and she considered all types of escape schemes, including jumping off the boat before it reached Natchez. She would, she decided, slip away from the *Delta Mist* and disappear. But she couldn't do it, for there was now something stronger than her fear of Lucas. She loved Virgil Cooper far too much to drop out of his life forever. She vowed to face Lucas Palmer and beg him for a divorce.

After the boat docked in Natchez, and after Virgil and Jaylene left, Emily went to her cabin. She felt bad about refusing to go ashore with Jaylene, but what could she do? She couldn't take a chance on Lucas seeing her and making a scene, or worse. Lucas might even harm Jaylene if he thought she was in his way. Besides, Emily felt safer on the boat. She knew he wouldn't be able to take her off the boat by force, whereas if he saw her downtown, he might feel no compunctions about kidnapping her. Emily knew that if she just waited on the boat, Lucas would come to her. She didn't want him to, but she would rather that he come to her than go to him.

Nearly an hour passed before there was a knock on her door. During that hour Emily began to entertain hopes that he wouldn't come at all, that this was all a nightmare. But the knock on her door dashed any such hopes.

Emily took a deep breath, held it for a moment as if preparing to jump into a cold stream, then walked over to open the door.

"So I have found you at last," a man said.

Lucas was standing there, leaning against the doorjamb, smiling triumphantly. He was about forty-five, with black hair and flashing dark eyes. A small, thin moustache was set above a well-formed mouth. His very handsomeness made his cruelty seem even more harsh.

"What do you want with me?" Emily asked.

Lucas chuckled. "What do I want? Why, I want you, my dear."

Emily turned away and walked back into her cabin. "Lucas, leave me alone," she said. "I've been out of your life for four years now. Please, just let things be."

Lucas followed her into the cabin, then closed the door behind him. He locked it and removed the key.

"Why did you do that?" Emily asked with a catch of fear in her voice.

"So we can talk, my dear, without being disturbed."

"I don't want to talk to you," Emily said. "I don't want to have anything to do with you. Please, just go away and leave me alone."

Lucas smiled evilly. "Why, I thought you wanted a divorce."

At the mention of a divorce, Emily looked at him with quick-building hope. "Divorce?" she said. "Lucas . . . you would really give me a divorce?"

"Yes," Lucas said. "That's what you want, isn't it?"

"Oh, yes, that's what I want more than anything in the world!"

"Then I think we can work something out."

"Work something out? What do you mean, work

something out?" Emily asked. "There is nothing to work out. We simply go to a lawyer and get a divorce."

"Oh, no, my dear, it isn't quite that simple," Lucas said. "You see, as the injured party, I'm entitled to certain . . . damages."

"Injured party? Damages?"

"Yes," Lucas said. "After all, you have abandoned my board and bed, and you have committed adultery. Now you did all this despite the fact that I, at great personal expense, made a home for you."

"I see," Emily said, sighing. "You want me to pay you for a divorce, is that it?"

"Well, my dear, some friends have helped to support me at the gaming tables. Now I owe them a bit of money, and these friends have become quite insistent that I repay them."

"All right," Emily said. "How much do you owe them?"

"Five hundred dollars," Lucas said.

"Five hundred? Why, that's a small fortune," Emily said.

"Yes, I agree. I know it is far beyond my poor powers to raise. That's why I am asking you for it."

"But that's all the money I have in the world," Emily protested.

"Unfortunate," Lucas said, unmoved by Emily's plea. "But if you want a divorce, and my guarantee that you will never see me again, you will give me the money."

Emily looked at Lucas for a long time while considering his offer. Finally the thought of her freedom was more than she could resist, so she sighed, and walked over to a trunk. Hanging from a chain around her neck was a key. She pulled out the key and opened the trunk, then took out a small box. She opened the box and removed a sheaf of bills.

"Here is four hundred and fifty dollars," she said. "It's all I have. You'll have to raise the other fifty somewhere else." She handed the money to him and he stuck it in his pocket.

"Well now, I just knew I could count on you," Lucas said, smiling broadly. "But I am disappointed that you are fifty dollars short."

"I'm sorry. You'll have to raise the rest of the money somewhere else."

"But the price of the divorce is five hundred dollars," Lucas said.

"Lucas, what am I to do?" Emily asked in an exasperated tone of voice. "I told you, I have no more money."

"Perhaps we could work something out," Lucas proposed.

"What?" Emily asked tonelessly.

Lucas smiled again, then began unbuttoning his shirt. "It's been a while since I've had a woman, and to be honest, my dear, I'm quite randy. Suppose you accommodate me?"

"No!"

"I could force you to accommodate me," Lucas said.

"You mean you would *rape* me?"

Lucas laughed in deep appreciation of the joke. "Rape?" he said. "Oh, hardly rape, my dear. After all, you *are* my wife. In fact, were you to make too much of a row, I'm quite certain the law would be interested in your adulterous affair with Captain Cooper. After all, that is against the law, you know.

327

You could wind up in prison for twenty years. Is that what you want?"

"No," Emily said, frightened at the prospect, not only of a potential prison sentence, but of the humiliation it would cause Virgil and Jaylene. "No, of course I don't want that."

"Then you will cooperate with me?"

"I . . . I suppose I have no choice," Emily said in a small voice.

"That's right," Lucas said, his smile broad and evil. He was stripping out of his pants. "You have no choice at all."

Emily went to bed with him, gritting her teeth and shutting her eyes to his brutal penetration of her body, trying to will herself into insensibility, the better to survive the ordeal. Lucas had just grunted out his obscene release when, suddenly and unexpectedly, the door was opened, and there, before Emily's horrified eyes, stood Virgil and Jaylene.

Emily was forced off the boat abused, degraded, and stone broke. Everywhere she went the evil that she did followed her. Jobs were denied and friendship was withheld.

Then came the war. Emily's acting ability could no longer be put to use on the theater stage, so she became a master of many disguises, playing many roles, living many pasts, anticipating many futures. She took comfort and satisfaction in her ability to be accepted as whoever she wanted to be, and realized that in playing these roles in these dangerous times, she was taking a great chance, for she could have been exposed as a fraud, taken for a spy, and shot.

There was something about living on the edge of such extreme peril which gave her pleasure . . . as if she were able to flaunt social behavior and flirt with danger at the same time. Society had turned its back on her, and in playing her roles now, she was turning her back on society. She moved with impunity on both sides of the lines, loyal to no cause, save her own. She played a nurse, a soldier's sweetheart, an officer's wife, a serving girl; once she even dressed as a young man and played a soldier. The challenge was great and the thrill of success invigorating.

Emily existed in her own world then, giving friendship or allegiance to no one, until she saw Jaylene, and she realized that, more than anything in the world, she wanted to regain Jaylene's friendship and respect. But she couldn't do that until she could make Jaylene understand what had happened, and if Jaylene wouldn't give her a chance to explain, then Jaylene would never understand.

But Emily had figured out Tony Holt's purpose in being here. She knew that Tony Holt was the liaison officer in charge of conducting the underground railroad. Emily also knew about Lucy Wade, the white girl who was in reality a negress and the property of Hamilton Culpepper. There could only be one reason for Tony Holt to be here, with Jaylene's assistance, and that would be to rescue Lucy Wade.

But the rescue wouldn't work if Lucy wasn't aware of what was going on. Therefore, Emily had waited all evening for her opportunity to speak with Lucy, to prepare her for the rescue attempt. Surely, that would make Jaylene grateful enough to listen to her.

Emily reached Lucy's door and tapped lightly.

The moment Lucy opened the door, Emily knew, she would be committing an act of espionage, an act punishable by death. But by now this was old hat to her. She felt the familiar excitement, the quickening of her senses, the increased awareness of being alive. It was a heady feeling that she liked, and she realized that she would probably be doing this even if she wasn't looking for a way to reach Jaylene. She was addicted to the excitement of danger.

CHAPTER TWENTY-SEVEN

The Confederate defenders of Yazoo City, under the command of Colonel Hamilton Culpepper, were enjoying a respite from engagement with the enemy. The Union troops had completely bypassed the town in order to swell the total number of forces under General Grant surrounding Vicksburg. The siege of Vicksburg was being pressed with every possible unit, as the knot at the head of the sack was being pulled tighter and tighter. Nothing was going in to the city, and no one was coming out. Vicksburg was slowly consuming itself, and it was only a matter of time until defenders and townspeople alike would be starved into surrender.

Some of Culpepper's staff officers thought that Culpepper should attempt to muster a rescue mission. After all, Culpepper had nearly one quarter as many troops under his command as Grant had around the city. A coordinated attack by Culpepper's and Pemberton's forces might break the siege.

Though the staff officers didn't realize it, this was also an idea conceived by General Joseph Johnston and approved by President Jefferson Davis. But when orders for the implementation of the plan were dispatched to Culpepper he refused, saying that his forces were too ill-equipped to carry out the mission. Culpepper also claimed that he had support of his staff in making his decision.

The organization of the Confederate government was such that Culpepper, though only a colonel, could refuse the order of a general and a president, because he was a military governor. The whole purpose of the war was to preserve the rights of state authorities. Therefore, as military governor, Culpepper could be requested, though not ordered, to cooperate with the overall defense plan of the South. That principle had already cost the South several significant defeats, and had led to the situation which now saw Vicksburg under siege and the entire Mississippi River about to fall into the hands of the North.

Because they were not fighting, the defenders of Yazoo City had a lot of time on their hands, and they were exceptionally anxious for the Edward Fox Troupe of Players to present their first show. And thus, on the night of their opening performance, the theater was packed to the greatest capacity ever.

Jaylene was sitting at her dressing table applying her makeup when the door to her room opened, and someone walked in.

"Uncle Edward, is that you?" she called without looking around. Whoever it was could not be seen in the mirror.

"No," a voice said and then, thrust in front of Jaylene, was a single long-stemmed rose.

For just an instant, Jaylene felt a quick thrill. It was Todd Kirk! Then, almost as quickly as the feeling had developed, she submerged it. After all, she

333

was now engaged to Tony Holt. She had no right to feel a sense of excitement over the sudden, unexpected appearance of Todd Kirk.

Jaylene turned and looked at him. Never had he seemed so handsome, though there was something different about him. At first she wasn't sure what the difference was, and then she saw it. The cockiness that had always been a part of Todd was gone. The resolution and self-confidence were still there, but now they were tempered with humility.

"I know I was ordered never to return," Todd said, grinning sheepishly. "But fortunately I don't take orders from Hamilton Culpepper."

The words were softly spoken, and without a challenge to draw a sharp retort from Jaylene, she found that her own words were equally as soft.

"I thought you never wanted to see me again."

"I was hurt," Todd said. "And grief-stricken." He gave a little laugh. "And, I suppose, too proud to cry."

"To cry?" Jaylene asked, as shocked at hearing him say the words as she would have been had he actually begun to weep.

"Yes," Todd said. "I thought men didn't cry. But I've learned that they do."

"Oh?"

"I've just returned from Vicksburg, Jaylene. There I saw grown men crying at the sight of starving children. They cried without shame, and I think it was one of the bravest things I ever saw."

Todd's simple words moved Jaylene deeply, so that she could find no immediate response. She looked at the rose for a moment, then raised it to her nose to smell its fragrant bouquet.

334

"I can see that you are busy," Todd said.

"I'll see you after the performance. I want to talk to you, Jaylene. There is something I want to ask."

"Jaylene, darling something has come up. There is a problem we must try to solve. Perhaps Edward will—" The voice was that of Tony Holt, who came into the room but stopped in mid-sentence when he saw Todd Kirk.

Todd was as shocked to see Tony as Tony was to see him. But Todd was armed, and Tony was not, and Todd recovered from his shock quickly enough to draw his pistol.

"Captain Holt, I believe," he said. He thumbed the hammer back on his pistol.

"Yes," Tony said. He put his hands up.

"Todd, no," Jaylene said. "You don't know what you're doing."

"Don't I?" Todd asked. "This man is a Yankee captain. Oh, but of course you know that, because you were with him in Winona."

"Please, Todd, you don't understand," Jaylene begged.

"Wait a minute," Todd said, suddenly seeing the light. "Did you call her darling, as you came in here?" Todd ran his hand through his hair. "Yes, I think I do understand. Madam, you are a Yankee spy as well, aren't you? I've been played for the fool that I am."

"She is not a spy," Tony said quickly.

"Oh? And I suppose you aren't either?"

"Yes," Tony said. "I am. And I am your prisoner, sir, so do with me what you will. But, I beg of you, let Jaylene go, for she is innocent of any wrongdoing."

335

"Tender words," Todd said. "The words of a lover, perhaps?"

"Our personal affairs are none of your concern, sir," Tony said.

Todd looked at Tony for a monent, and a blood vessel throbbed at his temple. Finally, with a sigh of disgust, he holstered his pistol. "All right," he said. He waved his hand. "It isn't the first time love of this woman has made a fool of me. Go on, make your getaway. I won't turn you in."

"Love of me?" Jaylene said in a small voice.

"Yes," Todd said. "I was going to ask you to marry me."

"I'm afraid it's a bit late for you to ask that question," Tony said. "I have already asked it of her, and she has consented to be my wife."

"I see," Todd said quietly. He looked at Jaylene and smiled a slow, sad smile. "Madam, I always seem to be around you when I'm not wanted. I pray that you will forgive me." He turned to Tony. "In the meantime, Captain, I suggest that you avail yourself of my offer of freedom. Should someone else discover you, he may not feel as lenient."

"Todd, he can't go," Jaylene said. "He's here to save Lucy."

"To save Lucy?"

"Yes," Tony said. "I intended to get her out of here and put her onto the underground railroad north."

"He's doing the same thing Sam was trying to do," Jaylene said.

"It got Sam killed," Todd said.

"Yes," Tony said. "And it may get me killed as well. But I am determined to try it."

Todd ran his hand through his hair in agitation. "Sam was a well-respected Confederate officer and he got caught. How do you expect to get away with it when Sam failed?"

"Sam was a brilliant cavalry officer," Tony said. "But as an espionage agent, he was totally incompetent."

For one quick instant Todd bristled at the words, but he realized their truth, and his anger never surfaced.

"You are right," Todd said. "I would never let him go on such a mission for just that reason."

"Todd, will you let Tony rescue Lucy?"

"I'll do nothing to stop him," Todd said.

"Perhaps you can do more," Tony suggested.

"More? What do you mean?"

Tony looked at Todd from the top of his head to the bottom of his boots. "It could work," he said. "You are about my size."

"What are you talking about?"

Tony looked at Jaylene. "Jaylene, I only have two lines to say in the third act. Do you suppose you could put Major Kirk in my costume and makeup and let him make that appearance for me?"

"What? Me go on stage?" Todd sputtered. "I'm afraid not."

"There's not that much to it," Tony said. "Believe me, the third act is the easiest part of the whole play." Tony looked at Jaylene.

"Because of the play, the guard has been changed," he said. "Instead of two guards in the alley behind the Lexington House, there is only one, and he walks around the whole block. There is about a three-minute period when I could get Lucy

337

out without being seen. But after the play the guard will increase again."

"Oh, yes, that's a magnificent idea," Jaylene said. "No one would suspect anything during the play. Especially if it goes on as scheduled."

Todd held his hands up in protest and backed away. "You are both crazy," he said, "if you expect me to get out on that stage."

"Todd, you must," Jaylene said simply. "For if you don't, we will have no chance to save Lucy."

Todd looked at both of them, then sighed in resignation. "Very well," he said. "I suppose I have no choice. What do I do?"

"There's nothing to it," Jaylene said. "You only have two lines, and Tony can tell you what they are and show you how to do it while I get you made up."

"I must be out of my mind," Todd muttered, as he allowed Jaylene to lead him to the dressing table.

When someone knocked lightly on Lucy's door later that night, she was ready. Emily had told her that Jaylene and Captain Tony Holt were going to try to arrange her escape. Emily warned Lucy that it would probably be dangerous, but Lucy didn't care. Even death would be preferable to what she was going through now.

When Lucy questioned Emily about the details, Emily admitted that she didn't know them, and that, in fact, she wasn't even acting as an official conduit of information. But she insisted that an attempt would be made to rescue Lucy, and so persuasive was she that even without details Lucy took what action she thought would be necessary to help in her own escape.

Lucy had packed a few belongings in a silk scarf and tied the scarf into a small, easily carried bundle. Next she put pillows under the bed covers, and arranged them in such a way as to make it appear to casual inspection that she was sleeping. Then she dressed in men's pants and a jacket. This would not only disguise her, but would also make traveling easier. Finally, she settled into a chair by the open window, and sat in the dark room, looking out over the alleyway and at the roofs and walls of the city.

From two blocks down the street, she could hear the sounds of the play. There was a surprising ache in her heart as the old familiar sounds of the crowd's reaction reached her ears: applause, laughter, an occasional cheer for the heroine or a boo and a hiss for the villain. Once she even heard Frank Hardenburgh's voice, his magnificent projection carrying it this far on a breath of air.

In the alley below her window, the lone guard trudged along, his footfalls making hollow sounds on the brick surface of the alley. Lucy watched him walk the entire length of the alley, then turn the corner at the far end.

Almost immediately after the guard disappeared a black shadow appeared, moving quickly and quietly through the alley, staying close to the wall. The shadow reached the wall just below Lucy and started to climb.

"No!" Lucy hissed down at him. "You stay down there. I'll come to you."

Lucy startled him, but Tony recovered quickly, then stepped back into the alley and looked both ways to make certain they were clear. "All right," he called up to her. "Come ahead now."

Lucy climbed out of the window and grabbed a brick outcropping; then, using loose bricks, molding, window ledges, and anything else she could find, she moved quickly and gracefully down to the ground.

Tony laughed quietly. "You did that better than I could have done it."

"I've had a long time to study the best way to come down," Lucy said. "But until now there was no reason to try it. Let's go."

"You knew I would come," Tony said. "How did you know?"

"A friend told me," Lucy said. "Don't worry, no one else knows."

Tony and Lucy slipped through the shadows until they came to Tony's two horses. Within seconds they were riding out of the city.

The curtain fell on the stage, and the audience gave a thunderous ovation for the players.

"Jeremy," Edward called. "Return to the stage for the curtain call."

Todd was standing in the wings, where he had been since his last exit. The fact that even Edward Fox didn't realize that he had changed places with Tony was encouraging, but no one had mentioned anything about a curtain call, and he had no idea what was expected of him. Then, to his great relief, Jaylene dashed off the stage and took him by the arm to lead him back on.

"We will form a tableau," she whispered. "When the curtain opens again, you lean over with your face to the rear. They will think it's part of the staging."

"All right," Todd said.

The curtain went up, and the thunderous applause washed over them. Todd felt the sweat popping out on his brow and under his arms. He had faced the mouths of cannon with less fear. Oddly, he knew it wasn't the prospect of being discovered that brought on the fear, as much as the idea of being on stage in the first place. He suddenly developed a new respect for Jaylene and the others who did this all the time.

The curtain dropped, and the people on stage began to move. It was only then that Edward noticed who Todd was.

"My God!" Edward said. "What is this?"

"I'll explain it later, Uncle," Jaylene said. "For now, help us to carry it through."

"All right. The presentation tableau—no, not that one, he would have to face the audience. Uh . . . how about the deliverance tableau?"

"The what?" Todd asked.

"Never mind," Jaylene said. "Just move over here and hold your arms over your head like this." Jaylene put him in position. "Now get on your knees and I'll stand so that no one gets a good look at you."

Todd assumed the position she suggested for him, and the curtain came up again. Again they were assailed by a thunderous ovation, until finally the curtain dropped for the final time. The charade had been successfully carried off.

CHAPTER TWENTY-EIGHT

From his position on the side of the hill, Todd could look down over the town of Yazoo City or into the fields around it. Culpepper's army, consisting of almost fifteen thousand men, was camped around Yazoo City in a large semicircle, and their campfires winked in the night like fallen orange stars. The songs of a dozen encampments reached his ears in an oddly mixed melange of sound. *How different this army is from Pemberton's besieged defenders,* Todd thought.

"I wondered what happened to you," a woman's softly modulated voice said, and Todd, startled by the sudden intrusion, looked around with a jerk. "Did I frighten you?" Jaylene asked with a little laugh.

"No," Todd said. "But I didn't expect you out here, either."

"Mr. Hardenburgh said he saw you come this way. I just started walking until I reached this hill, then I climbed it."

"Don't you know it isn't safe for you to be out here alone?" Todd asked.

"Who should I fear?" Jaylene asked derisively.

"There isn't a Yankee for miles. They are all around Vicksburg."

"Perhaps a Confederate deserter?" Todd suggested.

"Who would desert from Culpepper's army? He'll never lead them into a fight. They've no need to desert."

Todd laughed. "You have made a most astute observation."

Jaylene saw the hundreds of campfires winking in the night.

"Oh," she said. "Isn't this a breathtakingly beautiful sight?"

"Yes," Todd·said.

"Though the sight of so many campfires couldn't have been pleasant to Tony and Lucy. I hope they got through all right."

"I'm certain they did," Todd said. "If they hadn't, we would have heard something by now. Besides, these very campfires would have provided them with beacons as to what to avoid."

"But the pickets . . ." Jaylene said.

"Are few and far between," Todd interrupted. "After all, you said it yourself, the Union army is at Vicksburg. Even the lowest-ranking private knows that, so no one is apt to be too observant on a night like tonight. No, I imagine your Tony made it with no problem."

"My Tony?"

"Isn't he?"

"Well, he . . . he has asked me to marry him," Jaylene said.

"And you said yes."

"Yes," Jaylene agreed, but the word was barely audible.

"Is that what you want?"

"Oh . . . I don't know *what* I want," Jaylene said. "I'm so confused. First there was the business with Booth, then you, then Lucy was captured by Culpepper. And then there was Tony and then, out of nowhere, Emily McLean came back into my life. Todd, I just don't know what to do. I told Tony I would marry him because I thought I truly loved him. But I love you too, and when you came back it just made things even more complicated. Now I don't know . . ."

"Wait a minute! What did you say?" Todd asked.

"I said your coming back just made things more complicated."

"No, before that," Todd said.

"I said I love you too," Jaylene said.

"Jaylene, can this be true?" Todd asked. "Do you really love me, girl?"

Jaylene saw the expression of happiness in Todd's face. His eyes flashed as brightly as the campfires in the field.

"Yes," Jaylene said. "Yes, it *is* true. I love you, Todd."

"Then you won't marry Tony Holt," Todd said. "I won't let you. I can't let you."

"But I can't hurt him," Jaylene said. "Oh, Todd, you don't understand. Yes, I love you, but I love him too."

"Jaylene, you can't love both of us."

"And now you understand my confusion and dilemma," Jaylene said. "For the sad truth is, Todd

346

Kirk, I *do* love both of you. I don't know which of you I love more. And until I find out . . ."

But before Jaylene could finish her sentence, Todd took her in his arms and kissed her.

As before, Todd's kiss was able to sweep her out of her mind. She lost her train of thought, forgot who and where she was, and let her body melt against his. Her knees turned to water and she felt herself falling, or being gently lowered to the ground. She felt his hands on her, deftly and quickly removing her clothes, and then the kiss of the night air against her bare skin told her she was naked. She was surprised. It had happened so quickly, and yet she had no desire to fight against it, for never had her body been so filled with pleasant sensations.

Todd removed his clothes and within a moment they were skin to skin. Jaylene could feel the caress of the night breeze and the texture of the soft grass beneath her. Dimly, she was aware that they could be discovered by anyone who might happen along. This realization added a sense of excitement to the situation, though in truth no such excitement was needed to heighten the moment.

Todd moved over her then, and a second later entered her. She felt an exquisite pleasure, silken sensations unlike anything she had ever experienced. She raked his bare back with her fingernails, becoming as much the aggressor as he. She took his lips and tongue eagerly and arched her back to receive him, bound on the golden quest of rapture.

That rapture was attained with a spinning, whirling sensation of pleasure, starting deep inside and spreading out in waves, moving with more and more urgency, drawing her tighter and tighter, until finally, in a burst of ecstasy, her body gained the release and satisfaction it sought. She cried her pleasure into his throat as her body jerked in orgasmic, convulsive shudders.

Then came another, immediately on the heels of the first, a searing lightning bolt of pleasure that thrust her quickly back to the pinnacle of sensation, and then a third, which made her feel pleasure so intense that every part of her tingled. She was able to feel Todd's muscle-jerking release, the two of them sharing rapturous explosions.

"Do you want some coffee?"

Jaylene opened her eyes and saw the soft, golden light of early morning. The sun was a red-orange ball, barely above the horizon in the east, and she was bundled up in a sleeping bag. She knew immediately that inside the sleeping bag she was naked.

"Oh, my," she said, blinking her eyes and looking around. "I *slept* here?"

"That you did, girl," Todd said. He was tending a small fire. Hanging from a tripod over the fire was a coffeepot. The smell of coffee permeated the morning air.

"I've never done this before," Jaylene said. "I mean, spend the night with a man."

"Well, you want to do it again sometime?" Todd joked. "I'm willing if you are."

Jaylene smiled and sat up. As she did so the sleeping bag fell to her waist, exposing her breast to the morning sun. She flushed with quick embarrassment and then, concurrent with the flush, came the memory of the intense rapture of the night before. With the memory came a resurgence of the heat of passion she had experienced. Boldly, and without realizing she was going to do it, she opened the sleeping bag. "How about right now?" she asked quietly.

Todd took one look at her, gulped in surprise, then smiled in eager anticipation. "I think right now would be a wonderful time," he said, moving to her.

The sun had turned white and hot, by the time Jaylene left the hill to return to town. Todd had returned to his men, buoyed not only by the events of the night just passed, but also by the fact that Jaylene had told him that she would marry him. That meant she would have to tell Tony, a prospect she didn't relish; but it would have to be done. She hoped Tony would understand, and, more importantly, she hoped he wouldn't feel that she had merely agreed to marry him so that he would rescue Lucy.

How had the rescue gone? Surely it was successful, or by now she would have heard something. Though, she told herself, how could she have heard anything? She had been with Todd for the entire night, and they certainly hadn't heard any news.

Jaylene smiled as she thought of the night. Never in her life had there been one like it. But there would be many more. She and Todd had promised each other that.

"Well, well, well, if it isn't Miss Cooper," a rasping voice said.

Jaylene was startled by the sudden appearance of

Colonel Culpepper. He had been standing behind a building, and he stepped out in front of her just as she reached it.

"Colonel Culpepper, why must you startle me so?" she asked.

"I didn't want you to see me and run from me," Culpepper said.

"Colonel Culpepper, I do not find your company that pleasant, as you well know. But I scarcely think I would run from you."

"You might, if you knew what was in store for you," Culpepper said ominously.

"In store for me? What do you mean?" "Espionage, Miss Cooper," Culpepper said. "Tamara Gilbert has escaped, aided, I believe, by one Captain Holt. You know Captain Holt, don't you my dear? He is the one you introduced as Jeremy Tremont."

"I'm sure I don't know what you are talking about," Jaylene said, though her trembling voice was now evidence that she was quite shaken by the charge.

"I'm sure that you *do* know, Miss Cooper. I've already arrested your uncle, Mr. Hardenburgh, and Emily McLean. They, and you, Miss Cooper, will be hanged tomorrow morning. Take her to the guardhouse, men," he said.

From behind the building, two grim-faced soldiers emerged, carrying rifles. They stepped up to Jaylene and took her in custody. Jaylene fought hard to keep from fainting.

350

CHAPTER TWENTY-NINE

Culpepper had separated Jaylene from the others, taking her into another room for what he termed interrogation. He offered her a glass of wine. Because she was frightened and thought the wine would have a calming effect, Jaylene accepted.

"Now, my dear, I know you are wondering what is to become of all of you," Culpepper said. "The answer to that . . ."

Suddenly Culpepper's voice began to fade, and Jaylene felt the room spinning. Dots of light danced before her eyes, and she felt herself slipping away. *What is it? What's going on?* she thought.

"Ah, yes," Culpepper said, smiling broadly. "You are feeling the effects now. It's the drink, you see."

Jaylene looked at the wine, then poured the rest of it out. She wanted to do it angrily, to dash the contents in his face as a defiant gesture, but it was too late for that. She barely had the strength to turn the goblet over, and she watched the liquid slide out slowly as she slipped into unconsciousness.

When she regained consciousness, she opened her eyes and looked around to see that she was in the same room, in bed. She tried to sit up, only to discover that she was tied to the bed, and she was naked.

"What?" she said aloud. She jerked at the ropes as if unable to believe it. "Help," she called. "Someone help me!"

"Oh, my dear, it will do you no good to call for help," Culpepper said.

"You!" Jaylene said, raising her head up from the pillow so she could see him. "You did this!"

"Yes, I did," Culpepper said. He stepped out of the shadow and into the light of the flickering lantern. Jaylene realized that he was also naked.

"Oh," Culpepper said, looking at her with eyes which reflected the flickering flame of the lamp. "Oh, this is going to be good, girl. This is going to be better even than it was with the black wench."

As Culpepper spoke, he allowed his fingers to trail across Jaylene's body. The sensation, far from being pleasant, gave her chills, as if someone had grated their fingernails across a slateboard.

"That's why I was willing to let the black wench escape, you know." Culpepper explored the mounds, crevices, and curves of her body, and Jaylene, in an effort to dissuade him, tried to engage him in more conversation.

"You *let* her escape?"

"Oh, yes," Culpepper said. He laughed. "Do you remember the night I brought Emily McLean to identify Mr. Jeremy Tremont?"

"Yes," Jaylene said.

Culpepper chuckled evilly. "I didn't leave when you thought I did. After she 'identified' him, I merely opened and closed the door at the rear of the

353

theater, while I remained hidden in the darkness. I overheard every word spoken. Your Jeremy Tremont was Captain Tony Holt of the Union forces."

"But . . . I don't understand," Jaylene said. "If you knew it, why didn't you do something then?"

"Because I knew I could have you, Miss Cooper, just where I wanted you. Now you are my prisoner, a Yankee spy. Anything that happens to you will be too good for you. I can satisfy myself with you, then hang you and no one can stop me."

"And the others?" Jaylene said.

"They will hang too," Culpepper said. "All of them, your uncle, the rumpot, and the lying Miss Emily McLean."

"No," Jaylene said. "You have me where you want me, by your own admission. Let them go. I am guilty, not they."

"Oh, most noble of you," Culpepper said. "And does your plea for amnesty include even Miss McLean?"

"Yes," Jaylene said.

"Even after all she has done to you?"

"Yes," Jaylene said. "She has more than made up for having wronged my father and me. I have been wrong all this time. I have no right to hold it against her."

Culpepper laughed long and loud. He laughed so hard that tears came to his eyes and for the moment even his lust seemed interrupted by his rather bizarre sense of humor.

"What is it?" Jaylene asked. "What are you laughing at?"

"I'm laughing at you, Miss Cooper, and at your fool father, and your self-righteous sense of justice.

354

And at Emily McLean who has had to pay for all these years, yet who still sought your forgiveness."

"What are you talking about?"

"I'm talking about Lucas Palmer, Miss Cooper. Surely you have heard of Lucas Palmer?"

"No."

"He is a most undesirable character, to be sure. But he has pulled off the greatest feat of making others fools of anyone I have ever known."

Culpepper went on to tell Jaylene the story of how Lucas had trapped Emily into the situation in which Jaylene and her father had discovered them, and how everyone was so willing to believe evil of Emily that Lucas, rather than being the villain, turned out to be the hero of the affair, a husband who was equally as wounded as Jaylene's father.

"But I didn't know," Jaylene said quietly.

"Of course you didn't know," Culpepper said, wiping the tears of laughter from his eyes. "You never gave Emily the opportunity to explain it to you. But I knew, and so did many others. You heard only what you wanted to hear."

"Oh, poor Emily," Jaylene said. "How she has suffered on my account!"

"Lucas wouldn't have wanted to hear that," Culpepper said. "He used to enjoy taking credit for that himself. Until he got himself killed up at Shiloh."

"Colonel, please, let Emily and the others go," Jaylene said. "If you will, I will bargain with you."

The laughter left Culpepper's voice, to be replaced by triumph. "You have nothing with which to bargain," he said. "You have only your body, and I don't need you to give that to me. I am going to take it."

Now once again Hamilton Culpepper was the apparition from hell. He moved to her bed and Jaylene saw that he had quickly regained his lust for her.

"No," she said. "No, please don't!"

But Jaylene's pitiful entreaties fell on deaf ears as she felt the colonel's full weight upon her. She wanted to scream, but knew that to do so would be useless. He entered her brutally, and that which had brought her only pleasure before now brought her pain. It was so acute that it was all she could do to keep from crying out with the agony of it. How different this was from her sensual response to Tony, or her passionate hunger for Todd. Now there was only the obscene desecration of her body, painful and degrading beyond imagination.

Finally Culpepper let a grunt escape from his lips and shuddered as he finished. He withdrew with as little fanfare as he entered; then, as casually as if she weren't even there, he began to dress.

"Colonel," Jaylene said quietly, "when is the sentence to be carried out?"

Culpepper smiled at her. "When I have had my fill of your charms," he said. "I will be back," he added.

Todd's first inclination was to ride into Yazoon City as soon as he heard that Jaylene had been captured. But he knew that boldness without a plan was foolhardy and ineffective. He needed a plan, and after an entire day of consideration, he developed one. It was risky, and would require an unprecedented degree of cooperation between adversaries. For Todd's plan depended upon help from none other than Captain Tony Holt.

356

Todd sent a message to Tony, and asked for a midnight meeting near the covered bridge on the Canton Pike. He had specifically chosen this place because it was equidistant from Yazoo City and Winona, in what was actually no man's land. It also ran through the middle of swampland, so that there would be no way of approaching except via the road; therefore the opportunity to sneak in additional forces would be nil.

Todd had no reason to doubt Tony's sense of fair play, but there was, after all, a rather substantial reward out for him, so he couldn't be too careful.

Todd's sense of caution made him reach the covered bridge not at midnight but at nine, three full hours before the scheduled meeting. He took his horse down into a stand of trees nearby, tied it securely, then returned to the covered bridge. He climbed up into the top and sat on a rafter, completely invisible to anyone. And there Todd waited.

Tony arrived at about eleven-thirty. Todd watched him approach by looking through a venting window in the top of the bridge. The moon was bright, and he had an excellent view, not only of Tony, but of the four riders who were some distance behind him.

At first Todd was angry, because he thought Tony had double-crossed him. Then he realized that Tony didn't even know he was being followed, because the riders were making every effort to stay out of Tony's sight.

"Tony," Todd called quietly.

"What?" Tony answered, sitting upright in his saddle and looking around.

"Shhhh!" Todd cautioned. "There are riders following you, did you know that?"

"No," Tony said quietly.

"Get rid of them," Todd said. "Then come back and we will talk."

Tony turned the horse and galloped down the road for a short distance, then stopped when he drew abreast of the riders who had trailed him. From his distance Todd couldn't hear what was spoken, but a moment later all four riders were moving back down the road. Tony waited there for a long time, before he returned to the bridge. This time, Todd was standing in the road waiting for him.

"Thanks for telling me about them," Tony said as he swung off his horse. "'they weren't my idea. In fact, they weren't anyone's idea except their own. Somehow they found out about this meeting and sought a way to collect the reward on you. It is quite substantial, you know."

"Yes," Todd said. "Enough to keep me cautious."

"Now," Tony said. "What is the purpose of this meeting? Surely you aren't surrendering yourself to us."

"No," Todd said. "It's about Jaylene."

Tony sighed. "I see. Well, Major, if you have come to plead your case with her, then I have to advise you that it will fall on deaf ears. I love Jaylene, and I have asked her to marry me."

"I love her too," Todd said. "And I have asked her to marry *me*."

"Then you have come to tell me what I already know," Tony said. "We are competitors for her."

"No," Todd said. "Now we must fight together for her."

"What do you mean?" Tony asked, confused.

"Jaylene has been captured," Todd said. "She, Edward Fox, Mr. Hardenburgh, and Emily McLean are prisoners of Colonel Culpepper, and he intends to hang them all."

"Oh, my God," Tony said. He took off his hat and ran his hand nervously through his hair. "I thought the escape with Lucy went too smoothly. She is already in Cincinnati. How did it happen? How were they discovered?"

"I don't know," Todd said. "I know only that Culpepper has them and he intends to hang them. And I want your help in getting them out."

"Of course you shall have it," Tony said. "Though what can we do? Have you any ideas?"

"Yes," Todd said. He took a deep breath, then let it escape slowly, as if loathe to say what he was about to say.

"How many combatants can you muster from Winona?" Todd asked.

Tony looked at Todd strangely. "I can't tell you that."

"You must," Todd said.

"Todd, you are asking me to commit treason. *Real* treason!"

"No," Todd said. "I'm telling you that *I'm* going to commit treason."

"You mean by helping a few prisoners escape. Those are prisoners only because they helped an innocent girl escape. That may be Culpepper's idea of treason, but it isn't mine."

"Nor mine, sir," Todd said. He took another deep breath. "But what I am about to propose is. I want my forces to join with yours, to conduct a raid on Yazoo City."

Tony let out a low whistle. "Major Kirk, your name would be forever linked with Benedict Arnold's were you to carry out such a scheme. Whether the South wins or loses this war, people of both sides would hold you in low esteem."

"I know," Todd said quietly.

"And yet you are willing to go through with it?"

"Yes," Todd said. "For I feel that is the only way to rescue Jaylene."

"Would that even be effective?" Tony asked. "For I will tell you now that I could muster less than two hundred and fifty combatants. That is hardly enough to strike at the army Culpepper has in Yazoo City."

"If my men join with yours we could double the strength. If we attack from the south, Culpepper may be fooled into thinking that General Grant is moving toward Yazoo City with a sizeable army. Culpepper will do one of two things. He will either position his army in a blocking action, which would leave the northen approach to the city open, or he will withdraw from the city entirely. My guess is he will do the latter. In either case, I don't propose to do much more than make a demonstration against him, just long enough to allow me to slip into town with a few men and get Jaylene and the others out of jail."

"If you go into Yazoo City, I'm going in with you," Tony said.

"It will be safer for me," Todd said. "I can go in under the guise of helping to defend the city."

"I'm going in with you," Tony insisted. "That is,

if you want my men to participate in your demonstration."

Todd looked at Tony for a long moment, then smiled warmly and stuck out his hand. "Just remember," he said, "You'll be in my army, and in my army, I'm a major."

"I'm at your service, sir," Tony said, shaking Todd's proffered hand.

CHAPTER THIRTY

As the sun rose over the black dirt delta hills just south of Yazoo City, it illuminated a strange sight. Stretched from the river to the east was a long line of mounted soldiers. Some wore blue and some wore gray. Ropes stretched between several of the horses and branches were tied to the ropes. By stretching the riders out in such a way, the line gave the appearance of more soldiers. The plan was to drag the branches along the ground as they rode, thus raising dust clouds as if from a much larger force.

The advancing army was short of cannon, but several firing positions had been preselected, and the gunners were instructed to fire one round, then quickly move the guns to another position and fire again, thus creating the illusion of great artillery support.

Lieutenant Pearson, in charge of Kirk's Raiders, sat on a horse at the front of the line, dressed in the dark blue uniform of a Union general. A private rode beside him, carrying a general's standard. At the other end of the line sat the Union lieutenant left in charge by Tony, also dressed as a Union general, complete with a standard bearer. To the casual observer, the phantom army would be attacking Yazoo City with at least two divisions.

A red rocket arched through the early morning sky and at that signal the cannons opened fire. Because the cannons would have to be moved quickly, they weren't disconnected from the teams that pulled them, and because they weren't disconnected, they weren't well laid in. Therefore the cannon fire was inaccurate, but it was the noise and the illusion Todd was after, and in that they were exceptionally effective, for after the first volley the defending commanders in the field around Yazoo City believed they were under a major attack.

Culpepper was at breakfast when he heard the opening volley, but he didn't pay any attention to it. This was because he was thinking of the pleasure he had enjoyed with Jaylene the night before, and the exquisite pleasure he would enjoy this morning. It would be particularly sweet this morning, because immediately afterward he would have the guards take her and the others out and hang them. She would die with the smell of him still on her body, and the wetness of him in her womb.

As Culpepper thought that exciting thought, he felt such a jolt of pleasure that he nearly had an orgasm right there. He put his hand on the table to steady himself and switched his thoughts away. He must preserve his pleasure for as long as possible. It would be awful to spoil it before he even enjoyed it!

"Attack! Colonel, we are being attacked!" The bearer of the news was a young lieutenant, flushed with excitement and sweating from the exertion of running from the field.

Culpepper looked up from his breakfast, surprised by the sudden intrusion. It was only then that he heard the artillery firing. The defenders' artillery was returning fire, so that there was a sustained volley of firing. Though they didn't realize it, their firing added to the overall panic, for many thought that only the attackers had artillery.

"What is it?" Culpepper asked. "What is going on?"

"Colonel, the whole damned Yankee army is out there!" the lieutenant said.

"But they can't be!" Culpepper said. "They are all around Vicksburg, holding it in siege!"

"They have either captured Vicksburg, or they've broken off the attack. Either way, it looks like we're next."

Culpepper ran out onto the front porch and looked north. He could see the smoke from the cannon fire and in the distance, spread out across several hills, the rising cloud of dust from the advancing army.

"My God, there must be ten divisions out there!" Culpepper said.

"We make it two, sir," the lieutenant replied.

"Two? Are you mad?" Culpepper asked in fear-crazed anger. He pointed toward the hills. "Look at the size of that army! It stretches for five or six miles! I tell you, that's ten divisions!"

"No, sir, it couldn't be," the lieutenant said. "The line is long, but it isn't very deep. Besides, we've only seen two generals. Major Phillips has sent for reinforcements from the units north of town. We can block their entry that way."

366

"Reinforcements? What right has Major Phillips to issue such an order? *I* am in command here!" Culpepper screamed. "Me!"

Officers and soldiers were running to and fro on the street in front of him, and anxious civilians were gathering in clusters, shielding their eyes as they peered toward the developing battle.

"Colonel, we knew you would approve, sir," the lieutenant said. "We have to put men there to block the Yankees' advance. Otherwise they could break through and come into the city."

"Let them come!" Culpepper screamed. He threw both arms up in the air. "Let them come! Do you think for one minute *I'm* going to be trapped here in this godforsaken town like those dumb bastards in Vicksburg? No, sir, not a bit of it! I don't give one damn what happens to this town. You inform Major Phillips that I am moving my headquarters."

"Colonel, you can't do that!" one of the civilians shouted. "You can't abandon us to the Yankees!"

"If you had any sense, you would get out too," Culpepper said. "Aide!"

"Yes, sir?"

"Bring me my horse!"

The aide, a private who was still dressed in the white serving jacket he had been wearing while he served Culpepper breakfast, brought a saddled animal around to Culpepper and held it while the colonel mounted. The horse was highly spirited and made nervous by the cannonading, and he spun around a couple of times until Culpepper got him under control. Culpepper looked at the young courier who had brought him news of the attack.

367

"You go back and tell Major Phillips to hold them off long enough for me to get the headquarters moved. Then he can find me for further orders."

"Where will you set up the new headquarters, sir?" the lieutenant asked.

"Somewhere where there aren't any Yankees!" Culpepper replied, putting spurs to his horse and leaving at a gallop.

Culpepper's dash out of town precipitated a rout. The men of his army, like their commander, had no stomach for fighting. Those who did had long since transferred, discovering early the makeup of the army in which they had found themselves. The result was an army that consisted of slaggards, misfits, and cowards, perfect reflections of their commander. When he left, they did too, abandoning weapons, horses, wagons, tents, and everything else.

"I'll be damned," Tony said. Tony was wearing the gray uniform of a Confederate captain, and he, Todd, and four others were sitting on their horses on a hill just north of town, watching the disorganized exodus. "I don't believe I've ever seen a Southern army do this before."

"You aren't seeing a Southern army," Todd said derisively. "You are seeing Culpepper's Cowards." He raised up in the stirrups and looked toward the town. "We may as well go on down there now."

Todd slapped his reins against the neck of his horse and the six riders started into town at a gallop. Before they had ridden any distance at all they began to encounter fleeing soldiers, some mounted, but most on foot. Many were officers.

"Turn back," some of the soldiers called to Todd

368

and his men. "Turn back! General Grant and the whole army are comin' into Yazoo!"

"Get back there and fight!" Todd called to them. "Get back there, you cowards!"

"Todd, we don't want them back, remember?" Tony said.

"Yeah, I know," Todd said. He sighed. "I just wish I hadn't been right. This is the most disheartening thing I have ever witnessed."

"Come on, we've got to get into town and find Jaylene," Tony reminded him.

"They are probably in the jail," Todd said.

The riders tied their horses to a hitching post in front of the jail. "You two men round us up a wagon and team," Todd said. "And you two stay with our horses. If anyone so much as makes a move toward them, shoot them."

"Yes, sir," the soldier said.

Todd pushed the door open and went inside. There was no one there, though a pot of coffee was still warm, evidence of recent habitation.

"Hello!" Todd called. "Anyone here?"

"Back here!" a man's voice replied. "We are back here!"

Todd and Tony dashed quickly into the back of the jail, and there they saw Edward, Emily, and Hardenburgh, all in one cell.

"Where is Jaylene?" Todd asked.

"I don't know," Edward said. "Culpepper took her out yesterday."

"Look in the Lexington House," Emily said. "My guess is he took her there."

"Where are the keys?" Tony asked.

"They're over there, hanging from that hook," Edward said, pointing. "Get us out of here, please!"

"You take care of them," Todd said. "I'm going after Jaylene."

Before Tony could protest, Todd dashed out of the building and down the street toward the Lexington House, which was just two doors away.

When Todd stepped into the Lexington House, he saw several of the townspeople in the dining room. Contrary to the panic he had seen among the soldiers in the streets, the civilians were in a jubilant mood. Some were drinking wine, others eating bread and cheese, and still others had made bundles with the tablecloth and curtains and were stuffing them with food.

"Look," one of the townsmen called. "We've been starving, while this sonofabitch had all this food here!"

To the rear of the dining room a flight of stairs went up to the second floor. Todd pushed through the crowd to reach the stairs, but once there it was easy moving, for most were interested only in the food they could find, and few thought there would be any food upstairs. Todd took the stairs two steps at a time, then ran down the carpeted hallway.

"Jaylene!" he called. He jerked open doors. "Jaylene, are you here?"

"Todd, I'm here," he heard. He heard her knocking on one of the doors. "I can't get the door open. It's locked, and Culpepper has the key!"

"Stand back from the door," Todd ordered. He raised his foot and smashed it at the door, just next to the knob. The door, the doorjamb, and part of the wall exploded into the room, and he was just behind it.

"Todd, oh, thank God, you've found me!" Jaylene cried. She ran to him and threw her arms around him, and they stood there in a long embrace.

"We can't stay here," Todd finally said. "We have to get out."

"Uncle Edward and the others?"

"We've got them," Todd said. He looked toward the window.

"No good trying that way," Jaylene said. "When he finally untied me I thought to escape that way, but since Lucy left he's had bars put across the window."

"Then we'll just have to use the front door," Todd said. "Come on."

By now the crowd downstairs had reached enormous proportions, as news of Culpepper's food cache reached others in the town. It was all Todd and Jaylene could do to get through, but as they were trying to get out and the others were trying to get in, most of the crowd let them pass. Most neither noticed nor cared that a prisoner was being helped to escape.

A couple of Todd's men arrived out front with the wagon then, and all the escaped prisoners, including Jaylene, were loaded aboard.

"Let's go!" Todd shouted, and the entire party started out of town at a gallop.

"Cowards! Leaving us to the Yankees!" a civilian shouted, stepping into the road in front of them. He raised a rifle and fired as Kirk's band thundered by, and he just managed to jump aside before he was run down by the team and wagon.

"Keep 'em at a gallop," Kirk shouted. "We need to put as much distance between us and the town as possible."

They rode on for several minutes until the labored breathing of the horses told them they would have to stop and rest the animals. Finally Todd held up his hand and signaled the others to stop. "We'll rest here," he said. He smiled broadly. "Well, we made it."

"Todd," Tony said, and his voice had a strange, almost strained quality to it. "What will you do now?"

Todd laughed. "Do? Why, I don't know. I haven't made any plans beyond getting Jaylene out of there."

"Well, I did make some plans," Tony said. "You aren't going to be able to stay down here, you know."

"Yeah," Tony said. "Yeah, I know."

"I got you a commission in the Union army."

"Thanks," Todd said, "but no thanks. I know what you must think of me, but I can't fight against my own people."

"You don't have to," Tony said. He coughed. "Your commission is with the army out west. You'll be fighting Indians."

"I don't know," Todd said, looking at Jaylene.

"You can take her with you," Tony said. "There are quarters for officers' wives in the garrisons out there."

"Tony, you mean you'd release me from my . . ." Jaylene started to say. Then she screamed his name out in grief and agony, for she saw for the first time that Tony was wounded.

"Tony!"

Todd heard Jaylene's agonized scream, and he looked around. Tony had dismounted and was standing beside his horse. When he turned and started toward a tree to sit down, Todd could see that Tony was holding his hand over his chest, and bright red blood was spilling through his fingers.

"What happened?" Todd asked in surprise.

"You remember the fella who called us cowards and took a shot at us?" Tony asked.

"You mean he hit you?"

"Dead center," Tony said.

"Why didn't you say something?" Jaylene asked.

"I wanted to make certain that everyone got away," Tony said. He coughed, and blood bubbled from his mouth.

"Oh, Tony, no!" Jaylene said.

Tony put his hand on the tree to brace himself as he coughed, and when he sat, his hand slid down the tree, leaving a swath of blood painted on the trunk. He tried to hold himself up after he sat, but he couldn't, and he tumbled forward, spilling his blood in the dirt.

"Tony, no!" Jaylene said again. "Oh, no!" She sat beside him and cradled his head in her lap.

"In answer to your question," Tony gasped. "I do release you from your vow. Though, it was nice to think you were mine for a while."

"I was yours when I said that, Tony," Jaylene said. "I was."

Tony looked over at Todd, who was kneeling beside him. "You take care of her," he said. "You are in my army now. And in my army, I outrank you."

373

He tried to get something from his jacket pocket, but he couldn't do it. Jaylene got it for him. It was an envelope.

"That's your commission," Tony said. "It also authorizes you to enlist as many of your raiders as might want to go west with you. That will protect them as well."

"Major, count us in," one of the riders said.

"I guess I'm not a major any more," Todd said. He opened the envelope. "Why, I'm a captain, not a lieutenant. I thought you said you'd outrank me."

"Date of rank," Tony said. He laughed, then he coughed, and his head fell back.

"Tony?" Jaylene said. Then, louder, "Tony!"

Todd put his fingers to Tony's neck to feel for a pulse, but could find none. He looked at Jaylene and shook his head sadly. "I'm sorry," he said.

"What will we do with him?" one of the men asked.

"We'll take him to Winona," Todd said. "They'll decide what to do with him."

"They'll send him to Boston," Jaylene said.

"Maybe."

"They will," Jaylene said. "I will insist upon it."

Todd put his arm around her and pulled her to him. "We'll both insist upon it," he said. He looked at the others. "Put him in the wagon," he said.

Todd tied his horse to the wagon and drove it slowly along the road to Winona, with Jaylene sitting on the seat beside him. In the back of the wagon, Edward, Hardenburgh, and Emily rode with the body of Tony Holt. The outriders rode quietly alongside.

Jaylene turned on the seat and looked at Emily

for a moment, then held her arms out to her. Emily went to the younger girl and they embraced for a long, quiet moment.

"Emily, can you ever forgive me?" Jaylene finally asked. "Can you ever love me again?"

"I never stopped," Emily said.

"Niece, I suppose you'll be going out west to fight the Indians?" Edward asked.

"I hope I don't have to fight any Indians," Jaylene said. She slipped her arm through Todd's. "But I'll be going out west."

"Then I take it you'll have no objections to my signing Emily on with the troupe?"

"Objections? No, I think that's fine," Jaylene said. "Oh, but you can't! Uncle Edward, if you try to play now, surely you will be arrested."

"In San Francisco?" Edward asked.

"San Francisco?"

"A truly wonderful city," Hardenburgh said. "They have a great love for the theater. I've spoken to your uncle about it, and he has agreed to go."

"Oh, Uncle Edward, that is wonderful!" Jaylene said. "And if you are in San Francisco, perhaps we'll get an opportunity to come see you sometime. Would you take me to San Francisco, Todd?"

"Jaylene, you've made me so happy that I'll take you to the moon, if you've a mind to go there," Todd said.

"The moon? Heavens no, I've no desire to go to the moon," Jaylene said. Then she laughed. "For where on the moon could you find roses for me?"

"Like this one, you mean?" Todd asked, and to the utter amazement of everyone, he was holding in his hand a beautiful long-stemmed rose.

"Where did you get that?" Jaylene asked in surprise.

"Do you really want to know?" Todd asked.

Jaylene took the rose and held it to her nose to sniff its fragrance. "No," she finally said. "And I shall never want to know, so promise me you will never tell."

"I promise," Todd said, and even as he spoke he produced another one.

"What? Another? But this is impossible! Where do they come from?"

"I'm sorry," Todd said. "I promised a beautiful girl that I would never tell, and I never go back on a promise to a beautiful girl."

WIVES, LIES AND DOUBLE LIVES

MISTRESSES   ($4.50, 17-109)

By Trevor Meldal-Johnsen

Kept women. Pampered females who have everything: designer clothes, jewels, furs, lavish homes. They are the beautiful mistresses of powerful, wealthy men. A mistress is a man's escape from the real world, always at his beck and call. There is only one cardinal rule: *do not fall in love.* Meet three mistresses who live in the fast lane of passion and money, and who know that one wrong move can cost them everything.

ROYAL POINCIANA   ($4.50, 17-179)

By Thea Coy Douglass

By day she was Mrs. Madeline Memory, head housekeeper at the fabulous Royal Poinciana. Dressed in black, she was a respectable widow and the picture of virtue. By night she the French speaking "Madame Memphis", dressed in silks and sipping champagne with con man Harrison St. John Loring. She never intended the game to turn into true love . . .

WIVES AND MISTRESSES   ($4.95, 17-120)

By Suzanne Morris

Four extraordinary women are locked within the bitterness of a century old rivalry between two prominent Texas families. These heroines struggle against lies and deceptions to unlock the mysteries of the past and free themselves from the dark secrets that threaten to destroy both families.

Available wherever paperbacks are sold, or order direct from the publisher. Send cover price plus 50¢ per copy for mailing and handling to Pinnacle Books, Dept. 17-445, 475 Park Avenue South, New York, N.Y. 10016. Residents of New York, New Jersey and Pennsylvania must include sales tax. DO NOT SEND CASH.